ABOUT THIS BOOK

Ford:

I've never thought much about Orson Naples.
He's a cute guy who I'd seen around town a few times, but then one day he up and left and didn't reappear until a few years later. No one knows where he went or what he was doing, all this gossipy town knows is that he's a widower, owns the florist, and is friends with that divorced group that hang out at the Killer Brew all the time.
But then one day I step into his flower shop and go from rarely thinking about him, to him constantly being on my mind.
There's a restlessness to him that I'm dying to unlock answers to.
And his eyes linger on me a little too long for a straight man

…

Orson:

Ford Thomas is a pest. A delightful one. A tempting one. But I'm too old for games.

The ones I've played in the past have always led me to trouble which is why I vowed to settle down and live a quiet life.

So when Ford walks into my shop all uncontained energy and flirty quips in a pair of heavy work boots, I know I should show him the door.

I don't need fun. I don't need experiences.

Especially when those experiences have me questioning things I thought I knew about myself.

BUDDING ATTRACTION

DIVORCED MEN'S CLUB
BOOK 3

SAXON JAMES

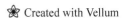 Created with Vellum

DEDICATION

This one is for my three boys.

I hope one day they're as fearless as Orson and Ford.

1

Orson

"AH, FUCK," I MUTTER, SPRINGING UP OFF THE GROUND. MY ass is tender from landing wrong, and my skin prickles with the uncomfortable dampness seeping through my pants and underwear. I twist around to get a good look, and *yep*. Between the water and the soil turned mud, anyone would think I shit my pants.

What a beautiful start to the day.

I pick up the pot I'd knocked over, upending more soil in the process, before going to get supplies to clean up. The shop is already open, but it's midweek and thankfully quiet, so there's no one around to witness this.

Silver linings. It's a minor inconvenience that no one will ever know about.

At least, that's what I think.

Just as I've finished cleaning the floors and am trying to work out what the hell to do about the mess on my pants, the bell over the door sounds, and I dart back out front.

Then almost trip over my feet.

Ford Thomas is standing in the middle of my florist, looking completely out of place.

He's tall and thick and covered in tattoos, wearing his heavily stained mechanics uniform and taking up more room in my little shop than should be physically possible.

Even being the only person in the room, he manages to make it feel crowded. It's not hard to see why people think he's scary at first glance, because when that intense stare falls on me, I feel like I might rattle out of my skin.

"Morning," he says cheerfully.

I snap out of ... whatever that was. "Hey. Ah ... flowers. Want some?"

"Is *that* what these fluffy little things are called?"

I eye him, thrown off by the genuine confusion in his tone, when—

He bursts out laughing. "Shit, you believed that?"

"No."

"Sure you did. Just how dumb do you think I am?" Ford's grin lightens his whole face.

A chuckle slips from me. "We haven't officially met before. I'm Orson. Florist, forty-five, and *extremely* gullible."

"Eh." He shrugs. "Are you gullible or just trusting?"

"Definitely the first one."

His intense stare is traded for an amused one, and when his eyes lock onto mine suddenly, the room gets warmer. Shit. Not good for the flowers. I drop his gaze and shuffle over to the thermostat to check the temperature—all while trying to keep my back turned away from him. I'm overly aware of the wet clothing clinging to my skin, and even without looking at him, I can *feel* him following my every move.

"Do you think it's weird?" he asks.

I have no choice but to glance back over. My hands feel awkward and cumbersome, so I tuck them into the front of my apron. "What's weird?"

"We've lived in the same town all these years and never actually met."

"There are a lot of people in this town. If you've never needed flowers before, you likely wouldn't have met me."

He nods. "You don't go out?"

"Rarely." I reach over and pluck a dying leaf from one of my arrangements. I used to go out all the time after my wife died, and it got me into a *lot* of trouble that I never want to relive. "Just not my scene."

He hums, and my attention flicks back to him in time to catch him openly checking me out. *Openly.* His gaze runs from my head down my legs and back up again. "You ever date?"

"*What*?"

His lips hitch up on one side. "You're cute. Figured I might as well ask."

"For … someone? Or for … you?" And I have no idea why my voice is coming out all stilted like this, but damn, I need it to stop.

There's something knowing in his eyes. "Me."

"Oh." My face burns. "But I'm straight though …"

His eyebrows lift, eyes still locked on mine. "Okay."

"Right. So, flowers?"

"The fluffy things. Yeah."

I throw him a *fuck you* smirk, finally able to focus on

something that doesn't make me feel like I've been hiked out of a plane. "What's the occasion?"

"My parents' fortieth anniversary."

"Congratulations to them."

"Yeah, their anniversary is always a great reminder that I'm a bastard."

Feeling emboldened, I ask, "You need the reminder?"

He rewards me with another of those loud laughs. "Just good to get confirmation it's not completely my fault."

"Once a bastard, always a bastard?"

"Exactly."

I circle him to get to a flower display, keeping my ass pointed in the opposite direction. "I don't think you're doing a very good job of upholding that image."

"Oh, *really?*"

"From what I hear, you're a total softie."

"First, they're lying. Second, you've heard about me, huh?"

I shoot down the interest in his tone. "I'm friends with Payne."

"I knew I never liked that guy." Ford's smile gives him away. "He's actually the reason I'm here myself. Usually my assistant runs errands and things like this for me, but since Payne left the garage, I'm an assistant short. Again."

"That sucks."

"You're telling me. I swear every time I get someone trained up, they move on to something better. But enough of me whining. Which flowers say *your bastard son loves you?*"

"Can't say I've heard that one. Nasturtium is technically for fortieth anniversaries, but I don't stock it because they turn bad so quickly. And I think they're ugly. Gladioli are used too, and I have some of those …" Of course, right across the room. "Ah, there …" I point to a bright bouquet that's closer to Ford than me. He glances in the direction and points at the wrong one.

"This?"

"The next one." As soon as he turns to look, I hurry over and angle my back away again.

Ford eyes me. "You all right?"

"Excited about flowers." I wave my hand over them. "Now, do we want to go traditional with this bunch, or there's the roses, or you could go simple and elegant with something in pastels …"

"What would you pick?"

I point to the one with the gladioli in it. "I'm a traditionalist."

"Easy decision, then."

"Right." I pick up the flowers, and then …

My gaze flicks to the counter on the other side of my shop. Shit.

Ford's watching me again, and there's something too shrewd in his gaze.

I wave my arm. "After you."

"No. After *you*."

Motherfucker. "Guests first."

"Actually, I'm a customer, not a guest, and the customer is always right."

My eyes widen. "I *really* insist."

"So do I, sweetheart." He leans in. "And I'm a stubborn guy. I can do this all day."

A curl of *something* shivers through me. "Okay, so, counter …"

"Ring me up."

I don't move. Sure, I could turn around and laugh it off, but there's something completely *wrong* with Ford having that picture of me in his head. Let's see him think I'm cute with shit all up my back.

"Actually, take them," I say. "They're on the house."

His expression has gone from amused to concerned to *what the hell is going on here?*

I force a smile.

His frown deepens. And he still doesn't take the flowers.

Ford steps to the side, and I jerk around, realizing a second too late that there was nothing natural about my movement.

"Normally I'd assume you're doing some kinda homophobic thing with not wanting to turn your back on the gay man, but …" His eyes light up with mischief. "There's something else going on here, isn't there?"

"Don't know what you mean?"

"Oh. So you *are* homophobic?"

"No, I'm …" I slump. "*Fine.* I was trying to save myself the embarrassment." I suck in and hold a deep breath, then turn and walk to the counter.

His laughter follows me the entire way. "What the fuck did you do?"

"I was watering some flowers, backed up into a pot, knocked it over, and went ass over tits into the mess."

Somehow, his laughter doubles.

"You good yet?" I try to give him a dry look, but my lips twitch.

"Funny how there's no mess left to corroborate your story."

"I cleaned it up!"

"Uh-huh, I'm sure."

"I *did*."

He lifts his hands. "I'm not questioning you."

"You are trying to stir me up though."

"What was that you said about me being nice earlier?"

"Ah … the true Ford comes out." And wow, the teasing note that comes with my words almost, *almost* sounds like flirting. But … why? I'm not interested in a date with him, but even I can recognize there's something about him that's comforting. Thrilling? *Both*? I'm not even sure that's possible. Just talking to him is like waiting in line for a roller coaster.

I ring him up and round the counter to hand over the flowers, but before he takes them, Ford shrugs out of his jacket.

"What are you—"

"Here." He steps forward and loops it around my waist, then ties the sleeves together. This close, I can smell … motor oil … aftershave … sweat … and I don't hate it. It speaks to long days working with his hands, surrounded by cars, getting filthy …

I tear my gaze from his chest and find him watching me. His hands have dropped from his jacket, but we're still way too close.

"Ah, thanks …" I shove the flowers at his chest. "I hope they like them."

He's slow to take the bunch, thick, rough fingers brushing my own. "I'm confident they will."

"Great. Have a …" Fuck, what do I normally say?

He smiles. "You too."

Then he's gone, leaving me with his warm jacket around my waist and a shop that smells like motor oil and … possibility.

2

Ford

I FINISH MY ORDER FOR THE PARTS I NEED SHIPPED IN WHEN A commotion outside my office makes me glance up. Three of my office walls have enormous windows, giving a clear view of almost the entire workshop, and I immediately spot someone who shouldn't be out there.

Orson.

Walking through my workshop with my jacket slung over his shoulder like he's strolling through the fucking daisies instead of between my grease gremlins. And hey, I'm not about to complain.

I lean back in my chair, not bothering to hide my grin as he walks into my office without knocking. Holy Corvette, he looks hot today. Well, *every day*, but today especially. His gray tee is stretched over his chest, silver-streaked scruff trimmed neatly, and fluffy dark hair all styled and shiny. It's tempting me to bury my fingers in it and *tug*.

He lays my heavy jacket over the desk, forearm muscles

bunching with the movement. "You know, most people at least *try* to hide when they're eye-fucking someone."

I chuckle. "You gullible enough to believe I was only trying to remember who you are?"

"Not even close."

"Worth a shot. Besides, I've always been told I can look with my eyes and not with my hands. Just following Momma's rules."

"Respectful mother."

"Bastard son." I give him a quick wink, wanting to move on from this conversation. He says he's straight, so I'm gonna go ahead and believe him, even if the way he eyes me makes me think there's at least a little curiosity there.

I'm not about playing games with men, so if he wants a piece of all this, he's going to have to get to that conclusion on his own.

"Thanks for the jacket," he says. He's got a nice voice. Deep, but not overly so. Kind, light, like he has no problems. Which is horseshit, given he lost his wife and … My gaze strays to the scars on his forearms before I jerk it away again.

"Always gonna help out a damned man in distress," I say.

"And there's the nice guy showing through again."

I grunt. "Determined to ruin my reputation, aren't you?"

"I think I'd have fun doing it. Showing the world what an upstanding gentleman you are."

"An upstanding gentleman who's been to prison?" The words are a test to see how he reacts.

"I've heard those rumors." He eyes me with interest, but the amusement hasn't left his face. Good to know he doesn't scare easy. "Is it true?"

"You're one of only a handful of people to ask me that directly."

"And let me guess, that's all you're gonna give me?"

"Smart man."

"Keep your secrets." He paces slowly, fingertips brushing the things on the edge of my desk as he looks at the framed car posters on the wall behind me. The only wall in my office that isn't almost all glass. "Interesting collection you have up there."

"Yup. Those are my babies."

He hums, eyes lingering a little longer. There are four cars up there. Three are absolute beasts of engineering, and the fourth ... holds more sentimental value than anything.

I wait Orson out, watching as he goes from inspecting the pictures, to the clipboard of jobs hanging by the door, to the filing cabinets sitting along the left wall. He seems to be stalling or ... something. I dunno, but I'm curious. I've been curious about him for a while.

I know Orson is friends with Art and some of the other guys I know around town. They have a group for divorced guys or something, which almost makes me wish I was divorced so I could join. Most of us have grown up in the area, but Orson moved here with his wife after college, then disappeared for a bit after she passed. I'm not surprised he needed to get away, but I was surprised when he returned, opened the florist, and got on with life as though nothing had happened.

"You like cars?" I ask.

"Not really. I mean, they're great transportation." He points at my posters. "And I know that the Bugatti, the Porsche, and the Ferrari up there are all a hell of a lot fancier than a Ford Thunderbird." He lifts his eyebrows. "Is this a name vanity thing? I would have thought you'd be the kind of guy to at least get off over the original."

"So you *do* know cars?"

He smiles. "Never said I didn't. Dad was into them."

"*Was*?"

"He died the same year as Tara."

"Ouch." I wish I'd never asked.

Orson waves my concern away. "I took my time processing it all. Mom too. I miss them, for sure, but it's all part of life." He leans his hip against this side of my desk, close enough that it feels like he's standing over me. I fucking like it. He points at the T-Bird. "So what's the story?"

"Thought I could have my secrets?"

"Oh, come on. I gave you my whole sob story."

"Unlike you, I'm not that gullible." I look pointedly at his scars, and Orson smoothly tucks his arms behind him.

He leans in. "Tell me about the Ford, Ford."

"Ahh … known you for two whole days and you're already a pain in my ass."

"I'm curious."

"Curious *and* gullible. Tell me, how many Nigerian princes have your bank account details?"

"No princes, but about fourteen princesses. They said I'll have the money any day now."

I rub my hand over my mouth to try and hide my smile. Because I'd always known the guy was hot; I'd just never realized he was fun as well. I'd clearly caught him off guard when I bought the flowers yesterday because today, he's a thousand percent more comfortable. Probably helps he doesn't have shit smeared up his back.

"The '73 T-Bird happens to be the car I was born in. My

name was supposed to be Alexander, got changed to Ford instead. I heard that story so many times growing up that the car thing must have been embedded in my brain, and so here we are."

"Huh."

I snort at the single-sound answer. "Well, I'm glad I relayed that story."

"I enjoyed it, if that helps?"

"Immensely."

Orson turns those gorgeous hazel eyes back toward the picture, and I watch as his tongue slides slowly over his bottom lip. My cock takes notice, hyper-interested in that man and his mouth and how all that rough hair would feel on my balls, but I force the interest back down again.

He could be a new friend. Probably shouldn't make this creepy.

But he still isn't leaving.

I lean over to pick up my jacket and get a waft of something floral. "Returned this fast."

"Don't worry, I washed it."

"I wasn't worried about that at all." I gesture to the grease stains all over my jeans. "Hazards of the job."

"Thanks. Again. For letting me borrow it. I got kind of busy, and it wouldn't have been fun to serve customers with my back to the wall all day."

"I could imagine."

"Hey, I know," he says, like he's just had an epiphany, but there's something too tense about his tone for me to believe that. "Why don't I take you out for dinner? As thanks."

"You asking me on a date?"

He laughs and pushes off my desk. "Straight, remember?

Though feeling pretty flattered by how desperately you want to take me out."

"Take you out." I grin evilly. "*Something* like that."

"I want to say thanks. Don't make this weird."

"I think you've done that plenty for the both of us."

He flips me off. "Friday?"

"That's my hookup night."

"Meet at eight at Killer Brew."

My smile is getting bigger by the second. "You gonna bring me flowers?"

"If you play your cards right, I'll even pay."

"Will you put out?"

"Not a chance."

I laugh. "Friday it is."

"See you then."

"Bye … sweetheart."

He shakes his head on the way out the door. "Not a date," he calls.

Which is a damn shame, but I can roll with that. I like having friends, and I'm not going to say no to a free meal. After just two conversations with him, I can already tell I'm going to like hanging out with the man, and the idea that I'm going to see him again is … exciting. I don't get excited about dates anymore—they're usually the lead-up to something transactional—but knowing we're going to go out with no expectations of ending the night in bed together means I need to turn up my personality.

Put in actual effort.

I like the idea of that.

DMC GROUP CHAT

Orson: *You guys know Ford, right? On a scale of one to ten, how likely is he to kill me?*

Art: *Easy nine.*

Orson: *What?*

Payne: *Jfc don't listen to him. He'd be lucky to be a one.*

Griff: *He's a total ten ... in hotness.*

Art: *Yeah, but your opinion doesn't count when you'd say that about anyone.*

Griff: *No way. Beau's a twelve ;)*

Payne: *Can I leave this chat yet?*

Art: *You pretend to be exasperated by us, but we all remember the Night of The Drunken Jealousy that you put us through.*

Payne: *please don't give it capitals.*

Griff: *Art's right, it was a real event.*

Orson: *... I'm sure none of this is what I opened my phone to talk about.*

3

Orson

I PACE FROM ONE SIDE OF THE ROOM, SPIN ON MY HEEL, AND pace back again. Art chuckles from behind the bar and slides a drink my way. Ginger ale, I'm guessing, since I don't touch alcohol. Haven't for a long time, which Art knows better than anyone.

At first, he wasn't sure about us always hanging out here at Killer Brew, thinking I'd slip back into that place where alcohol was my crutch, but I was never addicted, and I'm actually reasonably happy with the way my life is now. Going back to how I was holds no appeal.

"You're awfully nervous, considering this isn't a date."

I shake my head, ignoring the drink. "I'm not nervous."

"Eh, Ford has that effect on people."

My lips twitch when I think of Ford. Sure, he's big, but my nervousness doesn't stem from *that*. And like I said, I'm *not* nervous, more … unsettled.

Outside of my friends with the DMC, I don't have a life.

I work at the shop, hang out with Art or Griff or Keller, and … that's it. Adding another friend into the mix, one who I haven't met through Art, feels like a big thing.

I first moved to Kilborough when I was … twenty-seven? Twenty-eight? I made a few friends in that time, but other than Art, most of them were tied to Tara, and when she died, none of them knew how to handle me. I stuck around in town for a few months, but on what should have been her thirty-fifth birthday, I up and left with no plans to return.

If it wasn't for Art, I probably wouldn't have.

"Looking deep in thought over there," Art says.

"What am I *doing*?"

"What do you mean?"

I run both hands roughly over my stubble. "You're right. I'm basically taking him on a date."

"Relax, Orson. Grown-ass men can have dinner together. He does it with Barney at least once a month."

"*Leif's* Barney?" I don't know why that's so unexpected. Of course Ford has friends. He's always lived here, so he likely knows everyone. Barney and Art are the ones who started the Divorced Men's Club together, and Barney … he doesn't strike me as the type of guy who could handle Ford. Friend or otherwise. "I didn't know Ford and Barney were close."

"Eh, they went on a date before Barney and Leif were a thing."

A date? Of course they did. "And … now they still get dinner together."

"As friends. Which you're apparently doing, though you kinda sound like you want to get into a pissing contest with Barney."

"Don't be ridiculous."

"Can I give you advice?"

"Why are you asking when we both know you're going to give it anyway?"

His sly grin crosses his face. "Don't forget to douche."

"Fuck you, man."

"No, but for real. Payne's found his man, Griff's moving on with … whatever the hell Griff's doing. Ever since you've gotten back here, you've laid low, and hey, not on me to judge your journey, but you look *excited* over hanging out with Ford. That's good. It's breathing some life back into you."

"Still straight."

"I'm not saying this shit has to get romantic—though you'd be an idiot to draw some arbitrary straight line in the sand, if you start realizing there's more there—just pointing out that friendships can be strong too. And important."

"Course they are. Why do you think I haven't managed to shake you yet?" It's easier to address the main point than his random segue. *If* there's more. Straight men don't randomly turn queer. Not for one man. Well, I'm sure there are some exceptions, but it's not the rule. And I'm not an *exceptions* kind of guy.

But *if*—and that's a very strong if—there was something … maybe it wouldn't be the worst thing.

I haven't slept with anyone since getting back here. It's been a lot of long, lonely years on that front, and I'm hesitant to break my celibacy for just anyone. I've done the cheap hookups and one-night stands. The self-destructive sex for the sake of a high. It only left me feeling like dirt, and I made the decision that I'd never go back there.

So the thought of exploring more with anyone—let alone another man—is overwhelming. I can't picture it. It's been way too long since relationships were on my radar. So I revert to my default when things get too much; I let time happen and be there for the ride.

My eyes catch on the old clock above the bar. "Fuck. I should probably go down."

"*Yep.*" Art rounds the bar to plant both hands on my shoulders. "You're a strong, independent man. You got this."

I slap his hands away. "Maybe if I make friends with Ford, I can finally rid myself of you and your motivational quotes."

"I'm like herpes. Once you have me, there's no turning back."

I chuckle as I walk away. "Do you hear yourself sometimes?"

"All the time. I love the sound of my own voice."

I flick him a wave as I carry my ginger ale down the stairs, leaving him behind on the deserted mezzanine level. The bar below is already busy, and I purposely don't look around to see if he's here yet because if he is and he's watching me, there's every chance I'll trip over my own feet and end up sprawled at the bottom of the stairs.

Whose bright idea was Friday night? Friday nights are *date* nights. I'd been so confident the other day, strutting into his office like I owned the place, and now … I laugh at my stupidity. What am I even thinking? This obviously isn't a date when I have no interest in him like that. Damn, I need to get out of my head.

And not a minute too soon. I spot Ford sitting at a bar table across the room, talking with the guy who's stopped beside him.

He's kinda familiar-looking. Feminine name, I think.

Pretty. Younger. And … touching Ford's arm. All my attention narrows in on the supposedly casual gesture.

Stamping down my irritation, I slide onto the stool across from Ford. "I'm barely two minutes late and you're replacing me already."

His attention snaps from … *Molly*—that's it—and lands square on me. "You should see what I can do with three."

"I'm terrified already."

He chuckles and turns back to Molly. "Good seeing you again, darlin'."

"You too." That little fucker flutters his eyes.

I watch Molly leave, mostly with amusement. "Huh."

"Huh, what?" he asks.

"Here I was thinking you were serious all those times you asked me out, but apparently, I'm not your type."

Ford chuckles and drains his beer. "Molly's been trying to sleep with me for years. Still haven't gone there."

"Why not?"

"Not sure, really. I'm not usually too picky, can't be around here, but I get a vibe from him."

I'm leaning in. "A vibe?"

"Yeah, the kinda vibe where sleeping with him will just be fucking myself over. Pretty sure one time is all it'd take for us to have monogrammed towels and matching rings."

Wow. That's … I dunno how I'm supposed to react to that. One time with Molly and he'd be hooked for life? Maybe I should have walked away and let them have this.

"Huh."

He lets out that bark of laughter. "You like that sound."

"I'm … processing."

Ford nudges the menu my way. "Process away, but while

you do that, pick some food. Since you're paying, I might as well order one of everything."

"I didn't say I was paying."

"You said you were if I play my cards right, and when it comes to dates, I'm always on my A game."

"Not a date."

"Potato-pot*ah*to."

"It doesn't work that way."

His smile is crooked behind his beard, and no matter how many times I see him, I'm reminded of an overgrown child. An *evil* child who's plotting how to take out the babysitter, and as my eyes trail over him, they catch on the bump right above his nipple. It *almost* looks like he has a piercing. "You mean I wore my only pair of clean jeans for nothing?"

"I told you there would be no putting out."

"Ahh, you break my heart."

Fucking idiot. I nod Molly's way. "It's okay. You have options here."

"Don't need options when I'm focused on our date."

"Not a date."

"Geez, so fixated on the details." Ford pretends to turn his attention to the menu.

"I'm regretting this already."

"No, we can't have that. Quick, let's order drinks." He goes to get up, but I throw an arm out.

I'm never ashamed to tell people I don't drink, but it's not my favorite conversation after some of the reactions I've had over the years. "I don't, ah, drink …"

"What's that, then?" He points at my almost empty glass.

"Ginger ale."

"And that's not a drink?"

"It's not an *alcoholic* drink."

Understanding lights up behind his eyes. "Then you can still have *a* drink with me. It doesn't have to be a hard one."

It's an instant relief not to be questioned over it. "Sounds good."

"My shout. I never expect my date to pay for everything."

I don't bother answering him this time, and he looks way too smug as he walks away. He *is* wearing clean jeans. Tight ones. They're practically molded to his strong legs. I rip my eyes away and throw back the last of my drink while I wait for him. It only takes a few minutes before he's sliding in across from me.

"Okay, since apparently you're the expert on what's a date and what isn't …" He holds up one hand and uses it to shield him pointing with the other. "Those guys. Mates or dates?"

I glance at the two men a table over. They're joking around about something, and while I can hear them talking, they're not loud enough for me to make out actual words. The guy closest to us leans over the table and drops his voice to a barely audible murmur, and whatever he says morphs the other guy's expression from smiling to shocked.

"Umm … date?"

Ford bursts out laughing. "I hope not. They're brothers."

"Shit." I bury my face in my hand. "Best of three?"

"And if you lose?"

"Yeah, we're not turning this into a bet. I don't trust you not to lie."

"Damn, what happened to gullible?"

"I still have *some* self-preservation instincts working for me."

"Fine, I guess we'll do this for …" He shudders. "Fun?"

"Works for me."

Ford's dark eyes trail over the room and pause on a couple at the bar. "Those two."

"Date and married."

"Damn it." He sizes me up. "How did you know?"

"Because it's their three-year wedding anniversary. He came in today to buy flowers."

"Could have been his mistress."

"I like my chances."

"Good call. One to go though." Ford lifts his glass to take a deep sip, and I eye the dark color. Spirits mixed with Coke, maybe?

Before I can ask, he jumps. "Oooh. There. Those two."

I follow his gaze across the room to a pair of teenage girls. They're holding hands and giggling, but— "No fair."

"What?" he asks innocently.

"There's no way for me to know. Besides, I feel creepy staring at girls that young."

"Staring isn't going to get you answers anyway. Teenage girls are an anomaly."

"You basically cheated."

"Can't cheat when there are no rules."

I prop my chin on my palm and chance a quick look back at the girls. "Why do I get the feeling you live by those words?"

"I could confirm or deny, but I think it'd be more fun to stick around and find out."

Strangely, I agree with him. "Okay. The girls. Clearly … friends."

Ford makes an obnoxious buzzer noise. "And that's the game. Two-one to Ford Thomas. You owe me a lap dance, sweetheart."

My eyes fly wide, but maybe not for the reason he thinks.

He's quick to lift his hands. "Fucking joking. Calm down, hetty."

"Hetty?"

"You're my hetero-bro. Don't worry, I get it. The whole date thing is me lightening the mood. You don't need to worry about me coming on to you or taking advantage or whatever shit crossed your mind. I'm naturally flirty, but obviously, it makes you uncomfortable, so I'll quit—"

"Don't." My hand flies out to cover his forearm before I can stop it, and I quickly snatch it back again. "I'm not uncomfortable. It's not that. It's ..."

He eyes me like he's trying to read whether to believe me or not, and *screw it*. He has no idea how close he was with his lap dance joke.

A groan sneaks out, and I lean closer. "Promise to keep it to yourself."

Mischief fills those dark eyes, and he leans in too. "Pinky swear." He actually holds out his pinky, so I link it with mine. And just like when I touched his arm, he's so warm, so ... well, it just feels really nice to touch another person again.

"*Iusedtobeastripper.*"

Ford blinks at me. His mouth slowly inches open. "Come again?"

"I used to be a—"

"Oh no, I got that. I mean, I think I'm about to come again." He pulls a face and reaches down between his legs. "Fuck me, that's hot."

My head falls back on a laugh, and I point at him. "Our secret."

"You're telling me no one knows?"

"No one."

"Not even Art?"

"Do you seriously not know what *no one* means?"

"Wow. No need to get feisty ..." Ford still looks a little stunned, and it feels good to have caught him off guard. "Why'd you tell *me*?"

"Well, we're friends, right? Last thing I'd want is for you to think I'm some homophobic dickwad because you made a lucky guess."

He cocks his head. "So the flirting is still cool, then?"

"Well, I wouldn't want you to discriminate ..." I spread my hands like there's nothing I can do rather than tell him I *like* it when he flirts with me. It's fun. Different. He keeps things interesting.

"Tell me, does saying all I can picture is you taking off your shirt and thrusting on that bar top fall under flirting or creeping?"

"It definitely toes the line." We meet eyes. Smiling, always smiling. "But I'll allow it."

DMC GROUP CHAT

Griff: *So ... date with Ford, huh?*

    Orson: *Dammit, Art! Ignore him. It was a date.*

    Orson: *WASN'T. I meant wasn't.*

    Payne: *...*

    Orson: *I meant wasn't! Fucking autocorrect. We just met up for dinner and kinks.*

    Orson: *DRINKS!*

    Art: *Oh, this is gold.*

    Orson: *You know what, I don't need to explain myself.*

4

Ford

I walk into Oopsie Daisies—one of the only places in town not named after the Kilborough Penitentiary that drives our tourism—for the billionth time this month. And maybe that's a slight exaggeration, but considering I'd never stepped foot in here before a month ago, the place has become familiar.

Which could possibly be because of my sudden flower-buying obsession.

Even with a new assistant, I can't keep myself away.

Orson glances up from where he's leaning on his counter, doing a crossword puzzle. "Good timing. Motor part that starts with *P*."

"Pistons."

"So clever." He folds his arms over the counter rather than writing anything down.

"You already had it, didn't you?"

"First guess, yeah."

"Smart-ass." I turn my attention to the flowers rather than his knowing stare.

"What's the occasion this time?" he asks.

"Jeff's mother's retiring."

"And Jeff is …"

"My newest hire." I puff out my chest, daring him to call me on it, but Orson doesn't even laugh. I catch him biting his lip against one, though, before he schools his face and approaches me.

"In that case, daisies and daffodils. Something bright. Promising." He points to a yellow bunch that has a few purple tones throughout.

"Maybe something red?"

"Sure." He shrugs and points across the store. "I didn't realize you were trying to get her into bed."

I snort. "Even if I wasn't gay, I wouldn't cross those lines."

"What happened to not being picky?"

"I'm definitely not, but I also have standards. They've gotta be available, and they've gotta be interested. I don't chase."

"That so?"

And maybe we're only making conversation, but it's one of the truest things I've told him. If someone's with me, it's because they want to be with me. Sure, it's usually only sex, but whether it's one night or many, I like to know I have my partner's attention. I have a bit of an ego about that, so sue me. I lean over to nudge Orson. "Changed my mind. Show me something blue."

"Hope works."

"Sure. That." But we both know I'm gonna end up with those yellow ones he showed me first. We've done this a few times now, Orson leading me around his shop, making recommendations while I shoot down every one until we wind up back at the start. See, after the first two times of buying the first bunch he showed me, I realized that once I've paid, I don't have a reason to stick around. And those few minutes of his company aren't enough.

Neither is a solid half an hour of teasing, if I'm honest.

He leans down to replace the latest bouquet, and my gaze lands squarely on his ass. *Damn*, that's a booty. My gaze slips to his waist and follows the lines of muscle up to his broad shoulders, and while I've never seen him out of clothes, I can only imagine what he's packing under there.

The guy used to be a stripper? I don't think he has any clue how hot that image is.

He straightens and sets his hands on his hips as he turns to me. "Any other color you'd like to see?"

I grin, and his lips twitch before I've even said a thing.

"I've heard yellow's a good choice."

"Have you really? Follow me, then." He leads me back to the yellow and purple lot. "How about these?"

I don't even look at them. "Perfect."

I swear Orson almost rolls his eyes before he grabs them and returns to the counter. His movements are fast and practiced as he rolls the bunch in two layers of paper. One brown, one kinda clear.

"Got a busy day?" I ask.

"Wednesdays are mostly inventory than anything else. As far as I'm concerned, if it's not Sunday, it's not busy. That day kills me so much I need to take the next two days to recover."

Sundays, he has a booth at the market inside Killer Brew.

I hadn't realized how much of a business there was for flowers, but he says he's doing well for himself.

"Wanna meet me for lunch?"

He smirks. "You know my terms."

"But it was *totally* a date."

"Keep going," he says, handing the flowers over. Then he lets out a completely fake sigh. "I guess we'll never hang out again."

I'm so torn. On one hand, I love teasing him, and I've been carrying on about this date thing for so long it feels like losing to agree that what we had wasn't a date. Even though it wasn't. If we'd been on a date, there'd be no way to dispute it.

But Orson also said we won't be hanging out again until I admit it was just two friends having dinner, and after a couple of weeks, I'm running out of reasons for needing flowers. I'm gonna have to cave soon. Damn him for being someone I actually feel good around. For his confidence and his sneaky smiles and the way he doesn't shy away from meeting my eyes.

"Fine."

He lights up like he's won, and nope, can't do it.

"Mighty *fine* date we had."

He points at me. "You're a stubborn mule."

I tug a flower out of the ones I'm holding and pass it to him. "For you, sweetheart."

"And now I can resell it. Even better."

"Resell?" I splutter. "That's a friendship flower, and you better goddamn treasure it."

"For the handful of days it's alive? I shall."

And … that's it. I've paid, he's given me my things, and we're still no closer to hanging out again.

I linger, not wanting to leave but having no reason to stay. "Think I've got my cousin's boyfriend's aunt's thing next week. I'll see you then."

"Yeah." He crosses his arms over the counter again. "See you then."

As soon as I'm out of sight of the sweet-smelling shop, I hang my head back dramatically. What was that I said about not chasing men? And here's me after a fucking straight one. Even to be friends, this whole thing is a bit much. I don't *need* friends, I'm not lonely, I've got my shit sorted.

But that little seed of instalust I've always had for him has exploded into this buzzing desire to be around him. Just around. I don't get like that with men. I have hookups, and I have friends like Barney, whose company I enjoy, but I don't get this crawling under my skin after a few days of not seeing them. That's all Orson.

I'm aware that I've developed a bit of a crush on the guy, but that side of things is harmless. Crushes come and go. And maybe I should let this one fade away into nothing, but I have genuine fun around him. The kind that floods a truck-load of adrenaline into my veins.

I catch a woman about to walk past and hold the flowers out to her. "For you, darlin'. Turns out I don't need them anymore."

"Oh." She takes them stiffly. "Thank you?"

I don't blame her for phrasing it like a question. I can read the *what do you want* in her eyes, but I just give her a friendly smile and a nod, then keep walking. No point terrorizing people trying to make it through hump day.

Work is the same as usual, and once the bookwork and ordering is taken care of, I head out into the warehouse to help my grease gremlins look after our babies. The general population doesn't know how to look after their cars and doesn't show them the respect they deserve. They're incredible machines, useful, and if you look after them, they'll look after you.

I like that. The reliability.

"What's up with you?" Taylor asks, climbing out of the driver's side of an old Nissan.

"Nothing, why?"

"You're very introspective. I don't think I've ever seen you this quiet."

They're right. Normally, I'm the one singing my pipes out to the music, talking to the cars, or running my people through something they need to know. It's not often I'm still.

"I think I've gotten myself into a bit of a shit situation."

"Yeah?"

"Straight dude."

Their bubble-gum-pink lips form an O.

"No need for that judgment."

"Just saying, I thought you were smarter than that."

"Don't worry, I am. I'm not about to end up heartbroken or anything. I … I like him in general. To hang out with. But I can't stop flirting with him."

Taylor lifts an eyebrow. "Is there a single person alive you don't flirt with? You're not even interested in women, and I've seen you make them swoon."

"Fair point, but …"

"He's straight and hates it?" they guess.

"He's straight, and I think he might *like* it."

"Huh. Well, hey. He's not caught up in toxic masculinity, so yay him?"

I bite my tongue against mentioning the times Orson's eyes catch on me that bit longer than feels natural. For all I know, he's a visual kinda guy. A real lookie-loo who thinks nothing of staring at men like he wants to know what they taste like. Dammit. It's these thoughts that are making this friendship more complicated than it needs to be, but I can't make myself stop. The teasing is addictive.

Clearly, the gas fumes are getting to me.

"So what's wrong with this old girl?" I ask, focusing the conversation back to an area where I know what the hell I'm talking about.

"Starter clutch is fucked."

"Got a price for them?"

"On my way to do that now." Taylor hesitates. "Unless you need to talk some more?"

"Nah." I wave them off. "I'll be fine."

Not a lie either. Maybe I need to go to Oopsie Daisies tomorrow morning with a coffee offering and my tail between my legs, admitting that it wasn't a date and that any other times we hang out won't be either. It'd be the truth. And it'd get me what I want, which is more time with him.

Giving in shouldn't be this hard.

Maybe we could catch up Friday night again? Or for lunch one day this week? Saturdays are busy at the shop, so that day's out, and then Sundays, he's run off his feet at the market. He really should get some help with that.

Wait ...

I might have found my loophole.

A laugh spills from my mouth as I grab the remote and turn the garage speakers up, already looking forward to the weekend.

5

Orson

IT'S NOT EVEN DAWN WHEN I PARK MY VAN IN THE BACK LOT of Killer Brew and cut the engine. I'm still half-hazy with sleep, but I manage a smile toward the soft glow on the dark horizon. Even on the days that I'm not feeling it, I try to keep perspective. Life is so damn fleeting. Tara can attest to that. Or she *could* if it wasn't for the stroke, but since she isn't here, I live every day in her memory.

There are days where I fail. Moments I become too self-absorbed and focus on the negative. But being alive is a gift, and while I might not appreciate it every minute, I always *try* to do better.

So yes, I'm still tired, but I'm going to get out of my van and spend the day making a stable living doing something I love while I get to hear stories about other people's lives.

It might not be a big thing, but having those moments of connection throughout the day helps me feel like I'm living through them. Birthday parties and anniversaries, celebrations and apologies. The flowers bought for funerals are always the hardest, but I need those too. The moments to connect with someone grieving and remember what it's like, then the time after when I let the pain go. It doesn't get easier, but it reminds me of my resolve to stay positive.

Just as I reach for the handle, my door is yanked open, and the internal light floods the cabin, giving my heart a good jump start. It takes a second for me to recognize Ford standing in front of me.

"You gonna sit there all morning, or what?"

I grab my keys, then climb out, eyeing him. "You strike me as the sleep-in-on-Sundays type. Are you actually here, or am I still in bed, dreaming about my workday?"

"Naw, you dream about me?"

"Haven't yet."

He hisses like he's in pain. "Couldn't let me have it, could you?"

"Remind me, was that dinner or a date we had?"

That keeps him quiet. And while we both know what the truth of it was, I like the teasing. Him not giving in gives us *something*, and I wish I hadn't thrown out the spur-of-the-moment comment about not getting dinner with him again if he was going to get the wrong idea. Because now I'm stuck. Wanting to hang out but not wanting to be wrong. I call him stubborn, but I'm no better.

"Coffee?" Ford asks, holding a cup out to me.

"Why does this feel like a bribe?"

"Not at all," he says, taking a sip of his own. "But I figured we're gonna need them to get through today."

"*We?*"

The smug look he gets so often appears. "I figured it was this or sit around bored at home. Congratulations, you won over my couch."

"High honors." I round the back of the van and pull open the doors. "You're going to regret your decision, but I'll enjoy the help while I have it."

"I work in a garage all day. I think I can handle this."

"Did I say you couldn't?" Handling it isn't going to be an issue. The actual transaction of the flowers he'll be able to do with his eyes closed, but when people start asking about symbolism and which are the best for a dinner party and which will impress someone with understated elegance is when he'll struggle.

But hey, at least I can take a piss break this week without having to close everything up.

We load up the carts with buckets of flowers and head inside.

The other vendors are trickling in nice and early, getting their stalls ready for when the doors open at seven. Conversation and laughter filters through the brewery, along with the occasional thud of stock being shifted and whir of machines coming to life. This has been my every Sunday for years now. It's outside of a corporate nine-to-five, outside of me desperately counting calories to keep the only job I'd been able to hold down during my spiral—this is where contentment lives.

I smile at Amber and Steve, who are setting up their produce stand next to mine, and drop the buckets off. It takes us a few trips with the carts between the van and the booth to get everything, but having Ford's help makes the process much faster.

"You only came in once this week," I say to Ford as I get to work setting up my display. "Running light on events in Kilborough?"

"Got my receptionist's daughter's teacher chocolates instead. Had to give you a chance to miss me, after all."

"Chocolates? Wow. Why do I feel like you've cheated on me?"

"Now probably isn't a great time to mention the balloon bouquet I've ordered, then, huh?"

I pretend to shudder. "It's like you don't even care."

Ford laughs. "I don't get up at the ass-crack of dawn for just anyone."

"Technically, it's not dawn yet," I point out, trying and failing not to like his words too much.

"The gooch of day, then."

I snigger. "Do me a favor and don't wish anyone gooch morning."

"You're going to take all the fun out of today, aren't you?"

"I'll let you have fun. I'm just stating up front that I'm banning all mention of body parts."

"But what if someone says they want balls in their flowers?" He points at a bunch where most of the flowers haven't bloomed yet.

"Those are buds. The stick part is a stem—if you call it a shaft, I'll have to ask you to leave."

The grin he gives me tells me that's exactly what he was going to do.

"The prices will be on everything. All you need to do is ring each customer up, and leave the flower talk to me."

"Now I can't even talk to people?" He throws up his heavily tattooed arms. "I gave up *The Bachelor* for this."

"The … Bachelor?"

"Dumbass trash TV is my weakness."

"I don't even own a TV."

My confession is met with silence like it so often is.

"No … TV?"

"It's never been my thing. If I want to watch a movie, I do it on my computer, but …" I shrug. The bewilderment on his face doesn't fade.

"So you've never been exposed to the seedy goodness of reality show drama?"

"Never."

"Okay, I'm adding that to our list."

I cock my head. "Our list of …"

"Things to do together," he says like it should be obvious. "You know, when we're allowed to actually hang out again."

I finish getting my display right, then join him behind the counter in the booth. The doors will open soon, but right now, it's peaceful. "We're hanging out now."

"No, we're *working* now. We won't even get a chance to talk once it's busy, so we're not going to pretend like today is all fun and games."

Joke's on him, though, because working together or not, I'm glad he's here. We spend the next little while running through how to take payment, and I try not to be too focused on the way Ford's arm is pressed against mine. Or how much taller than me he is. I'm a reasonably tall guy, but Ford is enormous. It's … interesting.

I glance up at him to find him way closer than I was expecting. "Does that make sense?"

"Sure does." He offers a small smile. "I'm glad I came this morning."

And I can't bring myself to respond to that with anything other than the truth. "Yeah, me too."

Ford's smile turns wicked. "I didn't realize you cared that much about my sex life."

Of *course*. "Should have known that's what you meant."

"Uh-huh. And now I can check out your ass every time you bend over without getting boned up."

My head falls back on a laugh. "Still straight, Ford."

"Still gay, Orson."

I've been around more than enough queer men not to be uncomfortable by his flirting, but I never thought I'd actually enjoy it. "In that case, look all you want. But no touching."

"I've been aware of the rules since middle school, sweetheart."

I pick up my spare apron and hand it over. "Suit up. We're about to open."

After that, Ford's right. We don't get much time to talk. It's not that I'm run off my feet or anything, but I have enough of a constant stream throughout the day that when one customer wanders off, the next arrives, and whenever one of us ducks off for a drink or a piss, we come back to a few people waiting.

There's one other florist in town, but he's mostly retired and sells from his property, so business here is always hot. Today is less about the celebration gifts and more that when people pick up their produce for the week, they grab some flowers for their homes as well. I'm only too happy to supply that spot of happiness in their lives.

"… and the blue ones will be good for that."

I turn toward Ford's voice and find him chatting with a lady a little younger than us.

"Supposed to help with creativity, and hell, if it doesn't,

you've still got these things to look at while you work all day."

"Good point. I'll grab them."

He rings her up, and after she's walked away, I approach. "Creativity?"

Ford's face drops. "That *is* what you said, right?"

"Ah ... once. Weeks ago. You remembered that?"

"Not exactly hard information to remember," he teases before jumping to life to help someone else. But after that, I keep a closer eye on him, realizing that not only did he remember that fact about blue flowers, but he's remembered ... well, maybe everything I've ever told him.

"A triathlon coming up?" he asks, and his loud voice carries. "You'll want something fun. High energy. These orange ones are good for that."

My eyes narrow, and after the couple leave, I pull him aside. "Now, that's one I *haven't* taught you. You've been researching your flowers."

"Maybe." He pinches his thumb and forefinger a tiny bit apart. Then he sags. "Fine. You caught me. I might have a small issue with incompetence, so I brushed up on learning everything I could before today."

That's ... well, it proves this morning wasn't a spur-of-the-moment decision. My mouth goes oddly dry at the thought, and I scramble to find some way to tease him over it, but I've got nothing.

Ford chuckles. "You've got some dirt ..." He lifts a hand but freezes right before he makes contact with my face. I don't pull back, oddly on edge as I wait to see what he does. Neither of us breaks eye contact as Ford's large, warm hand rests along my jaw and his rough thumb rubs my cheekbone.

"There ... all gone."

"Thanks."

He doesn't move for another second or two, and then his fingers skim my skin as he releases me.

I clear my throat and turn to check if I need to move some flowers around, anything to get a bit of space from him and that overpowering presence he has.

"At this rate, I'm going to have to pay you double."

He snorts. "I'm not taking your money."

"But you're working. I'm not letting you do it for free."

"I told you, this is my boredom cure. An interesting way for me to spend my Sunday."

"I can't let you help me without being paid."

"I'm not here for a paycheck. I don't need it."

"Then what are you—"

The look Ford throws my way cuts me off. "Don't insult both of our intelligence by asking that question."

And as much as I love the implication that he only wants to spend time with me, I need to be clear about something first.

"I … I really like you, and I don't want you getting the wrong idea," I say in a rush.

"So you've said. You never had friends before, Orson? Sometimes people just like to hang out with people."

"Well, that makes sense considering I like to hang out with you."

Ford holds out his hands. "See? I'm doing us both a favor by being here. You're welcome."

"In that case, I'll take one for the team too. Dinner after this. My treat. I won't even make you eat your words about last time."

"I'd love that." His sincerity catches me off guard.

"Another date. Careful, Orson. You'll be falling for me before long."

Damn, the big idiot makes me laugh. "I'll try to control myself."

"Wish you wouldn't." He winks. "It'd be far more fun for both of us that way."

For the first time, those words give me pause. *Am* I controlling myself around him? The thought of walking up to Ford and kissing him is … I shake the image out of my head, but it bobs back to the surface. I'm not sure exactly what I'm feeling other than a weird mix of discomfort and curiosity, but I can't deny the way my pulse spikes over the image.

My friends kissing other men doesn't even register with me. Beau and Payne are together all the time, and I've seen Art hook up with way more men than I've ever wanted to, but I don't give those things a second thought. It's like when Keller hooks up with women.

It's a nonevent.

But planting *myself* in the image with another man is where things get murky.

Especially when that man is Ford.

I can deny my interest all I like, but there's definitely some kind of chemistry between us. I'm drawn to him. Want to be around him.

I said I'd let time happen and see how things unfold, but if I'm holding back, then how will I ever know?

So I make a resolve.

From now on, if Ford asks to hang out, I'm going to say yes. Anything more than that is down to my gut and how I feel at the time, but when it comes to friends, I'm in this completely.

Now, let's see how long it takes for him to get sick of me.

6

Ford

BARNEY'S WAITING AT OUR USUAL TABLE AT FREE TALK— named after Rodney Talkoma, one of the few prisoners who successfully escaped Kilborough Penitentiary—and I cross the restaurant to get to him. Normally I'm here first, straight from work and settled in with a beer, but not only have I been distracted all day, but we had a late shipment of parts, which required some calling around to a few clients whose cars are waiting.

"About time," Barney says, picking up the menu before I've had a chance to sit. I'm surprised he hasn't ordered already since he's usually starving by the time he gets here, but I guess his politeness won out over his belly.

"Got held up at work."

"I can see that. Let's order before we do anything, otherwise, I might launch across the table and devour your arm."

"I got something else you could devour."

Barney laughs. "I dare you to say that around Leif."

"Hey, he's the one who set us up on that date."

"*Before* we were together. He's very possessive of me."

"He knows he's got a good thing." And even though it sounds like I'm flirting, it's the truth. Barney is cool. Straw-colored hair, chunky, pretty eyes, and a naive sweetness that basically radiates from him. We both knew right away our date was a dud, but something else between us clicked. An easy friendship that led to almost weekly catch-ups.

With any luck, Orson and I will end up the same way. And after dinner with him last night, I'm confident we're heading in that direction. He's easy to talk to … and look at. And when I flirt with him, I mean it, even though my gut tells me it'll go nowhere.

Our server comes over and takes our order, allowing Barney to finally relax.

"Soda?" he asks. "I don't think I've ever known you to order that."

"Eh, trying something different."

He eyes me, confused. "Since when do you pass up a chance to drink?"

"Maybe I'm watching my weight."

"Uh-huh. Yeah. Me too," he says dryly, patting his stomach. "What's the real reason?"

"It's nothing deep. I had dinner with someone who doesn't drink, and it made me realize how much I do. Figured I'd see if I'm just as charming without it."

"That answer wasn't anywhere near as juicy as I'd hoped for."

I laugh. "Sorry to disappoint. Three things?"

"I'll go first."

Three things is something we came up with early on to make sure our dinners are never awkward. Each of us lists three things that are new or different since we last met up, which gives us shit to talk about, and even though we don't need it anymore, it's a habit. Plus, I think it gives Barney something to focus on throughout the week.

Barney holds his hand out and ticks off his things on his fingers. "We finally got those Build Your Own Kill Pen sets for the store." The tourists will love them. "I think I'm developing an allergy to coconut, and Leif bought a swing."

I almost choke on the water I've taken a sip of. The way the pink in his cheeks is deepening tells me it isn't your standard swing.

"Obviously, there's one of those things I want to expand on first."

He nods. "Yeah, the allergy came out of nowhere. I was eating and—"

"Swing. Details. Lots of details."

"What details do you want? Leif came home with it yesterday as a surprise, but we have to hang it properly, so we haven't tried it yet."

"Wow. What a tease."

"It is." A small shiver races over him. "I can't wait though."

"You gonna be comfortable with that?" When he and Leif first got together, Barney was self-conscious about his weight, but those issues have simmered down. Barney's got even more padding to love now, and he and Leif are stronger than ever.

"Yep. Hard not to be when Leif can never seem to get enough."

I chuckle. "Yeah, when I've got a man of my own, I'll be exactly the same way." And because I like to tease, I can't stop myself from adding, "Hopefully, he'll want to spread his legs for me as much as you do for Leif."

Barney's whole face goes red. "I regret telling you that every day."

"And yet, that doesn't deter you from telling me about your sex life."

He takes a long gulp of water, avoiding answering me. We both know he'll continue to do it because he loves talking about Leif. Leif and sex are his two favorite topics, no matter how embarrassed he might be getting the words out. He told me once that he checked with Leif whether he cared that people knew what they did in the bedroom, and Leif gave his full approval, so I have zero guilt about greedily listening to how happy they are together.

"Your three," Barney says, turning the attention onto me.

"Ah, right." I struggle to remember what I'd decided on telling him. "The soapbox derby got some good donations of parts this year, I hired a new assistant, and … I spent all day yesterday with Orson, and it still wasn't enough."

"Wait." Barney leans over the table. "*Our* Orson?"

"The one and only." Barney and Art both started the Divorced Men's Club and always talk about the members like their own little family. I swear hearing about the support and closeness those guys have almost makes me wish I was divorced. Almost. When I find love, I kinda want that to be it. My one and only.

Until then, I have my cars.

"Shit … he's straight though."

"He is."

"And …"

I lean back in my chair, ready to have this conversation. This reality check of going after a straight man and how idiotic it is. "It would be a total lie to say there's nothing there. He's hot, and I really like him, but I'm trying not to think about all that."

"How does he make you feel?"

Thinking of Orson, picturing his face and the way my cheeks hurt whenever we're together, makes my entire body prickle with awareness. "Alive."

Barney's expression fills with pity. "I'm sorry, Ford."

"Yeah, yeah." I wave a hand like I don't care. "He's a cool guy, and I'd like the chance to be friends. I just need these dumb little feelings to be on their way a bit faster."

"And if they don't?"

"Don't what?" I'm playing dumb and terrible at it.

"Go away, obviously. What do you do then?"

I shrug. "Deal with it. Give us space or whatever. The worst part is …"

Barney cocks his head for me to go on.

"I get a vibe from him. Only sometimes. But it feels like there's more there, and it gets me confused."

"Ford …"

"I know." I raise both hands. "Just saying what's on my mind."

"And if you're right and he's curious?"

That's the part I'm unsure of. If Orson asked me to suck his cock, I'm not so sure I'd say no. It's been a long time since I did the straight-boy thing, and never with anyone I've actually liked. Mostly, it was closeted guys in high school and a few I've met out wanting their first—so they say— taste of dick. Those times I was only too happy to help out because I got what I wanted out of the arrangement: an orgasm.

With Orson … I'm scared it wouldn't be so straight-forward.

"If he's curious," I finally answer. "I'd show him what he was missing out on."

Barney doesn't look convinced. Apparently, he's learned to read me better than I thought. "And you won't get hurt?"

"I never said that, but I figure the tradeoff of getting to see him naked would be worth it."

"Maybe, but … look, I know what it's like to be in love with someone and feel like they'd never love you back." He and Leif were both head over heels for each other for at least a year before they figured themselves out.

I chuckle. "I appreciate the concern, but no one said anything about love."

"Maybe not yet." His blue eyes get rounder. "But it's sneaky shit. You don't notice it coming, and *wham*, you're down for the count."

"I'll keep that in mind." Not that I need to. A crush is one thing; love is a whole other ball game that I have no interest in playing with someone so set on holding on to their straightness.

"And Molly?" Barney asks.

I sigh at the guy's name. "Cute, sweet, but too young for me."

"He's twenty-six now …"

"And I'm forty-two. Way too old to be babysitting."

"Fair enough."

Our food is brought out, thankfully putting an end to that conversation. Molly has been flirting with me for years now, and while I can acknowledge that he's attractive and I could probably go there, he's too inexperienced at life for my tastes. And while the age gap between us isn't a big deal for some people, it's too much for me.

Besides, how am I supposed to be interested in someone cute and young when I have a man a few years older than me, with quiet confidence, a quick tongue, and what looks like a sinful body hidden beneath his clothes.

Maybe Barney was right to be worried.

I may not be as in control here as I'd like to think …

7

Orson

"So what else is on your list?" I ask Ford, phone cradled between my shoulder and ear.

"List?"

"Yeah, you said you were adding reality TV to your list of things we could do together."

"Ohh … *that* list."

I smother a chuckle. "There's no list, is there?"

"No, there is! It's, uh, got things. A whole load of things. Things you'll have to be extra nice to find out about."

"I swear every third sentence out of your mouth is innuendo."

"Not at all," he says innocently. "I can't help if you're reading into it."

He's got me there. The low timbre of his deep voice on the line has my blood buzzing. "At least give me one other thing that's on this imaginary list of yours."

"Cooking dinner together."

"Deal. Anything else?"

"Why is it all down to me to plan our dates?"

"Okay, okay, good point." I switch my phone to the other side, and even though I'm starting to get stiff, I don't want to hang up yet. It's getting later, almost time to close up shop, and there's no one around. I could put my phone on speaker, but there's something special about having his voice in my ear. "We could … go out in Springfield …"

"*Ooh*, will I get to see those dance moves in action?"

"If you play your cards right."

"Now who's heavy on the innuendo?"

I laugh, loud and easy. "Dance moves, Ford. No innuendo there."

"I think you underestimate how hot I find you, in general. Seeing you dance might be all the sexy I can stand."

Something red-hot and consuming grows in my gut. I tug the string at the back of my apron and peel it off, feeling like it's getting hard to breathe in here. "So a night out is on the list."

"Can I add a lap dance to this imaginary list?"

"Eh. Not like I haven't given them to men before."

The smart-ass response I'm expecting never comes.

"Ford?"

"Sorry, I think I just swallowed my tongue."

I laugh. Again. And kind of hate how easily he makes me do that. "Don't get too excited. It was my job."

"Was it uncomfortable for you?" The rare serious tone makes me actually stop and consider the question.

"No, but … I've never been weird about that. Even in high school, I couldn't understand the shit this gay guy in our grade was given. I wish I'd done more to stand up for him, but there was a lot I didn't know back then. Some of the guys I worked with in the strip club refused to give dudes lap dances, but it was just another tip, you know?"

"Tell me if this is crossing a line. I'm gonna ask because I'm curious, but totally respect your right to tell me to fuck off. I know when I've had lap dances before, it's made me hard as a fire hydrant and about as ready to blow as one too. And most of those guys have nothing on you. So surely you've sat on a boner or two in your day …"

"Way more than two. It was weird. Never made me hard. Hence … *straight*." I shrug, even though he can't see me. "It wouldn't have worried me if I was queer. Maybe that's why it didn't occur to me to say no."

"And with the women you gave lap dances to …"

"Hmm." That's a bit harder to answer. "It was work, you know? A good ninety percent of them I wasn't attracted to, and it's not like you sit around getting to know the person you're about to grind on for the next ten to twenty minutes. Some of them were hot. I even sneakily let some of them grope me, but I could maybe count on one hand the number of times I got hard from it. I didn't view it as anything sexual. Just a paycheck."

"I still can't believe you used to be a stripper. Wish I'd known. I would have been front row for all of your dances."

"You pervy bastard."

Ford chuckles. "Back to the list. There is one thing we could, uh, maybe do? If you don't have plans tonight, but if you do, it's not important."

The uncertainty piques my interest. "What is it?"

"I'd rather show you."

"It's your dick, isn't it?"

"Nah, sweetheart. You'll only get to see *that* if you ask really nicely."

I tug at the collar of my T-shirt. "I'm supposed to be meeting up with Keller, but I'll text him and cancel."

"Ah, shit, don't worry. I couldn't ask you to do that."

"You're not asking," I point out. "There were a couple of us going over there tonight, so he won't miss me."

"You sure?"

"Yep." Even if I wasn't, I told myself I'd say yes if he asked to hang out, and every part of me wants to follow through on that. If I blew him off and went to Keller's, I'd have spent most of the evening trying to get it out of him what his plans were anyway.

"Okay, well, I close up here in an hour or so, then I can swing by your place and pick you up. Does that give you enough time?"

"Plenty."

"Sweet. Wear clothes you can get dirty in."

"Should I be worried?"

"Always." I can picture the dangerous grin I assume he's wearing. He hangs up before I can question him further.

"So let me get this right."

Ford hums from the driver's seat of his truck, *Momma T*, as he calls her.

I stare out at nothing but blackness. "We're driving somewhere you can't tell me."

"Yes."

"In the middle of nowhere."

"Kinda."

"And I'm supposed to trust you aren't going to dismember me and leave my parts for the wildlife to find?"

"Correct."

"Okay." I settle back into my seat. "I'm glad we got that cleared up."

"Me too."

"I guess I should probably let you know I'm not afraid to fight dirty. I'll pull hair and gouge eyes like nobody's business."

"Noted." Ford's lips twitch. "And oddly turned on by that imagery."

"By me kicking your ass?"

"Uh-huh. But in my mind, you're doing it naked."

"Good to know you're not opposed to a few participation awards during sex." I don't register what I've said until the words are out there, hanging in the silence between us. *Good to know*? Fuck, Orson, why? *Why* is that good to know?

Ford's tattooed hands tighten on the steering wheel, and for the first time maybe ever, he doesn't seem to know what to say.

"I have no idea why I said that," comes out before I can stop it, but thankfully, it relaxes him. Good for him, at least. My heart is still hammering madly behind my sternum at the implication that … that I need to know anything about Ford's sex life.

I keep slipping. Keep flirting and having these out-of-body reactions to the man beside me, but even picturing sex with someone who has a cock is kinda blowing my mind. My mouth is too dry for me to continue any kind of conversation, but I wish Ford would break the silence. Because I think I'm attracted to him—I *know* I like him a whole lot—but the thought of a hard dick doesn't do anything for me. Is it possible to like the guy but not all his … bits? And even if it is, what the hell do I do with that information?

I close my eyes for a moment with the reminder to get out of my head. I'm overthinking, worrying about things that I have no reason to worry about. I'm here. He's here. We're going to spend the night hopefully doing something fun and *not* having him murder me, and all I can think about are what-ifs and maybes.

Nope.

That's not me.

The truck slows, and Ford pulls into a parking lot. The building up front is dark and abandoned, but floodlights are on behind it, illuminating the area. We're about ten minutes outside of town, and there's nothing else around.

I cut him a look that he misses. "This isn't going to be some kind of underground fight ring, is it?"

"What? You don't think I'd be good at that?"

He looks like he could physically throw any man around, but from what I've learned about him, Ford isn't a fighter. "I'm not interested in trying to bandage up a bloody nose or whatever."

"Well, it's not a fight ring, but I can't guarantee there won't be any bloody noses. They're pretty competitive."

"Competitive?"

The truck stops, and he cuts the engine, then slaps my thigh as he clicks open his seat belt. "I'll show you."

That's reassuring. Even with my apprehension, I follow him, half tucked behind his broad frame until we round the abandoned building and I take in the scene waiting for me.

Maybe ten … fifteen kids, surrounded by piles of scrap metal.

"Ah …"

He glances back over his shoulder at me. "Orson, meet the Race Warriors."

8

Ford

THE SHEER CONFUSION ON ORSON'S FACE LIGHTS ME UP inside. He might not be a car man, but he clearly knows enough to help me out here, and while it's not exactly the kind of environment where we can spend time getting to know each other, it'll tell me more about him than any one-on-one time we've had so far.

How a man treats cars and kids is all the info I need on him.

Taylor's already here, along with some parents of the kids who like to help out. This isn't a paid gig; everyone's here because they wanna be, and helping my Race Warriors build the best damn soapbox cars to race is payoff enough. I love seeing their punk faces light up when they get to drive something they've created with their own two hands.

"What is this?" Orson asks curiously.

"These are our entrants into this year's soapbox derby."

"Soapbox derby?"

"Takes place outside of Springfield at the Thanksgiving festival. The kids have just short of two months to build their racers, but the younguns will be done before that. Thought you might like to help out."

His smile spreads slowly but takes over his whole face. "Yeah, where do we start?"

That's exactly the answer I'd been waiting for. We've got three groups here. The younger kids around eight to ten, then some barely in their teens, then three sixteen-year-olds who are determined to build the whole thing from scratch this year.

They might not have engines or any real power behind them, but helping stoke a kid's love of cars is something I'll happily spend the night doing.

Orson follows me through the old lot I use as a car graveyard. Empty shells are stacked on the other side of the lot, stripped of anything useable, and on this side are all the parts these kids are going to need to get on with their build. The younger ones have official soapbox kits, the middies will use the kits as a base, then customize however they like, and these older three will start from the chassis up.

Taylor and I are here to make sure shit goes smoothly and assist the older ones with their builds.

I step in close to Orson. "That lot over there will be straightforward. A lot of the kids here have their parents to help out, with the exception of a few whose parents work nights or whatever, so that's where you'll come in. They're cluey—they've all done this before—but you'll need to keep an eye on the instructions and make sure they're set. Got it?"

"Aye, aye, Captain."

I chuckle and clap my hands together loud enough to get everyone's attention. "Hey, gang, who's ready to get into it?"

There are a few cheers and some nods. "We've got another helper on hand tonight. If anyone needs Orson, yell out. He's not an expert like Taylor, but we'll take what we can get." I bring my hands together again. "Right. Let's build some winners."

Clusters of people immediately form, and it fills me with warmth every year. Parents helping out the kids here solo, kids swapping tricks and tips on what helped them last year, and my sixteeners, already sorting through the pile of chassis and parts on offer for them.

This isn't an official thing. Friends of mine mentioned a few years back how they were building a soapbox car for the race and asked if I could take a look at it. After asking around, I found there were a handful more people I knew who did this kinda thing both for themselves and their kids, so it only seemed obvious to offer up this site so we could all build together.

I'm not in charge here, even if I do pull strings through work to get us what we need and, in return, slap some Ford's Garage bumper stickers on whatever these kids come up with.

Orson splits off to help a group while I approach my sixteeners. They were only fifteeners last year, and there was one more of them, but apparently, she didn't want to return with Erin, Daryl, and Crispin. Her loss. I bet she grows up and buys a Prius.

Bitter? Not at all.

I just don't understand how anyone can *not* be interested in cars.

The next hour and a half, we work to the sound of light conversation, fast music, and the soundtrack of metal hitting metal. There's energy in the air, raw focus, and the hum of working toward a goal. My sixteeners don't waste a second. They know the basics of the build but need my supervision on the tools, and everyone is motivated and excited as they make progress.

I do everything I can not to keep glancing over at Orson. I didn't bring him here for the eye candy for once; it was only because I legitimately wanted him here and thought he'd have a good time. And from the glimpses I've been allowed, my hunch is confirmed.

He's jumped right into it, is getting along with the kids and the parents, and seeing him concentrate on putting the things together is a fucking turn-on. My competency kink is in full overdrive that my florist slash stripper can talk cars with Taylor and hold his own.

Our time is up way too soon. Even though it's unlikely it'll rain, the kids cover the start of their soapbox cars with plastic covers and pack away the spare parts they haven't gotten to yet.

Taylor says bye as they leave, and I wait for the trickle of people to make their way back to their cars and watch that every kid is picked up. It's not until the final door closes and the red brake lights dim that I let myself turn back to Orson.

"Not a bad way to spend the night, huh?"

Orson's arms are crossed loosely over his chest, shoulder pressed against the chain-link fence he's leaning into. His soft smile makes my gut give a violent backflip. "That was really nice. It's super cool of you to run this."

"I don't. Run it, I mean. It's nothing official; I had the space, so I made the offer."

His dark brown eyebrows creep upward. "You *were* running it. It's your place, your tools, your equipment. They waited for you to get started and asked you whenever they had questions …"

"Ah." My feet scruff the gravel, shifting under his scrutiny. "Just my area of expertise."

"So, like I said. It's cool."

"Or selfish. I don't have any kiddies of my own, so this gives me a chance to hang out with the little ankle biters, doing something I love."

Orson shrugs, eyes shooting away across the yard. "Do you *want* some of your own?"

"Nah. I like teaching them, I like that they're interested in what I'm interested in, but full-time isn't something I could do." Orson looks like he's thinking about something. "You?"

"No real feelings either way. I always thought I'd have some, but then I lost Tara, and it's … well, I've learned to love my life the way it is."

"Don't feel like something is missing?"

He looks at me again, right in the eyes, but all attempts he makes to speak are swallowed.

I try for a reassuring smile that I'm not sure I manage to pull off and step forward to squeeze his shoulder. "You okay?"

"Yeah. Very. Tonight was nice."

"Only nice?"

"I caught you checking me out a few times," he says, a mischievous spark in his eyes.

"Hey, couldn't let you think I'd gone total choirboy. Had to keep you on your toes."

His stare travels from the top of my head all the way down to somewhere around my thighs. "There is no way anyone is mistaking you for a choirboy."

"That so?"

"Someone who owns a motorcycle, maybe."

I pretend to gasp. "Those two-wheel hellions? Never. I like me a big baby with a deep purr."

"It's so lucky I know you're talking about cars."

"Technically, I could be talking about men too." I start toward the gate to the parking lot, and Orson follows me. "Nothing better than a thick man turned to Jell-O."

"That your type? Bigger guys?"

"Nah, like I told you before, I'm not too picky."

"That makes sense since Molly isn't big at all."

I frown, wondering why he's bringing him up. "Pickings are slim in Kilborough, but I've always done all right. Just wait until we go out in Springfield. I'll take you to a gay bar, and then you'll get to see how hot men find me. We'll have to make you a 'hands off' sign, though, because you can bet your ass the queer men will be on you like your cock is a magnet."

"I've already told you I don't care if other men touch me. I don't have to have sex with someone because I dance with them."

"I can hear their little queer hearts breaking already."

Orson tips his head, watching me as I slide the gate closed and secure the lock. "*Really*? Over *one* dance?"

"Fine. You'll make their dicks weep. Better?"

He cracks up laughing. "That's dramatic."

"Think about a time you've been left with blue balls. They're no one's friends."

"True, but I'm sure there are a lot of available people in a gay bar."

"There are, but when you're dancing with a hot man giving off all the signs, and then the sexy body you've been grinding against for the last hour is suddenly off-limits—not a fun way to end the night. I'm all for consent, but I'm also about not leading people on."

"Okay," he relents. "Hands off sign, it is."

My tongue swipes over my lips as we head for the truck, and I know I shouldn't steer the conversation to where I want to steer it, but fuck, I can't help myself. "You really wouldn't care?"

"What's that?"

"About men touching you? A sweaty dude pressed up against you who wants to suck your cock. You ... you wouldn't give a shit?"

"Nope. Been there, done that."

"I think there's a big difference between work and a night out though."

He crosses his arms again and leans against the driver's-side door so I can't get in. "Why do you think that?"

"Because someone paying to touch you is clinical, trans-actional. Someone doing it because they *want* to is another thing."

Orson's jaw ticks, eyes following the same path over me as earlier, and then he pushes off the truck. "Prove it."

"Huh?"

He turns us and backs me into the door, arms boxing me in but not touching. He's grinning, playful, biting his bottom lip against a laugh. "Touch me because you want to, and I'll let you know if it's weird."

"It's already weird."

"Shit. Sorry." He steps back, but I grab him and flip us, slamming his back into Momma T as I step in closer than he was before. The top of his head reaches my eye level, and I have to look down at him. The familiar curious expression stares back at me.

"You really inviting me to touch you?"

"Do you want to?"

I sneer. "That's like asking a thirsty man if he wants water."

Orson blinks up at me, a sweetness shining from his eyes. "Only if you're comfortable. You're, uh, I enjoy spending time with you, and I wouldn't want things to get … you know."

"'Preciate it, but a sexy guy is offering to let me feel him up, and you will never hear me complain about that."

"If you're cool, I'm cool. Just maybe no between the legs action."

"Ass?"

"It'd be groped on the dance floor, right?"

"Constantly."

"Then go for it."

I watch him, trying to read if this is for real or if he's about to freak the fuck out, but he just watches me back, waiting. Looking completely at ease that I'm about to paw him until I have my fill of every one of those muscles his clothes have been hiding from me. I wasn't lying when I said I'd *never* complain about touching him.

I swallow roughly and settle my hands on his shoulders.

Orson rolls his lips to hold in his amusement. "Are we going to a club in the 1800s? I didn't realize gay bars were so polite."

"Fine, smart-ass." I let my hands drift from his round shoulders, over his impressive pecs, and along every groove I can feel on his stomach. "Comfortable now?"

Some of the teasing leaves his face, but he nods. "Totally fine."

"And now?" My fingers duck beneath the bottom of his T-shirt, and it's like having pure fucking heat in my hands. Smooth abs, no body hair that I can feel, and skin that's like silk.

"*Hoo*." Orson lets out a shaky breath that my cock takes note of. "Wasn't expecting that. All good though."

And maybe I should have expected more resilience from someone who used to make a living from showing off his body, but I'm completely fucking gobsmacked that he's letting me stand here and grope him. My biggest worry right now is that he'll regret it, or it'll mess shit up between us, but then his hands cover where mine are resting under his shirt, the thin material separating us. He guides my hands up to his pecs, and I can't help my thumb flicking over the small bump of his nipple.

I let out a long, slow exhale, trying to ignore the way my cock is thickening.

He swallows, and I swear it's heavier than usual. "Totally fine."

"Hmm …" I step in so my body is pressed to his. Toe to toe, thighs pressed close, stomach flush with his abs. My hands are trapped between us, fingers exploring the light hair on his chest. "It's not only the touch though, is it?"

"What do you mean?" His smooth voice has dropped deeper.

"I mean, physical touch is one thing, but it's also your mind. It's knowing the guy with his hands on you wants more."

"That's nothing new."

"It's knowing his blood is rushing south. His pulse has kicked up a notch. His cock is rock hard in his pants."

Orson smirks. "Think you're making me uncomfortable, Ford?"

I lock eyes with him. "It's knowing the guy's gut is flipping out with want and excitement. The expectation of where things are heading next."

"What else?"

Damn, that question almost makes me groan. "It's knowing that even though you're together now, he's already picturing later." I slide one hand out from under his shirt to run my fingers over his lips. "He's picturing you on your knees, these pretty lips stretched wide around his cock."

Air rushes past my fingers as he sucks in a breath.

"He's picturing you stripped naked, maybe gripping his hair as you drill into his mouth. Maybe he's bent over for you. Or maybe … maybe he's got you bent over, sexy ass in the air while he fucks the life out of you."

Our faces are closer now, his eyes wide, lips wet and parted. "Is that what *you're* thinking?"

Holy shit. An exhale bounces from me. My cock is making it hard to think, but I do know that question wasn't curiosity. I do know the way he's looking at me is inviting more. But I also know that Orson wasn't prepared for whatever this situation is doing to us both.

So I give him honesty. "No." My jaw tightens at his surprise. "Because I won't fucking let myself."

I shove away from him, leaving Orson's shirt askew, a sliver of those delicious abs on display as he reorients himself.

He gives his head a shake and focuses back on me. Then he smiles. "See? Told you I don't scare easy."

I'm torn on whether to laugh or cry because no, he certainly doesn't. And I don't know whether that's a good thing or not.

I give his ass a solid slap. "Get in the truck. We've had enough playtime for tonight."

9

Orson

FORD DROPS ME BACK AT MY PLACE, AND EVEN THOUGH I'M acting normally around him, I think I'm freaking out. No matter what I said, having his hands on me was nothing —*nothing*—like any other man before.

He's right that work and play are two totally separate things.

I try to keep up my *it doesn't change anything* mentality. That drive to go with the flow and see what happens, but if "what happens" is anything like how I felt with Ford's hands on me, I'll be entering a whole new realm of possibility.

The question is do I want to?

The memory of Ford standing over me, his dark eyes fixed on mine, strong hands pressed to my skin, sends fizzy bursts of lust into my bloodstream. It didn't take much to get me hard, but the cynical side of me is wondering whether that had less to do with Ford and more to do with the fact I haven't had sex in years. There's no way to deny that having his body pressed against mine felt good. Too good.

I trudge up my two front stairs and open the front door of my sweet little cottage. It's just off Main Street and needed some serious repairs when I first bought it, but after a few years, my charming little one bedder feels like home. If it's up to me, I'll spend the rest of my life here. I mentally scoff at my naivety because I've had that thought before.

There's a loud clunk as I drop my keys in the glass bowl by my front door and turn to lock up. The house is dark, but I make my way through the open living area easily and flip on the light.

Everything in here is white, navy, or brown, which helps me to relax.

I'm having a moment over nothing. That much is obvious even to me. Being with a man doesn't freak me out; this isn't some kind of gay panic. I think it's more … general panic. I'm not sure how to be with *anyone*.

My friend Griff is going through the same thing after his split with his ex-wife, but where he feels like he *has* to have sex to get it out of the way and off his mind, I'm happier going on without it. My spiral after Tara died led to a lot of cheap and nasty sex, and I swore I'd never go back there. I don't need it. When I'm with someone, I want it to matter. I want it to mean more than an orgasm and a bit of sweaty fun.

And I think that's the issue.

The thought of seeing Ford's dick doesn't get me excited, but the thought of Ford taking his time, touching me like I mean something to him, *that's* the part that gets me all twisted up inside.

So far as I can tell, Ford is a casual man. He mentions settling down one day like it's a future thing, something that will slot into place when the time is right. It's great confidence to have. I wish I could be more like that. But the next time I have sex with someone, I'm going to be dating them.

I'm not confident I could be in a relationship with another man, so dragging Ford into my mess is fucking crazy when we've got a good friendship going as it is.

The more I think about it though, the more it occurs to me that I *am* ready. To date. To maybe find someone I can love again.

My only problem is this overwhelming curiosity when it comes to Ford.

Who the hell knows what I'm going to do about that?

I take a quick shower and get changed into some pajamas, then hunt down dinner. I enjoy my quiet, simple life, but I also remember enjoying having someone to share all this domestic shit with. It's getting to the point where that part of my life feels like so long ago I'm not even sure I'm the same person.

Actually, I'm not so sure I'm the same as any of the previous people I've been before.

A nerd in high school. A stripper to get through college and earn my degree in accounting. A married accountant. A grieving widower. A man so completely lost that I turned to anything I could find to take the world out of focus. Then someone beaten down and full of regret, and now … whoever this new Orson is.

I want to be someone patient and at peace with the world when, in fact, I'm just a horny man standing in his kitchen, waiting for leftovers to heat up.

It sounds pathetic, but is it still pathetic if I enjoy it?

Fuck, I'm too in my head.

I grab my dinner from the microwave and head out into

my small backyard. It's mostly bare except for one garden bed and a small bench, where I take my dinner to sit and eat.

Then I tilt my head back and look at the sky.

I can make out a light smattering of stars shining back at me, helping me refocus my perspective. Instead of letting all of this get ahead of me, instead of freaking out about what's next, maybe I need to lean in.

I'm holding on to the word *straight* because it's who I've always been, but maybe that word is what's holding me back from who I *could* be.

It's not like I didn't enjoy the lap dances I've given men in the past. They might not have done much for me sexually, but they were fun. I enjoyed the rush of knowing it was my body turning them on, and hell, maybe that's all tonight was.

Because Ford *was* turned on.

The hard evidence trapped between us gave that away.

A day at a time, each moment as it comes. I can do that. It's fine.

I just have to be careful because leading Ford on when there's no chance between us isn't something that I ever want to do.

I can already feel the shift taking place. My willingness to date, to open up, maybe not be secluded all the time. My friends are great, but even though I'm close with Art, Keller, and Griff especially, I still feel like I'm on the outer. Like they have their people, and I'm the one who came in last.

It's all bullshit negativity trying to feed on me because I've never done a thing to try and change the perception I have. My friends never make me feel unwelcome. They've had my back—especially Art—since I returned to Kilborough, and when the Divorced Men's Club started, Art pulled me into the group without me even needing to ask.

I smile at the memory and start shoveling my food down. I've been incredibly lucky in life to have been loved the way I have been. My family, my wife, my friends. And I still have so much ahead of me.

This thing with Ford … maybe it'll burn, or maybe it'll fizzle away to nothing.

Might as well be game for the ride.

Balancing my dinner on my knees, I pull my phone from my pajama pants pocket and type out a message.

Me: *Thanks for inviting me tonight.*

I have no idea if he'll write back or not, but I leave my phone faceup on the bench beside me anyway. Nerves are dancing in my gut, and I actually laugh at myself for being such an idiot. It feels great, this hint of possibility. Of … *want.* I want to see his name on my screen; I want to talk to him, and hang out with him, and resist the urge to roll my eyes when he says something flirty and gives me that smug look of his.

Am I going through a midlife crisis? Is that what this is?

The skin over my stomach zaps and sparks at the memory of his rough hands spread across it. I shovel more food in my mouth, ravenous from what felt like a long night, and have to admit to myself that it felt good. Really good. And if I freak out or hide away in a hole, I won't get that again.

And I think I want that again.

I just don't want to mess with Ford's head while I figure this out.

My phone dings beside me, and my gut jumps in excitement.

Ford: *You're welcome. Gonna make it every week?*

Me: *If I'm invited.*

Ford: *It's a volunteer thing, so technically you don't need an invitation.*

Hmm … less flirty than I'd expect from him. Is *he* freaking out over what happened? He'd been fine during the drive home. So is this standoffishness for my benefit or his?

Me: *Might not need one, but it'd be nice to know I'm wanted.*

The nerves that come with writing that sentence are sickening.

Ford: *I'd say by the fourth bunch of flowers, you should have gotten that message.*

Fuck, I even read that text in his flirty tone. My brain might still be confused by what's happening, but my body is apparently excited by it.

Me: *In that case, I better get busy. Can't let you be the one to plan two dates in a row.*

I bite my lip as the dots on the screen that show he's typing dance and disappear again and again. Was that too far? Is he going to tell me that I need to back off? That tonight was a mess and we need to wake up to ourselves?

I should know Ford better than that.

Ford: *Technically the next one will be our third. And you know what they say about third dates ;P*

10

Ford

"Why did I agree to this?" I grumble, watching as Orson slides the canoe into the water.

I blew off work early for this too since our days off don't line up together, and now I'm seriously questioning my sanity. But then I glance at Orson, and I come to terms with what a sucker I am. He wants to go canoeing, so I guess we're going canoeing.

"You sure that thing's gonna hold me?" I ask.

"Nope." He pops the *p* sound.

I do a double take. "I swear, if we sink—"

"Then we'll be swimming instead of canoeing." His hands land on my shoulders and massage gently. "Just relax and get in the death trap."

"Your sweet voice isn't fooling anyone." But despite my objections, I do exactly what I'm told. The canoe rocks alarmingly, and Orson cackles, the asshole, but as soon as I'm steady, he climbs in after me.

"You good?"

"Why anyone would want a boat when they can take a car is beyond me." That said, it seems like a sturdy enough thing. Big and a fancy-looking bright blue against the dull water. Two comfy seats with goddamn cupholders. It'd be a professional canoer's wet dream.

"Because we're doing something different, you old grump."

"There are plenty of different things we can do on dry land," I throw back.

I'm met by Orson's laugh. "And when you plan our next date, you can introduce me to all of those wonders."

Maybe he's only going along with my ridiculous date thing, but I love him joking about it. Probably more than I should, but I'm not about to put the brakes on now. I'm a glutton for punishment, I guess, though spending time with Orson isn't exactly a hardship.

"Okay, if I have to do this, I'm going to do it well. How do we get started?"

"The paddle beside you."

I turn and find one shiny metal pole with bright white paddles clipped to the side of the boat. It detaches with a tug, and Orson does the same with the one on the other side. It looks easy enough. I've seen people do this shit on TV. Not wanting to be out here longer than I need to be, I dig the paddle into the water and out again.

Splosh.

"Wait. *Stop.*"

I glance back to find Orson shaking water off his face.

"You trying to drown me?" he gasps.

"Ooops?" I give him an innocent shrug. "Let's remember, anything that happens out here is your fault."

"Are we back on possible murder again? Because it's less cute out here with no witnesses and a large body of water."

I grin, even though he can't see it. "I guess you better be nice to me, then."

There's an echoey thud, and the canoe sways as he shifts behind me, and before I can glance back at what he's doing, his warmth presses to my back. "I'm an incredibly nice person." His voice by my ear makes all the little hairs on the back of my neck react. Orson's arms wrap around me, and his hands cover mine. They're steady and large and warm. Softer than mine, but when I look down at his light skin against mine, the sun glints off his scars.

"Like this." His grip tightens, and he steers my paddle through the water in smooth strokes, expertly propelling us forward with little effort.

"You're good at handling a stick," I say.

He chuckles, still so close. "Guess I'm a natural."

"You're not going to feed me bullshit about doing this for years?"

"Only once before. I'm a *very* good student."

"A very good *tease* too."

"I think you like it," he responds.

"Wouldn't be here if I didn't."

"Someone has to keep you on your toes." And the bastard releases one of my hands and tweaks my nipple. "I *knew* it."

I flinch at his loud words. "Knew what?"

"You have your nipple pierced. I thought I spotted it through your T-shirt."

"Yeah, yeah. We both know you only wanted to cop a feel."

"Am I that transparent?" Orson playfully snaps at my ear before releasing me and dropping back into his seat.

Even the sun hasn't warmed my skin as much as his arms did. "Careful, smart-ass, or I'll drown you again."

"Hey, unlike me, you've had plenty of years' experience with a stick, and I expect you to use them."

I smile as I set the paddle in the water and go through the motions the way Orson guided me. I hear him do the same. "Well, I *am* an expert in stroking sticks. Plenty of experience getting men all wet too."

"I can tell."

"Many a-men have complimented my skill."

He sniggers. "You've got the patience down pat. Not rushing it."

"No point rushing through the enjoyable things in life."

"Ah, so you agree this is enjoyable?"

Fuck, he's got me there. "There are better ways to stroke a stick, but this isn't bad."

We leave the sheltered side bank and hit the river, where the current helps us drift along lazily.

"Put the paddle up and turn around."

"Paddle is doable. The moving, not so much."

He clicks his in beside me, and I try to do the same on the other side, but Orson ends up having to help. When I feel steady enough to turn around, I find him sitting across his seat with his shoes kicked off. His feet hang over one side of the canoe while his elbows lean on the other.

"I have a cooler there with some food and drinks in it."

That gets my attention. I open it to find some sandwiches, cut-up fruit, and bottles of water.

"Never had a picnic lunch on a date before," I say, and then, even though I'm still sure I'm gonna fall out, I kick off

my flip-flops and mimic Orson. My feet hang over the opposite side to his, and propped up on my elbows, I have a clear
view across at his handsome face.

"Technically, *late* lunch," he says.

"Whatever you wanna classify it as, my point stands.
This is the most wholesome little outing I've ever had."

"Including me pinching your nipple?"

I wave a hand at him. "What's a little tweaking between
friends?"

"I suppose it depends what you're tweaking." He pumps
his eyebrows at me, stare steady, and the look heats me
beneath the collar.

"Well, let's start with one of them sandwiches and go
from there."

His tongue swipes over his lip before he reaches down
into the cooler to grab one. He hands mine over, along with
some water, and we drift along, eating and thinking, in
perfect silence.

"Favorite childhood memory?" he asks.

"Breaking my arm."

Orson's mouth drops. "You're going to have to explain
that one."

"It was almost the end of summer in middle school, and
I'd been showing off to the boy next door. I had an inkling I
was gay but never really thought about myself in those
terms. He was so impressed by how high up the tree I made
it, but then he tried to throw the ball up to me, and I slipped,
fell straight to the ground, broke my arm in two places." I'm
still smiling, even though Orson looks horrified. "He thought
it was his fault, looked after me for the rest of the summer,
and one day, when our parents were both at work, he
kissed me."

"How romantic."

"All very PG with him, but that's where my obsession with guys started." I tilt my head. "You?"

"My favorite memory or my obsession with men?"

"Memory, obviously. We both know when your obsession with men began." I drop my tone suggestively, and Orson's gaze finds mine again. It's intimidating, looking him right in the eyes. He doesn't seem to feel the same weight of it that I do, but connecting like this feels a thousand times more intimate than when I had my hands all over him.

"I have two."

"Oh yeah?" I'm more interested in his answer than I should be.

"Tinkering with cars in the shed with Dad, and on cool nights, Mom would make me a hot cocoa with marshmallows, and then we'd sit in front of the fire while she painted my toenails."

Neither of those answers is what I expected. "You still do that? Either of those things?"

"No." He bites his thumb, gaze far off. "Don't even do the hot cocoa thing."

"You should." I've never much thought like that. I'm pretty go, go, go with anything fun, whereas Orson likes the soft moments. The quiet ones. Ones like we're having right now.

It warms my chest that he brought me here.

"I've changed my mind."

He narrows his eyes. "About …"

"Canoeing. It's awesome."

Orson's lips hitch up on one side behind his scruff. "Yeah, I'm enjoying myself too."

Movement to my left makes me glance down in time to

see a small turtle swim up to the side of the canoe. It extends its neck, trying to get a good look at me before ducking down again.

"Turtle."

"Oh, where?" He carefully shifts to my side of the canoe and leans over the side.

"I think it's gone."

He moves closer to the water, and I cringe at the thought of him falling in. Only when I go to grab his shirt to steady him, he jerks at my sudden movement, the canoe gives a sharp rock, and then he topples overboard. I only just manage to stay upright.

"Fuck, *Orson*."

The splash is loud, and ripples are cratering the surface of the water, making it impossible to see where he's gone. Every second I'm expecting him to pop up passes longer and longer until— Shit. I don't think he's coming up.

Heart pounding, I prepare to jump in after him when a shadow stirs beneath me, and I see him a moment too late to react.

Orson bursts out of the water, wraps his arms around my shoulders, and pulls me in after him. Cool water rushes up all around me, and for one suspended second, it's bliss.

Then my head breaks the surface.

Orson is chuckling as he swims after the canoe to stop it from drifting away.

"You're a dick," I call after him.

"You pushed me."

"I was trying to grab you to stop you from falling overboard."

He makes a skeptical noise. "The falling overboard part I believe."

Water is running down my face, sticking my hair to my forehead, drenching through my shorts, and even though I'd been reluctant about falling in at first, this is nice. Thank fuck we left our phones and wallets in the car.

I take my time catching up with him, and then I hold the canoe steady so Orson can climb in, and he helps pull me up after.

We're both soaked through, gripping each other, slightly out of breath and … so much for that quiet moment.

I laugh, and he joins in.

"I'm getting you back for that," I say, trying and failing to be grumpy when I'm feeling so good.

"It was your fault."

"*You* leaned over too far."

"And I was fine until *you* scared the life out of me."

We break into laughter again, the kind that makes me feel lighter, carefree, and when it drifts away into a happy smile, Orson and I meet eyes again. His are shining in the late-afternoon sun, and it's easy to believe he's as happy as I am.

"Should we go back?" I ask, not wanting to break the moment but knowing we can't kneel here clutching each other all day.

His eyes drop, cheeks reddening above his stubble. "Yeah. But …" He gestures to his dripping clothes.

I take my seat and grab the paddle. "My place is only ten minutes from here. We can change there."

"Good plan."

It takes us twice as long to get back as it took to get out there. We're too busy horsing around and splashing each other, and he keeps leaning forward to snake his arm around and pinch my piercing whenever he thinks I'm not ready for it.

What he doesn't realize is he's now made it my mission to find something to use against him. Maybe he's ticklish. Or has some secret fetish.

By the time we get back, we have to drain the puddle of water out of the bottom of the canoe, and Orson's shoulders have gotten red. I press my forefinger to his skin and watch the pale mark bloom.

"Need some aloe for that."

He glances down to follow my gaze and then looks up at me with a wicked smirk. "Got any at your place?"

"Sure do."

He whips his shirt off and tucks it into his shorts. "My back feels burned too though." He turns to show me his completely-not-burned back, and I'm confused for a second before he glances back over his shoulder. "I might need some help with it."

And while my mind is saying, *holy shit kill me now*, my mouth says, "I got your back, sweetheart. Literally."

Orson

FORD LIVES IN A STANDARD, WELL-KEPT BRICK HOUSE ON A huge block of land. He's got a monster shed behind the house, and I wouldn't be surprised if that's where he spends the majority of his time.

"How many cars do you have out there?" I ask, nodding toward it.

"Guess."

"Umm … twenty?"

He slaps a hand over his heart. "*Wow*, do you overestimate me."

"How many, then?"

"Guess you'll have to come out there one day and see for yourself."

I know if I pushed for him to tell me, he would, but it's obvious what he's doing. Another excuse for us to spend time together is fine by me.

It was a short drive back to Ford's, and even though I

took my loose tank off, my shorts are still uncomfortably wet. Ford almost had a fit over us sitting in the car like this, and I swear if he'd driven us out here in Momma T, we'd still be sitting around, waiting to dry off.

"No dripping on the floors," he teases as he opens his front door.

"And how do I stop from doing that?"

"I bet you'd drip less if you were naked."

"True, but I think I'd traumatize your neighbors."

"Hmm, good point." Ford steps aside to let me past.

And given how understated the outside is, I'm not expecting his interior. Dark timber hardwood, light brown walls, sturdy furniture. It's modern and masculine, clean, but definitely lived-in.

"Bathroom's down the hall."

I glance over as he closes the door behind us. "Not going to show me?"

"Thought I'd grab us some clothes first."

"Who says we need them?"

Ford's eyes narrow in on me. "I've had a lot of naked men in here but can safely say none of them were straight."

"There's a first time for everything."

He groans and palms his face before shoving me toward the bathroom. "Get in there. I'll pass the clothes through the door."

"Prude," I shoot back and head in the direction he pushed me. Teasing Ford is fun, and since I've given myself permission to relax into this spark between us, there's been a lot less overthinking. I still can't actually picture anything happening with a man, but I'm open to it if it does.

The hypothetical doesn't do anything for me, but moments when we're together, when his hands are on me or my arms are wrapped around him, get me hot under the collar. My blood buzzes, and the prospect of what *could* come next makes me want to try it.

The only thing holding me back is fucking up what we already have.

I only half close the bathroom door as I drop my shorts onto the tile and grab a towel that's been neatly folded under the sink. It's soft, overly fluffy, and expensive, I'd bet. I think of Ford, the enormous wall of tattooed man, and picture him walking into a store to buy the best towels they sell. Who knew he was a creature comforts kind of guy?

The creak of a floorboard outside lets me know he's back, and I quickly sling the towel around my waist before he can cop an eyeful. As much as I'd love to stand here, pretending to dry my hair and do the whole *oops, is my dick hanging out?* thing, I don't want to make him uncomfortable.

He nudges the door open, leaning against the opening, and without a word, his eyes roam greedily over my body. Seeing such raw appreciation sets my skin alight, fizzes up the nerves in my gut, and makes me want to step closer and offer for him to take a closer look.

"Didn't want to be a prude," he says.

"You good now?" I ask, holding back my smile.

He hums. "It'd be better without the towel."

"You've gotta earn those kinds of privileges." My gaze snags on the small bump beneath his T-shirt. "Besides, I still haven't seen that nipple piercing."

"That's a privilege you'll never earn."

The sweats he tosses me hit me right in the face. I laugh, removing them and resisting the urge to hold them to my nose and inhale. I get a good whiff anyway. Washing powder and his scent. "You're underestimating how persuasive I can be."

"That so?" His eyes narrow. "Just how do you plan on being persuasive?"

"You'll have to wait and see."

He hangs his head back and steps out of the room. "Get those on, and I'll grab the aloe cream."

I listen to his heavy footsteps disappear down the hall, then drop the towel. I'm all twisted up but *so alive*. It feels like a whole other world since I got nervous and excited over someone. Since I craved their attention. Their company. And while Tara will always be with me and I'll always regret that she was taken from me too soon, I think it's okay to be feeling this way again. To ... live. Tara was a big-hearted person, and seeing this solitary shell I've become would have disappointed her.

Sure, both of us would have preferred things turned out differently, but I'm here now. In Ford's home. With a dry mouth and clammy hands, feeling the beginnings of *something*.

I tug the sweats on and have to roll them at my hips a couple of times to make them stay up.

"You decent?" he calls, coming back down the hall.

"Wish I wasn't," I call back.

Ford walks into the room, and it's only when he's right in front of me that I'm aware of how small his bathroom is. "Wanna turn around?"

Instead of giving him an answer I'm not sure I can come up with, I just do it. Turn in the tight space, put my back to him, and ignore the way my body tingles, overly aware of his presence.

The click of the cap of moisturizer sends shivers down

my spine, and every nerve ending prickles with anticipation of him touching me. There's a long moment, stretched out between us, where nothing happens apart from his soft breathing behind me, and then … his hands close over my shoulders.

I try to stay still as he massages the smooth cream out along my skin. His fingers work the muscle, thumbs driving into the knot between my shoulder blades before lightly sweeping up my sunburned neck. His hands are large, rough, confident, quickly turning me to jelly.

All of my self-control is being used to stop me from making shameless noises under his massage, especially when he reaches my back, where he can increase the pressure. This isn't helping someone out with a sunburn; this is the kind of touch that I've craved for years without realizing it. Not the same as hungry groping, but deeper. The kind of touch that holds respect, need, and the aim to make the person you're with feel incredible.

Ford's breathing has gotten heavier, his hands moving slower but firmer over my skin. Traveling lower on my back, leaving no muscle tense.

I'm so lost in his hands that it takes me a moment to realize that the good feelings are pooling in my groin. I'm hard, cock pressing against the sweats, but the lusty need isn't all-consuming. It's … nice. Constant. A pleasant ache I haven't felt in a really long time.

My self-control fizzles away, and my moan spills out between us.

Ford chuckles, but it's humorless. "Enjoying this?"

"Sunburn never felt so good."

His answering sound is low and gravelly. "Never massaged a straight man before."

Ford's unasked question is loud between us. "You mean this isn't something friends do for other friends?"

"Not in my experience."

I smile, even though he can't see it. "You need to get better friends."

He leans in, and the air shifts behind me. "Why would I do that when I have you?" The deep voice in my ear makes me shiver. Brings the skin along my neck alive. I'm so overly aware of his closeness, drunk on the idea of him dipping his head, pressing his lips to my throat, scraping his stubble along my skin.

Huh. So apparently, the hypothetical *does* do something for me.

"Did, uh … did *you* get sunburned?"

"Not a spot." He abruptly pulls back, and I'm left cold. "Some of us have heard of sunblock."

Fucking smart-ass. I gulp down a few breaths and try to get my dick kinda under control before I turn around. "If you want to turn down a free massage, that's on you."

"Nothing is ever free."

"That's a cynical take on things."

His lips hitch at the corners as he checks me out again. "Everything comes with a price, and sometimes you have to work out if it's a price you wanna pay."

He could be talking in general, or about what's happening between us, but I get what he's saying. "So how much would you pay for a massage?"

"Haven't worked that out yet."

"You know …" I walk my fingers over his chest until I can flick that barbell that's taunting me. "I'm shirtless right now, so it's only fair that you are as well."

His eyes are searching. "That so?"

"Quid pro quo."

"Nah." He grins. "Think I wanna make you work for it a little more."

"You're so mean."

"Because it's fun."

"That so?" I echo him. Then I grab the bottom of his shirt and tug.

Ford works out what I'm doing a second after I move, and pins my hand to his side. We struggle against each other, shuffling and bumping around the small room as I try to lift his shirt, and he tries to stop me. We're both half laughing, half panting, until Ford gets me in a bear hug from behind and slams me face-first into the wall.

"*Oomph.*"

"Feisty, huh?"

"I want to see it."

"And you will when I'm good and ready."

"Something tells me it won't take you long." I push back, but it doesn't get me far. Ford's strong arms have me locked in tight, his solid body boxing me in. "Invite me to stay for dinner."

"Was gonna make some fried chicken and coleslaw. You hungry?"

"Starving."

He eases his hold on me and steps back, letting me off the goddamn wall, and when I turn to take him in, his face is flushed, and his eyes are darker. It's a fucking sexy look on him.

"Don't want to know what I'm planning?" I ask.

"Nah. It's more fun to wait and find out."

12

Ford

TURNS OUT, ORSON IS IMPRESSED BY A MAN WHO CAN COOK. And I say "cook" lightly because all I do is make up the chicken coating, set it in the pan, and chop up the shit for the coleslaw before cutting up and throwing some fries on as well. I learned early on how easy it would be for me to rely on takeout and ready meals since I have no one but me to cook for, and so I made it my mission to learn how to do this properly. And enjoy it.

Spending that half an hour or so every afternoon preparing whatever the hell I want to eat makes it taste that much nicer. Normally I'd have a beer while I cook, but I didn't pick any up this week, and I don't miss it.

"I've got some ginger ales, seltzer water and lime, or sodas in the fridge if you're thirsty."

Orson throws me a look. "Ginger ale?"

"Kinda picked up the taste of it lately."

"It just so happens to be one of my favorites."

"What a coincidence." The look he gives me makes me all fluttery. It's so easy to do when he's around. The kind eyes that get crinkles in the corners, the silver-flecked scruff, the way he holds himself all tall and confident, in a way that tempts me to bring him to his knees. Whatever that was in the bathroom was definitely coming from the both of us. Interest, flirting, that hum of possibility on the air— unspoken but so thick it coated my tongue.

For a supposedly straight man, Orson's the one toeing the line more often than not. I'm firmly planted on my side, observing and hoping but not sure how to proceed.

He opens the fridge to the sizzle of hot oil and inspects the inside before pulling out the seltzer water and some lime. "You know, I don't care if you drink. Art and the guys do around me. It's not a temptation thing."

"Nothing worse than being sober around a drunk person, but ... I never realized how much of it I did until you said you didn't. Most people naturally gravitate toward alcohol in social situations, and with you, I assumed you'd be the same. Sorry about that."

"Don't be. It's normal." He opens two bottles and slides a ginger ale over to me. "You know what isn't normal?"

"What?"

"You didn't ask why."

I shrug and check the chicken. "It's not like it's my business."

He chuckles darkly. "Other people don't understand that. Whenever I say I don't drink, I get odd looks and the third degree."

My frown settles deep.

"Do you want to know why I don't?" he asks softly.

"Only if it's something you want to tell me." I cross my

arms and face him. "You don't need to give me an explanation."

He shuffles slightly, not meeting my eyes. "I, uh … After I lost Tara, things got really dark for me. I ran away from where people knew me. Got into alcohol and drugs, sex with people I didn't like. I went back to stripping to survive financially, but I didn't enjoy it like I did the first time around. Instead of it being a job and good exercise, it was more like I was punishing myself. And I made some … messed-up choices. *Especially* when I was drinking."

My gaze falls again to his scars, but I look away quickly. The fact he shared any of that with me is a big deal. I'm not entitled to know these personal things, so him wanting to share them with me is something I won't take lightly. "It was brave of you."

"What? Running away and hiding?"

"No. That you saw you wanted better and did the work for it."

"That's … not a perspective I've had before."

I remove the chicken from the pan. "Not surprised. I am an incredibly clever and insightful man." And I'm pretty damn proud of my cooking right now because the chicken skin is perfectly crispy.

We sit at my table, plates piled high, talking about work and whatever shit comes into our minds, while I try to ignore the pornographic way Orson is moaning over the chicken. The way he licks his fingers into his mouth, over and over and fucking *over*.

It gets dark, and we finish eating, but neither of us makes a move to get up. The lights are on, but the house is silent, and with the way we've angled toward each other, we're sitting closer than we were originally.

"Question," he says after a sleepy silence. "Why the garage?"

"I really love cars. I swear, growing up, it was always *oh, Ford like the car?* and it just seemed like me and cars always went together. I knew how to rebuild a motor at fifteen. Doing oil checks. Changing flats. For my sixteenth birthday, my parents bought me this old VW Bug, and Dad helped me restore it. Taking that thing from a rusted scrap heap to something shiny and roadworthy lit a fire under my ass. There's only ever been one job for me." I watch him, trying my hardest to ignore his bare chest. "What about you? Why flowers? Because you didn't do that when you were here the first time, right?"

"Nope. And, well, they're … *important.*"

"Go on."

"Unlike you, I didn't have that one thing. All I knew was that I needed to go to college and get a job that would support my family. I did that. I married the girl. I bought a place. We were planning kids, and then …" He doesn't need to finish. "I lived my life exactly by the book, and the whole thing was slammed on me. So, screw it. I wanted to try something I never, ever considered for myself, and I landed on opening a flower shop. And I *love* it. Flowers are there when you're born, they're there for anniversaries and milestones, and they're there again when you die. I like the idea of being a very, very small part of that."

"That's a lot deeper than flowers are pretty and they smell good."

He laughs. "Yeah, and there's that too."

"You're … not like I thought you'd be."

"You know what? You aren't either."

I tilt my head. "What did you think I'd be like?"

"Not even really sure. But whatever it was"—he waves a hand over me—"this isn't it."

"Right back at you, sweetheart."

I know exactly what he means too. I'm not sure what I'd been expecting from Orson. Someone quiet? Shy? Hurting? But while he's not boisterous like me, he keeps me on my toes and is the furthest thing from the shy and bumbling guy I'd met when his ass was covered in mud. Which is good. Because fuck do I like this guy.

"So …" He shifts his body toward me, letting his legs fall open in a way that immediately catches my interest. "I think I still owe you."

"Owe me for what?"

"Don't you remember our first date?" He runs his thumb from the center of his chest all the way down to the rolled-up band of my sweat. "I lost the game we were playing, and you named your prize."

My gaze snaps up to his. "You've gotta be shitting me."

"Try me. Say you want to cash in."

"And what happens if I do?"

"Then I put all those years of training to good use."

"Technically, we never agreed there'd be a prize …" I'm not even sure why I'm arguing the point here because Orson is literally offering me a lap dance, and if I thought he was actually serious, he'd be in my lap already.

His eyes are bright as he leans forward and rests a hand on my knee. "I'm *very* good at them."

"You've also said many times that it was a chore to do it for the men who paid you."

"But you're not paying me." He picks up his phone, thumbs through for a moment, and then Def Leppard's "Pour Some Sugar on Me" starts to play. He sets the phone on the table, presses both hands to my knees, and leans forward so his face is an inch from mine. "Should we see if giving you your reward feels like a chore?"

I swallow thickly, sure I should say no but not able to make the word form. Because … I think he *is* serious. "More than happy to be your test subject."

The smile Orson gives me is wicked as he slowly parts my knees and sinks down between them. He hovers there for a second, on his heels, knees spread like mine, dick imprint against my sweats as he looks up and locks eyes with me. Then he rolls his hips as he stands, and it's that moment when I realize I'm a goner.

Orson can *dance*. His body is loose, fluid, hitting every beat. And between those sexy-as-fuck hip rolls and booty shakes, he doesn't take himself too seriously. He pulls faces and winks, throws in some lassos and dabs, a few finger guns, and he has me smiling like a goddamn fool. Drinking in his impressive body. Holding back from touching.

What Magic Mike shit is this?

Orson dances a step closer. And closer again. Some of the humor has left his expression, eyes darker, locking with mine, holding. His lips part as he reaches up to run his hands slowly through his hair, flexing his biceps, knees bumping with mine.

My grin is long gone as I swallow past the gargantuan lump in my throat.

Then the chorus kicks in at the exact moment Orson grips the back of my chair, jumps his feet out to straddle my thighs, and rolls his body. Over and over again to the music, close but not touching. Scent filling my nostrils, abs clenching, sweats sitting low and showing off the dip of his V and a hint of his pubes.

I'm desperate to press my thumbs to his cum gutters. To link them under his waistband and slowly drag the sweats down.

"Eyes on mine," he says.

I immediately follow directions. My gaze snaps to his, and the air punches from my lungs at the way he's looking at me. Unmasked lust, pure want, that snakes down my spine and pools in my belly.

His lips hitch up on one side, and then his ass lands in my lap. My eyes almost roll back at the friction.

Orson's sinful hips don't stop. Rolling and swaying, grinding down into me. He grips my shoulders to arch backward, showing off his body, and I'm fucking lost in him. I control myself enough to not touch, but fuck me, it's a real challenge by this point. His muscles are tempting me, his scent is driving me crazy, and the slight bulge I'm trying to ignore is making my blood hot.

Orson reaches for the bottom of my shirt, teases his fingers along the hem, lighting the skin he touches on fire. When he shoves my T-shirt up, I lift my arms, helping him rid me of it. His chest to my chest. Skin on skin. Warm, delicious, addictive.

Then Orson stands, hooks one leg over my shoulder, and the bulge I've been doing my best not to look at is right there in my face. Bobbing and hardening beneath the soft material, begging for my mouth, making my cock so stiff I'm practically cross-eyed, stare glued to the performance happening a few inches away.

"Holy *fuck*." The words come out a thousand times louder than I mean them to, but I'm in serious danger of being *too* turned on. What's the deal here? Just a fun bit of teasing? Will it be too weird if I *actually* blow my load?

Not like it'd be my fault when he's an inch away from grinding against my fucking face.

Orson's leg releases me, and his cock disappears, only to be replaced by his ass. That fucking round, perfect booty twerking up and down in a hypnotic rhythm. I want to lean forward, sink my teeth in. Warn him that this is a game I can play all night, but before I can move, his ass lands in my lap. Right over my cock. There's no way he doesn't know what he's doing to me. No way to deny that his body is turning me on.

The friction is sweet relief and agonizing torture all at once. I'm trying to keep it together, trying to be good and not get lost in him, not freak him out, but at this point, if he doesn't realize I'm this fucking close to the edge, the man is an idiot. He knows what he's doing to me.

And he's still going.

So he *wants* to be doing this to me.

That thought almost turns me on as much as this lap dance.

"Orson …" I gasp, trying to warn him. To let him know that soon, I won't be able to stop myself. My hands are aching to grab his hips, my cock desperate to thrust up against him.

Instead of backing off though, his fingers link through mine, and he steers my hands to his chest. My palms make contact with all that warm, smooth skin, marveling at every ridge as he drags my hands down to his hips and back up again.

Motherfucker, it's on.

I pull him against me, back to my chest, hips getting in on the action as I grope every part of his torso I can reach. His neck is right beside my face, and I bury my nose into it, inhaling the smell of his hot skin, scraping my blunt nails over his pecs, grinding my cock against his ass with only one goal in mind.

I need to come.

My brain is a lust haze where nothing else exists but getting there.

Orson's movements get faster, harder, more desperate. My eyes flicker open for a second to see his hand dive beneath the sweats and close around his cock. The mouthwatering, dark pink head peeks out as he jerks himself fast, and I have to slam my eyes closed again.

My hands clamp down on his hips, and I rut against him like I'm possessed. Like I'll die if I stop. The uncontrolled grunts coming from me mix with the music and that staticky type of feeling taking over my brain, reaching all the way down every limb. Making them float.

"Oh, yeah," he breathes.

And when I look down, thick ropes of cum spurt from his cock. My balls pull tight, zaps going off at the base of my spine, and it's not even a second later that I follow him over the edge in a wave of mind-numbing relief.

It isn't until some of the buzzing goodness and brain fog recedes that I realize I've just come in my pants.

For the first time in my adult life.

I groan and press my face to his shoulder. "That was … one hell of a reward."

To my complete relief, Orson cracks up laughing. "Can confirm that wasn't a chore. Not even close."

We both sit there breathing for a second before Orson reaches over and turns off the music.

We're plunged into sudden silence, and that awkwardness I'd been expecting kicks in. At least, that's what I think is happening.

When Orson turns in my lap, he's wearing the type of smug smile I'm usually giving him. I'm about to ask what he's looking so cocky about when his eyes very slowly travel to my chest.

Then he flicks my pierced nipple. Hard.

"Ah, fuck." I hurry to cover it. "Jerk."

"Told you I'd get to see it."

"You went to all that effort to see my nipple piercing?"

Orson gestures at his cum-splattered abs. "Apparently, we were both rewarded for the effort."

We laugh, but mine dies quickly. "Are we … is this okay?"

"Sure." He shrugs, trying to be casual, but my bullshit sensors are on high alert.

"Okay. Well, we should probably shower—"

"Actually, I'm going to head off." He stands to grab the dishcloth off my counter and uses it to clean up. Then he hands it to me with a smirk. "You're good to wash this for me, aren't you? *Sweetheart*?"

I take it, wishing I knew where things went from here. "It's the least I can do."

EMOTIONAL SUPPORT CHAT

Orson: *I need help.*

    Keller: *What's up?*

    Orson: *So ... you know how I'm straight, right?*

    Keller: *I don't think I want to answer that until I know where this conversation is going.*

    Orson: *I just got off with a guy and I didn't hate it.*

    Keller: *... what do you need help with? If you tell me experience, we're going to have to re-evaluate what friendship means.*

    Orson: *No, not that. I think I just need to talk to someone.*

    Keller: *Door's unlocked. I'll see you in twenty.*

13

Orson

KELLER STARES AT ME, EYES WIDER THAN USUAL, BUT NOT saying a damn thing.

"*Any* words of encouragement would be great," I point out.

"I ..." He shakes his head like he's trying to shake himself out of the shock he's gone into. "*Ford?*"

I sigh, nodding, expecting this reaction from just about everyone. Well, except Art, who'll probably offer to show me the ropes. Hence why I was pounding on Keller's door at ten at night instead of hunting Art down at Killer Brew.

"Seriously," I prompt. "*Anything* encouraging."

Keller finds a grin. "Was it good?"

My whole face flushes. I headed home to grab a shirt and clean up properly before coming here, but I'm still in Ford's baggy sweats, not wanting to rid myself of the memory yet. "What am I supposed to say to that?"

"It's pretty simple. Did you nut like your life depended on it?"

"I couldn't have stopped myself if I'd tried."

He chuckles, low and deep. "I take it we can say sex with a man was successful, then?"

"We didn't have sex."

Keller's dark eyes study me. "You were both … intimate. You both came. Not sure how you'd call it anything else."

"No." I frown. "Sex is … well …"

"Intercourse?"

"Exactly."

Apparently, that's the wrong thing to say because he roars with laughter. "Damn, you really were a straight dude."

I huff. "Still am. I think."

"Yeah, I'm not going to tell you how to identify, but I can guaran-fucking-tee you start spouting that *straight* shit around Ford and you'll piss him off."

Worry swirls in my gut. "You don't think I'm straight?"

"Well." He gestures toward me with both hands. "Taking nuance out of it, you got off with another man. What would you call it?"

A bone-headed decision that I couldn't stop myself from making?

"And if you say the word 'mistake,' I'm kicking you out of my house."

I run a hand over the scruff on my jaw. "I definitely wasn't going to say that. I knew what I was doing."

"You were the one dancing, so I should hope so. I also hope you can *actually* dance and didn't embarrass the hell out of yourself, but that's a conversation for another day."

Or never. Keller's a cool guy. He's another member of the DMC, and unlike Art and Griff, who I'm closest with, he's levelheaded. Art is all about theatrics, and Griff is a ball of anxiety half of the time, but Keller listens and gives me time to think. Let's me get to the answer on my own, without trying to fix all my problems for me. Art is a fixer, a hero type—look at the DMC, for example—and Griff hates seeing anyone he cares about struggle.

Maybe Keller just doesn't care about me as much as they do, but he hasn't kicked me out of his house yet, so I'm taking that as a green light.

"Where do I go from here?" I ask.

"Where do you *want* to go?"

Fuck. Maybe I should have gone to one of the others. Even Payne would have made some foolish suggestions, but I've only been getting to know him over the last few months, so I assume a late-night house call would be confusing and pushing the boundaries of our friendship. Plus, who knows what he and Beau are up to?

"I want to keep our friendship, no question. I *like* being around him. He's fun and hardworking and always makes me laugh."

"Do you want to be friends, or do you want to marry the guy?"

I flip him off. "Friends can make other friends laugh."

"It's not your words, my man. It's your face. You pregnant? Because you're glowing."

I slap my hands over my cheeks, but they don't feel any different than usual. "Can you concentrate?"

"Sure. But for what it's worth, I think I'm paying more attention than you are."

"You're barely on topic."

"What topic do you want us to be on?"

Okay, I take it all back. This whole sorting through things myself sucks ass. "Will sex ruin things between us?"

"Quick question first: You said you want the friendship to continue. What about the orgasms?"

Heat runs down my spine again at the memory of his hard cock pressing against my ass. "That's a solid maybe. On my end. I have no idea what he's thinking because I all but bolted once it was over. Does he regret it? Is he going to be weird now? Will we even be friends, or did he get what he wants out of me, and now he's not interested anymore?"

He hums, thinking through my billion and one questions. "You know who would have answers for you?"

"Who?" I ask, perking up at the thought.

"*Ford*, you idiot. You're how old? Go home, get some sleep, then call him in the morning. Or go and see him. Talk this shit out. You're allowed to have feelings about everything, and he's gotta expect that after what happened. Maybe he's right there with you, maybe he doesn't give a fuck now he's spilled a load, but sitting here and stressing about it isn't going to help."

"How are you still single?"

He pumps his eyebrows. "Why? You interested?"

"Not even a little bit. Sorry, but one guy is more than enough man trouble for me."

"They always are."

"Seriously though. You have all this …" I gesture around the enormous house. "And you're a cool guy. Why aren't you all loved up?"

Something flits behind his eyes. "I'm waiting on the right man."

"Man? Not woman?" As far as I know, Keller's pansexual.

"We'll see, I guess."

The front door slams, and I nearly jump out of my seat. "Who—"

"Dad? We're hungry!"

Keller lets out a long, controlled exhale. "There's pastries in the kitchen."

"Your son?"

"And his best friend, I'm assuming. Those two are inseparable, I swear." He raises his voice. "And for some reason, they choose to raid my pantry instead of their own."

A head pops into the room. And I say *head* because the rest of him is hidden behind the wall. "We're growing boys."

"You're twenty-six."

"Maybe when we're as old as you, we'll stop eating so much." The guy is tan, with sandy-blond hair and what I think might be a hint of Southern twang.

"Go eat and go home," Keller says.

"No can do. We're crashing here tonight."

Keller groans, and the guy laughs before disappearing again.

"Your son?" Even after being friends for years, I know next to nothing about his son except that he's been away at college.

"Nope. His friend."

"So …" I don't know how to ask this. "Are they, you know. Like Heath and Griff inseparable?"

"*No.*" He clears his throat. "They're not like that. At all. I'm sure."

Huh. Okay. I would have thought twenty-six was too old to be all protective papa bear, but what the hell would I know? Your kids are your kids, I guess.

"I'm going to leave you to it," I say, pushing out of my

seat. "Should probably try to sneak in some sleep between the restless turning I'll do all night."

"Enjoy your stress dreams."

"I fully intend to."

But walking out of Keller's house, I finally allow myself a moment to process what the hell went down tonight. The excitement over meeting Ford for our … well, I was joking when I called it a date, but that's exactly what it was. A date. With a man. Who cooked me dinner and made me smile and gave me all of his time and attention. A man whose body I couldn't stop eyeing. A man who made me feel *alive*, whose deep tone and steady eye contact and overwhelming presence made me hard. So hard I'd wanted to tease him, and deny it all I like, I knew where I wanted that teasing to end up.

I'd *wanted* to make him come. And somehow, I beat him to the line.

My thoughts cycle back around to Keller's genuine surprise over me still thinking of myself as straight.

I guess in the most clinical sense of the word, I'm not, am I? The whole notion makes my head spin. Sure, I'd wondered about all the different versions of me, but this is one I never would have seen coming until very recently, and even when I'd questioned it, the going through with things felt way too big to ever attempt. But I did. Almost without question. As I sat there at Ford's table, inhaling his scent, letting his voice drift over me, I'd been wrestling with how to close the distance between us. At that moment, him being a man didn't register, him being my friend did. And even with all the flirting between us, I couldn't convince myself that he wouldn't turn me down. Not having sex for years can fuck with your head, apparently.

Not that it mattered in that moment. In that moment, I felt it. Bone-deep. A desperate need to have his hands on me. To drag my body over his. To look into his face as he came.

I didn't get to do the last one, but as Meatloaf said, two out of three ain't bad. I'm also torn on whether that would have made things better or worse. In the moment, better of course, but now? After? It's probably a good thing I missed something so … intimate.

Giving someone a lap dance has always made me feel powerful, but tonight was next-level. Taking a man like Ford to the edge … just by using my body. A shiver races through me.

Oh yeah, I've never felt so high in all my life.

My mind tugs at that thought, disrupts it, tries to lay the guilt on thick. *Don't forget about Tara.*

I wrestle the horrible feelings down. Somehow, getting off with someone I like feels more disrespectful to her memory than all the sleeping around I did right after she died.

That had been a grief-filled spiral. A way of punishing myself. Of increasing the pain. And there was *so much* pain.

This … whether Ford writes me off as a fun time or not, this was calculated. Consensual. *Wanted.*

I had sex with Ford because he made me feel *good.* She would have wanted me to move on. To feel happy again.

Logically, I know that.

Emotionally, I'm conflicted.

But there's no point stressing about it all now. I remind myself to be patient. To go with the flow. Take it as it comes.

I don't think that mentality has ever been harder.

14

Ford

I clutch the coffees I'm carrying maybe too hard as I cross the street, but fuck me, I'm nervous. I've never been this nervous in my life. I don't *get* nervous, so it's easy enough for me to compare.

But messing around or not, Orson's special. I've already decided. There's no way I'm letting him run off scared because of a little friendly fire, and if I know him at all, that means me taking the first step.

If we're keeping on with a platonic friendship, I'll selfishly take it and make more of an effort to stamp out all these sexy thoughts. Which won't be all that easy when I've spent the past twenty-four hours replaying that lap dance instead of sleeping.

Orson opens the shop early on a Saturday, so even though I should still have my lazy ass in bed, I push through Oopsie Daisies' door just past seven. He must be out back, and I hope like hell that he's busy and didn't see me and bolt.

It seems like a waste that I've never been in here before this all started. The shop is welcoming, calming. Timber floorboards, stark white walls. A brown leather couch with blue cushions on one wall and rows and rows of flowers literally everywhere else. The door behind the long counter leads out back, so rather than hang about here waiting, I let myself back there.

Orson is standing at a long counter, hunched over something, every line of his body looking tense. It doesn't fill me with confidence over my visit.

"Morning," I say as chipper as I can make it.

Orson almost jumps out of his skin. He glances around like he's forgotten where he is, then lets out a long breath. "Hey, I didn't hear you come in."

Thank fuck for that. I step close enough to hand over his coffee and inspect his face for any sign of discomfort.

"Thank you." His words are sincere, but I definitely detect a guardedness in his eyes.

"I was in the area."

That relaxes him. His smile stretches before he takes a sip of his coffee and turns back to his phone. The same tension from before rolls over him.

"Everything okay?"

"Nope. My driver called off sick, and I have a huge wedding delivery to make. The planner has already called me twice for updates, and the shop gets busy in an hour. If he'd called earlier, I could have delivered them before I opened, but now—"

"I got you."

His head snaps up toward me, heavy frown crossing his forehead. "Ah, no. I'm not complaining so you'll do it."

"I want to."

I swear Orson's eyes almost fall out. "You gave your day off last week to help me. I can't ask you to do it again."

"You didn't ask. I also didn't offer. I made a statement, and that statement stands."

"Ford—"

I step right into his space. "Don't make this any more difficult than it needs to be, sweetheart."

He swallows, rough and thick, and I love the way his Adam's apple bobs up and down. "I'll feel bad."

"So gimme an IOU, then." I slap his ass. "Now, giddy up, pony, and tell me what to do."

Without waiting for his direction, I walk over to the cool room and slide open the heavy door. Buckets of flowers sit on pallets, but by the door is very clearly the wedding order. A handful of bouquets and a buttload of large flower arrangements.

Orson appears at my side, close enough that I can feel his body warmth. "Maybe I should take them."

"You want me to watch the store?"

His face contorts as he thinks, and I wait patiently. I'm happy with either option, but a quick drop-off sounds easier.

"I'm torn." He chews on his thumbnail while he thinks. "The shop is going to be busy. Very busy. And people don't just buy off the floor; they want things made custom. But a wedding is important, and this planner is … well, let's say she scares me."

"I should get along well with her, then."

He glances up at me in surprise, and I can't control my laugh.

"I scare most people. This isn't news to me. If she thinks she can intimidate me, she's in for a shock."

"I guess …"

"Wow. Such confidence in me. You better stop with the compliments before I get a big head."

He shifts anxiously. "You know it's not like that. I'm overly conscious that this is a big day for the couple and would hate it if my flowers were the reason their day wasn't perfect."

And this is why I've decided he's special. This is why I'm cool to hang around, even if *more* isn't on the cards for us—because Orson has a big heart. Hell, it's why I'd even consider a *more* with him in the first place.

I have no real opinion on relationships. Some are shitty, and some seem like they were always meant to be, but from what I've witnessed, most relationships have ups and downs. They require work. It's not the kind of thing I'd jump into with just anyone—I've rarely ever had that itch to even try— but I know what I feel for Orson isn't all about sex.

I *enjoy* him. Our time, our jokes, our *dates*.

With one hand over my heart, I raise the other and say, "I swear to be the most attentive and thorough delivery driver you've ever had, and then after your shift tonight, we can go for a walk along the boardwalk, and you can buy me some gelato."

"You're not going to drop this, are you?"

"Might as well give me the keys." I send him a grin, then go to reach for the nearest bucket when Orson's hand lands on my arm.

"Hey, I …"

I straighten at his serious tone. "You what?"

"Should we talk about it?"

Nerves—*fucking nerves*—spring to life in my gut. Deep, winged little fuckers making me all shivery. "Do you want to talk about it?"

"I don't know."

And somehow, I know that's an honest answer, not one simply to blow the conversation off. "Well, let me know when you do, then."

"Don't you want to talk about it?"

I shrug. "What's to talk about? I'm so irresistible I make even the straightest guys thirsty."

"*Ford.*" His cheeks pinken. "I'm … I'm not sure—"

I press my fingers to his mouth because if his brain is going wild, it's all going to fall out of his mouth. When we have this conversation, I want it to be purposeful. "You don't need to be sure of anything, sweetheart. We're friends. That's important to me. The rest I won't say no to, but I'm never gonna push, and if there are things going on in your mind that you need to work through, then work through them. There's no time limit. And there are no rules that you have to be one way or the other."

His mouth closes under my touch, and I draw my hand away. "I hate you."

"I get that a lot."

"You're very smart."

My laugh echoes off the walls of the cool room. "That's one I *don't* get a lot."

I'm about to turn and start grabbing the flowers again when Orson grabs my arm and hauls me into a hug. I freeze at first, caught off guard, because while we wrestle and invade each other's personal space often, and he literally rubbed up all over my cock the other night, we've never just … hugged. Embraced. It's a whole different dynamic to what I'm used to with him, but before he can freak out and pull away, I swamp him in my arms.

His chin tucks over my shoulder, arms around my back,

chest flush with mine. And fucking hell, it's *nice*. My nerves are back, along with this happiness radiating out into my limbs and making them all light. It's a new feeling. One I could get addicted to. Crave. The high from sex I can get anywhere, but *this*. This is so rare I can't remember if I've ever felt it before. All I know is it's worth sticking around and seeing where this goes.

"As much as I love being pressed up against you, my cock can't even rally for the occasion it's so cold in here."

He steps back, and it's like looking at another person. No more awkwardness or doubt, just Orson exactly the way he normally is. "Okay, let's get this loaded up. I still can't believe you're wasting your Saturday morning doing this, but you're saving my ass."

"Happy to. I like your ass."

"That definitely hasn't escaped my notice."

We work together to load up the van; then Orson gives me the address and directions on what to do once I get there. He's precise with every detail to the point I'm sure I can pull this off.

Right before I'm about to leave, he grabs my hand and drags me back inside.

"Wear this," he says, grabbing an apron. He steps forward to loop it around my neck, and then his arms wrap around me as he ties it behind my back. "Now you'll look like you belong."

If this wedding planner is anything like the anal-retentive prissy mess I'm expecting, I can guarantee my full sleeves and neck tattoos won't give that impression. "Admit it. You wanted to feel me up, didn't you?"

He tilts his head, hazel eyes catching the light as the lines in the corners of them deepen. He leans in, closer and closer again. Our lips don't touch, but he's so close I can taste his mint-scented words. "You know what? Maybe I did."

15

Orson

IT'S BEEN TEN DAYS. TEN DAYS SINCE WE HAD SEX. TEN days since I felt his body against mine. Ten days since I saw his nipple piercing, and now, I'm hungry to taste it.

The wedding delivery went off without a hitch, and then the next day, Ford showed up to help at the market as well. I helped out with the soapbox cars again, we got our gelato, and we've had dinner together twice.

Even with us finding pockets of time to spend together in between all our work, it's not enough. I want to be around him constantly.

That's not good.

As for the sex, I'm so boned up half the time that I don't think I'd stop him even if he threw me over a table at Killer Brew and went to town on me. That's a big sign that I'm okay with a repeat, but every time I imagine it, *he's* doing stuff to *me*. His hands or his mouth—holy fuck, it's hot. But his dick? I can't picture it. I can't picture touching it, let alone giving him head, and if we started something, I'd have to get comfortable with that pretty quickly. I don't have it in me to take and not give.

"I need queer advice," I say suddenly, raising my voice to be heard over the conversation. I'm at a DMC catch-up, but this one is smaller since it was one of those times Art jumped in the group chat and invited everyone down for drinks. All of us who are local are here though, and once Payne moved back to town, it became a five-five split between us straight guys and the queer ones, but it looks like the gay agenda is taking over, and we're about to become the majority.

Thanks to me.

"You've come to the right group," Payne says.

Griff looks lost for words. "When you say 'advice,' what kind of advice do you—"

"I had sex with Ford."

Keller hides his laugh behind his glass as Art, who was heading for Barney and Marcus, pulls up with an obnoxious screech.

"This sounds like my kind of conversation," he declares, dropping the drinks he was carrying on the bar table and climbing onto a stool. "I knew it. Men who turn down a date by saying they're straight instead of no are always leaving that door open a teeny bit."

"You can't possibly know that," Keller says.

Art shrugs. "Just speaking from experience."

"If the experience is talking out of your ass, yes, you do that a lot."

"Fucking A," Art says, then turns to me. "You. Talk. None of us will say no to details."

Payne lifts a hand. He has full-sleeve tattoos like Ford. "I'd be okay without them."

Griff gives him the side-eye. "None of us will say no to stories about Beau either."

Payne flips Griff off, but he's smiling. "You have Heath now. This horniness of yours shouldn't be an issue anymore."

"I can't see it ever going away."

"At least you won't have to invest in Viagra." Art sits back, dopey smile on his lips. "Living the dream."

"Really?" Payne asks skeptically. "No Viagra is the dream? Out of *everything* else, that's your nirvana?"

"Hey, sometimes when you're taking on more than one guy at a time, the little boxer gets tired."

"Believe it or not," I cut in before they can keep going, "Viagra *isn't* the thing I needed advice on."

Art cocks his head. "It isn't? So why are we talking about it, then?"

It's like herding cats, I swear. I love these men, but staying on topic isn't a strength of theirs. "You guys brought it up."

"*I* didn't bring it up," Payne points out.

"I think it's safe to say it was all Art." Griff smirks at him. "If it's sex related, it's *always* Art."

"You're the one who brought up Beau," Payne throws back.

"In *general*. I didn't mention anything sexual."

"We all knew you meant it though. I thought you were going to give it a rest with teasing me about him."

Griff holds out his hands like there's nothing he can do. "Sometimes you just need to gamble a punch in the face."

I choke back a laugh because that will only encourage

them. "Purely because I want to avoid seeing Griff knocked out, can we please get back on topic?"

Three blank faces stare back at me, which makes Keller sigh. "You're going to need to remind them."

"Don't make me say it again."

"You'd think hearing that our token straight friend crossed swords with Ford would be enough to keep them focused."

"Apparently, that was too much to ask."

"Oooh, that's right." Art rubs his chin. "Sometimes I forget straight people exist."

I wave to the other guys in the room. "Go tell them that."

He cringes. "Have you seen Silas? Unlike Griff, I'd like to not be punched tonight."

"What about your straight bartender?" Griff teases.

"*Damn.*" Griff really does want to be carried out of here on a stretcher. Like it always does when the hot bartender is mentioned, Art's jaw tenses for a second.

"We're having a nice conversation. No need to bring up that little punk."

"I wouldn't call him little," I say. Sure, the guy is lean, but even I've clocked the way his biceps are hugged by those tight bartender T-shirts. "Wait. Is the fact I've noticed Joey's muscles gay?"

"It could be," Payne says at the same time as Art snaps, "What are you looking at his muscles for?"

A silence sinks in, broken only by Keller trying to hold in his laugh.

Art clears his throat. "S'pose it's hard to miss when he insists on wearing a shirt two sizes too small."

None of us have the energy to fight him on it. Art is purposely obtuse when it comes to Joey, which is hilarious to witness when Joey's flirting is so over-the-top it borders on ridiculous.

"And still my questions are going unanswered," I say.

"Sorry." Art claps his hands and points at me. "I'm focused. Go."

"Obviously, things happened with Ford, and I enjoyed it. I don't think I'm having any kind of gay panic, and I *think* I want to try again, but I'm worried that I'll instigate something and then not be into it."

"If you're curious, you'll be into it," Griff says.

"Not necessarily," Keller corrects. "It's like anyone. If the attraction's there though, there's a high likelihood that the body parts won't matter. First time I was with a guy, it didn't even factor in that it was any different to being with a woman."

"It was different for me." Griff rubs a hand over his face. "But I think it would have been different even if it was another woman I slept with after Poppy."

"If it helps, start out slow," Payne says. "There's something really hot about feeling a cock pulse in your hand as it goes off. Especially that first time."

"I have a cock. I'm familiar with that feeling."

He shakes his head, grin taking over his face. "Nah, it's completely different with someone else."

"I'm up for a handie if you need practice," Art offers.

I give him a blank look. "Has anyone else told you how generous you are?"

"Frequently. Especially in the bedroom." He reaches for his fly.

"*Fuck* no." I hold up my hand like I'm trying to cover the view. "I mean, uh, no. It's fine. I think I'll stick to figuring this thing out with Ford."

"Have you actually talked to him yet?" Keller asks.

"Kind of."

"Okay, so what convoluted half conversation did you have?"

"I said I didn't know what to think. He said to take my time, but he's open to things happening."

"And you didn't say anything to that?" Griff asks. "It's not like you to hold back."

"I don't want to say the wrong thing or lead him on." Ford's ... special. "We flirt a lot though. I like that."

"Ford flirts with everyone," Art says.

"Doesn't mean I don't like it."

"Well, my offer is there if you change your mind."

"Hey ..." Griff says. "When I needed experience, you said you were busy."

Art laughs. "Because you're a stage-five clinger, my friend. Look at what happened to the first person you slept with as a single man: you've basically shacked up together."

"But you'd get your dick out for Orson no problems."

"I do anything for my boys."

Payne drums his fingers on the table. "So you've said to all of us, but seriously. Were you actually going to get your dick out?"

"It's only sex. If one of you needs me, I'm going to help out." He points at Griff. "Except you."

"Help out Joey," Griff half cough, half says into his glass.

Art ignores him, even as we all snigger.

"I've known Ford a long time, and Keller's right," Art says. "If you talk to him about it, he'll be understanding. And hey, if you leave him with blue balls, it'll only take him one phone call to have someone ready to fix that problem.

We used to go out together, and all the twinks are weak for him, I swear."

That immediately reminds me of Molly. And how sure Ford was that it would only take one time with him to change things. Does he still feel that way now with how things are going between us? Should I ask him about it?

He hasn't mentioned Molly once since that night, but then, why would he?

All I know is that remembering how Molly looked at Ford—like Ford was the greatest thing he'd ever seen—fills me with jealousy. I'm ... *threatened* by him.

He wouldn't hesitate over getting on his knees for Ford. Am I going to push myself into sex to prove I'm better than the guy?

I let the panic go.

No.

I'm definitely not going to do that.

But I am going to take Keller's advice. It's time to stop being chickenshit and actually talk to him.

16

Ford

THE MUSIC IS POURING OUT OF THE GARAGE INTO THE YARD, where I'm working with Murray on restoring a '63 Corvette. It's unseasonably warm for fall; my armpits are soaked, my hands are caked with engine grease, and my hat is damp over my hair, but I love it.

I have the best job in the world.

Between here and helping out Orson, I haven't had a day off in weeks, but it doesn't feel that way. Opposite, actually. I have more energy than I've had in a long time.

I worked all day yesterday and then had dinner with Barney last night, so it's been a whole day since I've seen Orson's face. He's not at work today, but I'm already itching my brain, trying to come up with a reason for needing flowers tomorrow, so I can go in there. I'm going stupid over a man in a way I never have before.

Fuck me, I like it.

We haven't talked about what happened between us since

the day I did the deliveries, but somehow, it doesn't matter. I told him to take his time, and I mean it. Questioning your sexuality isn't an easy process, even if you are an ally. For Orson, I get the feeling it's not about him crossing lines with a man but that he's struggling to work out what that means for *him*. As a person. This process has nothing to do with me.

Mostly.

I've caught the way he looks at me when he thinks I'm not paying attention.

And maybe that's what's making it so easy to wait him out. He's attracted to me. It might not come to anything, but it feels good all the same.

Besides, while he sorts his shit out, we've been having a boatload of one-on-one time, and it's just … fun.

Instead of focusing on my maybe-love life, I should be focused on replacing *another* assistant, but … that whole thing's low on my list of priorities right now.

"Wait, you're a *mechanic*?"

A smile hits my lips at the sound of the familiar voice behind me. I straighten, turning from the Sting Ray's engine and fixing eyes on the man who's been on my mind nonstop for weeks now. "Something I do in my spare time when I'm not coming to the rescue of cute florists."

He laughs, his whole face lighting up. I'm so fucking glad that brief hesitance of his is gone, and we've fallen back into an easy friendship.

"Geez, they let anyone back here, don't they?" I ask him.

"Security *did* pat me down on the way in. Insisted on a strip search. Slightly uncomfortable but worth it to see you."

"Wow. I probably shouldn't tell you this … I don't have security."

"So who had their paws all over me?"

I cock an eyebrow. "Think we'd both like to know the answer to that."

Orson steps close enough to rest his hand on my chest. "Maybe I made that up so you'd think about me naked."

"Who says I don't do that already?"

And while I know not to look too deeply into his flirting, I like hearing it all the same.

"You good out here, Murray?" I ask.

"Yeah, boss. Go with your boyfriend."

I'm about to correct him when Orson's hand closes over my arm, and he all but drags me back inside. Some of my people send me quizzical looks on the way through the garage, but I follow along like a good little puppy. Something's gotten into Orson today, and I'm interested to see what it is.

We reach my office, and as soon as we're inside, he closes the door behind us.

Not that it matters.

I catch Taylor throwing a curious look through the large windows, and I'm sure others are doing the same.

Ignoring them, I find a rag to wipe my hands on, then round my desk and drop into my chair, loving the feel of the cool leather beneath my heated skin. I'm expecting Orson to sit down across from me, but instead, he casually moves closer and leans against the desk right beside me. I take off my sweaty hat to see him better and toss it onto the desk.

He chuckles and runs his fingers through my hair. "You're a mess."

"I can imagine."

"Should probably take your shirt off too. It was hot out there."

I eye him for a moment, curious about where he's taking this. It's not like the usual subtle flirting, but I might as well see where we end up. I reach back and grab my shirt, tugging it over my head. Then I drop it on the desk beside my hat. "Much better."

His gaze drops to my piercing. "Good. I'd hate for you to be uncomfortable."

I give him a moment to let his gaze wander. Removing my shirt hasn't done any good in cooling me down because the hunger in Orson's stare is setting me on fire.

"Were you here for a reason, or did you just miss me?" I ask, breaking the tension.

He grins guiltily, knowing he wasn't being subtle. "Can't it be both?"

"Sure."

"Then both."

"Missed you too, sweetheart."

His eyes meet mine, and the nerves in my gut take off at a gallop. "It's only been a day."

"I don't see why that matters. Now, what were you here for?"

"Ah." He drops his butt onto the desk, squarely facing the back wall. "Maybe here isn't a great place to do it, but I'm back at work tomorrow, and you hadn't written back to my text to see you tonight."

Text? I slide open my desk drawer and tap my phone screen. Huh. There it is. "Sorry, I don't bother taking my phone out with me."

"It's okay. I was … anxious."

I shoot forward in my chair, every protective instinct on high alert. "Anxious about what?"

He bats at my shoulder. "Calm down. I decided that I had

to talk to you about what's going on in my head, and I've been worrying over how to do that."

Okay, not what I was expecting. "You don't have to have any conversation you're not ready for."

"And that's why I do. You've been patient and kind, so I owe it to you to open up."

"You don't owe—"

He laughs. "It's called mutual respect, Ford. Surprisingly, it's something I have for you."

"Yikes. Poor judgment skills on your end."

His hit to my shoulder is harder this time. "You're making this hard."

"You make *me* hard all the time. I'm only returning the favor."

"Sometimes it's like I'm talking to Art."

"Makes sense. We used to hang out a lot."

"Did you two ever—"

"Once."

"Ah." He scrapes his fingers through his hair. "That shouldn't surprise me."

"It shouldn't. It's Art. He'll offer it up to anyone, and after leaving the club alone, I wasn't in the mood to say no."

"When did it …"

That's a good question. So long ago I can barely remember specifics, though the alcohol doesn't help with that either. "We were … late twenties, I think? Fuck me, like fifteen years ago."

"Wow, you're old."

"Screw you, you're older than I am."

Orson shrugs. "Maybe, but I've aged better."

I reach up to rub his salt-and-pepper scruff. "Like fine wine."

"I'm told it's distinguished."

"You won't hear any complaints from me." It's one of the things I like about him. "But I'm confident you didn't come here to ask about my past hookups."

"*Oh*. Nope. Did you want to head out for lunch, or …"

"If you want our private conversation spread all over town, sure."

"Good point."

He still looks a tiny bit worried, so I wheel my chair over until I'm right in front of him. "This is a good place for a private conversation. And so is my place later."

"Here's fine. So … I think it's obvious I'm attracted to you. It's new and caught me totally off guard, but I like it."

A little burst of happiness goes off in my chest. "I like it too."

"Good." His eyes crinkle up in amusement. "The thing I'm confused about is … well, what happens from here?"

"What do you mean?"

His tongue swipes over his lip. "Well, our friendship comes first for me, and I know you said you'd be fine hooking up again, but I … I'm not …"

"A hookup guy?"

"Yes. I don't want to be either."

"So if anything progresses between us, it won't be casual?"

A long gust of air leaves him. "Exactly."

"Okay, I can agree to that."

"You …" He startles. "Just like that?"

"Sure." I can understand him being confused when dating isn't something I've done a lot of, but surely after the last month, he has to know this isn't fun and games for me? I rest my hands on the outsides of his thighs. "Does this mean we're in a relationship?"

"There's one more thing."

"Which is?"

Orson traps his bottom lip between his teeth for a second, and fuck, it's exciting to think I might actually be able to do that myself. "I don't know how to give you everything you'd want in a relationship."

Ah. Sex. Disappointing, but not a deal breaker. I'm not sure what kind of relationship he's envisioning for us—a romantic one, but open to others sexually, complete celibacy, occasional spontaneous orgasms?—but whatever it is, I don't want him to think that's all I want from him. "Look, I'm happy to cook most of the time, but I'd be lying if I said it wouldn't be nice for you to make me the occasional dinner."

Another whack to the shoulder, followed by a huge smile. "You know that's not what I mean."

"Yeah, I do … so what's your concern?"

"I think I'd be okay with it, but it's kinda confronting to think about your cock. And touching it and …" He swallows. "I'm worried I'll freak out and ruin things."

As much as I want to assure him that would never happen, it's also a legitimate concern. I've been with guys who were curious and into it before things got real.

"I get that."

"You do?"

"Sure. And you won't know how you feel until you're in that position, but at least I know where your head is at. We can work through it together."

"You're right." He steps forward between my legs and towers over me in a way that makes me squeeze his thighs tighter. "I won't know until I do it."

Orson sinks to his knees.

Holy fucking shit.

I do a quick scan of my office windows, but no one is paying us attention anymore, and the desk is blocking Orson anyway.

Except when I glance back down to where he's slowly reaching for the button on my pants, his eyes flick up to mine for a second, and I read the look in them.

Determination mixed with fear.

"Hey." I cover my fly with one hand and tilt his face up to mine with the other. "While I appreciate you wanting to jump right in, this isn't how I want it to go."

"You don't want me to blow you under your desk at work?" His voice is full of doubt. Accurately so, because when he says it like that, it sounds crazy.

I help him to his feet, and this time, I join him. Standing close, me looking down at him this time. "Why don't we table that idea for another day? I'm dirty and sweaty, and trust me when I say you don't want that for your first time."

He narrows his eyes. "So what do I want?"

I smirk and throw his answer back at him. "Mutual respect. We're gonna take it slow, okay? Why don't you come over for dinner tonight, and we'll see where things go. No pressure on anything happening. We'll hang out, eat, cross the reality TV bullet point off our list, maybe cuddle."

He laughs. "Cuddle?"

"I *love* to cuddle."

"Is it weird that makes me more nervous than thinking about the sex stuff?"

"Nope. Not weird if that's how you feel."

"Okay. You're cooking though, right? You might have only been joking before, but it's not my favorite thing."

"You like fish?"

"Sure."

"Then I got you." I take a chance to reach up and cup his face. His scruff is scratchy and warm against my palm. I lean in until our lips are a breath apart. "People can see us," I remind him, giving him the choice to pull away.

He nods, then tilts his head up and seals his lips over mine. The kiss is soft, hesitant, full of promise. It sends shivers rippling along my spine. There's no tongue, no hunger, but it's the type of kiss that takes my breath away.

Then pain shoots through my nipple.

I hiss and pull away. "You're gonna have fun with that, aren't you?"

"I think it's a new obsession of mine."

As I gaze down into his face, happy but uncertain, I think I know exactly what he means. "You good?"

"Yeah. Pretty sure."

I stroke his cheek. "Just so you know … I'm nervous too."

17

Orson

IT TAKES A PEP TALK OF EPIC PROPORTIONS TO GET MY ASS out of the car. Ford's plain, little brick house somehow feels a thousand times more intimidating than the last time I was here. Maybe it's because I know he's inside. Maybe it's because of what happened here last time. Maybe it's because of what I think is going to happen next.

All I know is I *want* to get out of the car; I'm just having trouble making that happen.

Pushing past the building weight of who I *was*, I click open my door and gather the courage to walk up to the house.

The main door is open, and I knock on the security screen and wait.

"Come in!"

I almost expected Ford to be waiting at the door for me, but I get the impression he's giving me space. Letting me come to him in my own time. As much as I'd love him to shove me into this, I appreciate the way he's always thinking of me.

I kick off my shoes outside, then follow the smell of cooking fish through the house and find Ford out on his back deck, standing at the grill.

"You came," he calls.

"Just how scared do you think I am?"

Ford shrugs as I step outside. "I gave you good odds."

He's already got a drink waiting for me, along with stuffed baked potatoes and mushrooms on a plate. "This looks amazing."

"Fish is almost done."

While he finishes up, I take a seat at the outdoor table and watch him work. It's cooler out now than it was earlier, and Ford's wearing a long-sleeve T-shirt that hugs every line in his big body. I'm shameless about checking him out. About imagining him pressed against me again. Impressive chest and arms, stocky middle, round ass that leads to legs like tree trunks. How he holds himself, how he moves, everything about him is all hard, rough, unrefined. I've never been attracted to someone like him before.

All afternoon, I've been on my computer, looking up stories that mirror my own. Words like bisexual, pansexual, demisexual, and split attraction filled my head, but I couldn't pin it down to one thing. From what I read though, my situation isn't unique. For whatever reason, there's story after story out there where one relationship ended, and then the person became attracted to someone they'd never imagined being attracted to before.

There are all sorts of theories about why, but one stuck with me. "I learned something today," I say.

"What's that?"

"It's a pretty dense psychological conditioning type of thing. I might bore you."

"Eh, if you bore me, I'll spend the conversation checking you out instead."

Of course he will.

Ford plates up our fish, and I wait until he's sitting across from me to keep talking.

"I've been researching, trying to figure out how the hell I can be forty-five and only now realize being attracted to men is possible. A lot of what I read doesn't apply to me, but I did find an interesting explanation. I have no idea if it's what happened, but it's the closest I've gotten."

Ford's full attention is on me. It's unwavering, like he's interested, and I can't help comparing how he's just letting me get it out, to how much effort the conversation with my friends was the other night. This is a nice change.

"I think I'm bisexual, but not the half-and-half type. You heard of the Kinsey scale?"

To his credit, he doesn't laugh at me. "I have."

"So I think I'm like a one. Mostly straight but could swing to another gender under the right circumstances. But because the attraction is so rare, I've been taught to ignore it. All my life, it's been *girls girls girls*, and I realized I can't remember a time before hearing about growing up and getting a girlfriend. It was always expected. It stayed with me. In my mind, there was no other option, so I didn't even think about it. But since everything with you … I've been thinking back on things more. Really evaluating them. When I gave other guys lap dances, sure, I never got hard, but there was definitely a rush of endorphins. A feeling of power and accomplishment over turning them on." My lips turn down as I consider that maybe my body's been trying to tell me the truth about myself for years.

"That makes a lot of sense," Ford says.

I exhale loudly. "Can I be honest for a second?"

"You can be honest forever."

"It really pisses me off." The words are out before I can stop them. "If my parents, my aunts, my uncles, all those people on TV hadn't pushed the concept of husband and wife down my throat every fucking day, would I have picked up on it earlier? Would I have been able to be myself? Experiment? Experience the things that were my right to experience?" I scowl in an attempt to discourage tears. It's crushing, all the what-ifs, but I don't want to turn our night into something negative when it could be the start of a whole new positive for me.

Ford reaches across the table and gently rests his hand over mine. "I agree. It's not fair."

"What was it like for you?"

He chuckles darkly. "Torture. Every day. It doesn't help that our parents grew up in the time before us, when there was a lot of media focus on how unsafe it was to be gay. I knew they loved me, but I also knew, deep down, that while they'd accept me, they'd be scared. And worse … disappointed. They wouldn't be able to *help* being disappointed. Still, I came out in my senior year of high school, and we got through their feelings on it together."

"It's so bullshit."

"I've always thought the same."

I stare at his hand for a moment, working through the mix of emotions rushing through me. Then I flip my hand over and hold his. The smile I get makes the doubt smaller.

"Wanna race?" he asks.

"What do you mean?"

"Let's see who can get through their dinner one-handed first."

"Joke's on you," I say, waving my fork. "I'm right-handed."

He sneers. "Leftie, baby. I'm not going to go easy on you."

"And if I win?"

"I'll blow you."

A laugh bursts from me. "No way. You'd do that anyway." I nod toward the large, newish shed. "I want to see your cars."

"Ooh … Introducing you to the girls is a big step. They're my pride and joy. Might get them all confused to see a strange man with Daddy."

"There's an easy solution, then."

"Are we back to the blow job?"

I shake my head. "Nope. You don't want me to meet them, you better win."

"Deal."

"So what do you win?"

His face goes blank like he wasn't expecting that. "Ah …"

"Blow job?" I tease, though I have no fucking clue if I could follow through. My research today also extended to porn, and apparently, I wasn't even ready for *that* because I can't remember the last time I voluntarily sat through such an awkward half hour.

"Nope, I don't want you stressing over that while we're enjoying our night together. I want … to pick what we watch tonight."

"Okay, then. Let's do this."

Ford calls out *go* suddenly, as though it'll give him a head start.

And it only takes a moment to work out why.

Ford *isn't* left-handed.

The mess he makes reminds me of something I'd expect from a toddler. There's food on the table, smeared all over the plate, and even specks of it in his short beard. He goes to remove his hand a couple of times, but I tighten my hold all the way up until I clean the last scraps off my plate.

Then I throw both hands in the air. "Winner!"

He gives me a few unenthusiastic claps. "I'm very impressed."

"Thank you, thank you." I bow.

Ford rounds the table and plants his hands on my shoulders. "You can meet the kids. *After* you do cleanup." He waves a hand toward the mess he made.

I pluck a chunk of potato out of his beard. "Should I start with you?"

He groans and takes a fast step back. "Nope. Because everything you say is innuendo, and my body can't handle it."

"Pity." I turn and lean over the table, pretending to pick up the mess when my sole focus is on making sure my ass is at a tempting angle.

"I know what you're doing," he deadpans.

"Cleaning? Of course. Just doing what I'm told like a good boy." I bounce my ass twice for good measure.

"You're going to be the fucking death of me."

18

Ford

ORSON WASHES UP BY HAND INSTEAD OF USING THE dishwasher and refuses to let me take over drying any dishes. He's whistling and relaxed, but I'm still keeping an eye out for any sign that he's not comfortable with our situation. The fact he's been researching all day and trying to understand himself instead of running from his feelings is a good sign.

It gives me hope that he isn't going to run the second things get real. Orson's gorgeous hazel eyes flick toward me. "What are you looking at?"

"Ah, I have a sexy man cleaning my kitchen. Tell me you're gonna fix my pipes and it's a porn video come to life."

"Which pipe?" He winks, and then his gaze dips to my crotch and back up again.

"Someone's playing games he's not ready for."

"We'll see."

"We will. In time." I step forward and take the dishcloth

off him. "But for now, you get to meet my babies. My pride and joys."

"If that garage is empty—or full of, I dunno, Nissans or something—I'm going to lose every ounce of respect I have for you."

"We better get this over with, then."

When I bought this place, I did it with building a shed in mind. I knew I wanted something big, and I eventually wanted to fill it with cars, but so far, my collection is still small. Like, four cars small. There's a lot of extra space to fill.

We walk in, and Orson lets out a long whistle. "This is … not what I was expecting."

I laugh, planting my feet wide and stuffing my hands in my pockets. "Eh. I'm getting there."

"Is this *the* Bug?" He walks toward the closest car. It's in the best condition out of the four because I've had it the longest. "The one you and your dad worked on?"

"Yup." I shrug. "Darleen has … sentimental value."

"Sentimental value or not, you probably shouldn't park her next to this beast. A '68 Dodge? How do you go from *that* to *this?*"

"Hey, hey. She can hear you." I hold out my hands like I'm soothing a spooked animal. "You're not giving them a great first impression."

Orson smirks and pats Darleen's hood. "Sorry, baby. Just teasing Ford. I didn't mean it."

"Better," I grunt. I pace toward the Dodge. "This little darlin' came into my life by pure dumb luck. I'd just opened the garage, some out-of-towner was taking a cruise in her, and she broke down on him. Apparently, she did that a lot. Just one glance at her and I could tell why. He wasn't looking after her, and she was throwing a tantrum because of it. He said she was costing him more than she was worth in repairs, so I paid him fifteen gs to take her off his hands."

"Good price."

"I've put a lot of work into her since then, given her a lot of love. Now she's hardly recognizable."

"Her name?"

"Rose."

Orson moves on to the next two, which are both in various stages of repair. The Sprite is missing pieces, but the old Jag is barely more than a body at this point. "Names?"

"The Sprite—that little one there—is Rita, and the Jag is Missy."

He laughs. "Missy?"

"Yeah, 'cause she's missing so much."

I fucking love hearing Orson laugh. It's deeper than his voice and … *happy*. Some people laugh under pressure, and some people try to control their laughs or don't let themselves enjoy the moment enough. With Orson, even the smallest laughs have heart behind them.

"You're not the type to jerk off over your cars, are you?" Orson asks.

"Nope. But I've always pictured fucking someone over Rose's hood."

His gaze snaps to the Dodge. "Really?"

"Yep. Hard, fast, dirty. Maybe we've been fixing up one of the cars together and can't bear to wait until we get inside and cleaned up."

He's silent for a moment. "Have you ever wanted someone that badly?"

"Are you asking if I've ever been horny?"

"Not necessarily just horny though. Like, that need to

have someone. To be with them. Sure, you're horny too, but it's more than that as well."

Given I can't relate to what he's talking about, my answer is easy. "Not more than fucking." I don't ask him the same question though. It goes without saying Tara was that for him, and I can't imagine what it would have been like to lose that kind of connection.

"No Thunderbird," he says, but it comes out like a question.

"Nope, but it's top of my list. These four I sort of came across by accident, and as you can see, I haven't been able to give them the time they deserve. So I haven't put the effort into finding a T-Bird."

"You should."

"I know, but every time I mean to, it's like the days get away from me."

"The days aren't coming back, you know," he says softly.

I'm reminded of his wife again, and I assume she's a part of why this is so hard for him. From what he's said, Orson's been with other people since her, but none of them had feelings involved. If he's starting to feel something for me, something real, it must be confusing for him.

I'd be an idiot if I thought things between us were going to be easy, so it's lucky I came prepared to do the work. I move a step closer and squeeze his shoulder. "Tell me about your dad."

That brings a smile to his face. "He worked in insurance and hated it. Used to come home swearing like a trooper about his bosses, pacing the kitchen and ranting to Mom while she cooked dinner." Orson rubs his scruff, staring at Missy. "I can't picture him without a cigarette in his hand. It was always there. His gruff face constantly surrounded by a cloud of smoke, whether he was eating dinner, kicking the ball around with me, or tinkering with the old pickup out back."

"What kind of cars did he like?"

"All of them." He chuckles. "For him, it was mostly the engines. He loved the mechanics behind it, even if he didn't actually know what he was doing. He'd roll out diagrams and have stacks of books for reference. He got the pickup going one day … made it halfway down the block before it conked out and we had to push it home again."

"My kinda man."

"Yeah." Orson's eyes flick my way. "He would have liked you."

"Cars have a way of bringing people together."

Orson shakes his head. "Not just because of the cars."

"Ah, you think he'd love my winning personality, huh?"

"Who wouldn't?"

Well, that question puts a damper on my mood. Many, many people give me a wide berth. I sigh. "It's not my personality that's the issue."

He turns to face me. "Do people *really* find you scary?"

"Apparently."

"Because of the tattoos?"

"And my size." I clear my throat. "And apparently, I have RCF."

"Which is …"

"Resting criminal face."

Orson cracks up laughing. "That's not a thing."

"You tell that to Mrs. Cleary. I swear she thinks I'm going to steal something every time I need to run into the general store."

"You're kidding."

"I'm not."

The amusement seeps from his face. "I thought everyone liked you."

"The people who get to know me, sure. But there's lots of people in this town who don't want to get to know me." I reach up to run my fingers lightly over his jaw. "Took us a while."

"I know. But that wasn't because I didn't *want* to."

"Did I scare *you*?"

He immediately shakes his head. "Never scared. Intimidated, maybe."

"What did it?"

He thinks for a moment. "You have this ... presence."

"Presence?" I echo, trying to work out what the hell that even means.

He nods. "You command a room. You're confident and self-assured, even before I knew who you were. I paid attention when you were around. There's something about you that had my attention. Made me want to keep looking."

I crack a smile and lean in. "Did it ever occur to you, sweetheart, that you've been attracted to me this whole time?"

"Not until I *just* finished talking."

We both laugh, and I summon this confidence he thinks I have and step in closer. Every move I make has this giant question mark hanging over it, forcing my limbs slower, giving him a chance to pull away. I wrap an arm around his shoulders. "I've been attracted to you for a while too."

"You have?" His hands settle on my hips.

"Yeah. There's a presence about you too."

His eyelashes flick up, gaze landing on mine, and the

need to lean in and kiss him is strong. The way he's got me all twisted up is addictive. I love it and hate it. Wish I could tell what he's thinking, even as the unknown between us is so exciting.

"I'm ready to go back inside if you are." His words come out on a whisper.

I take his hand, slotting my fingers through his, squeezing lightly. "I've been waiting for cuddle time all night."

19

Orson

MY HAND TIGHTENS IN FORD'S AS WE MAKE OUR WAY BACK inside. I hadn't been lying when I said he has a presence, and it's that overwhelming awareness of him that has my whole body feeling shivery as we walk back inside.

My dick can't decide whether it wants to get hard or hide, but there's no letting go now. I want to see this through. Whether something happens or we do end up sitting there *snuggling*, I don't fucking know.

But I want it. I want to see how things play out.

And when we reach the living room and Ford flicks off the lights and turns on the TV, the smile he gives me makes my heart give an extra *du-dum*. I inhale sharply, then try to shake my nerves as I flop back onto the couch. Ford joins me a moment later.

"What do you want to watch?" he asks.

"Don't care. With any luck, we won't be watching it anyway."

His deep chuckle stirs my want. "Slow down, Romeo. We've got all night."

"Put a series on, then. Something funny."

"You know if we start a show together, we have to finish it, right?"

"Good with me."

"Below Deck? It has nine seasons ..."

I can hear his unasked question. Will I still be here after tonight? "Eh. We'll find a longer one next time."

Ford takes me at my word and switches it on before sitting back against the couch. He shuffles around so he has one leg running along the back of it, other foot still planted on the floor, and opens his arms to me. "I'm super comfy."

"I'll be the judge of that." I slide over the cushion to lean back against him, and Ford's arms immediately close around me.

It's so foreign to be hugged like this, to be held close and ... surrounded. It's like he's holding me together, and as I sink back against his large, hard body, all my muscles let go of their tension.

"There we go," he murmurs, squeezing me tighter for a second. "I like when you're relaxed."

"Me too."

"Shh ... you're interrupting."

I smile and wriggle against him until I've found a position that works, and he's right. He is comfy. We lie there watching the show. Thankfully, Ford wasn't serious when he told me to shut up because we're both vocal throughout. The ridiculousness of reality TV is apparently something I've been missing in my life. It's fun. So fun, I don't notice at first how Ford's hand has started to roam. His fingers trail up and down my side, flirting with the bottom of my T-shirt and the small amount of exposed skin there. It's light, seemingly innocent, not pushing my comfort levels but making me *want* to push my comfort levels.

My hand rests on Ford's thigh, and I run it up and down, loving the feel of all that strength beneath my palm. It's new and exciting.

I let out a long, pent-up breath.

Lips press against the side of my head. "You doing okay?"

"Yeah … this is nice."

His hum has a roughness to it. "I agree."

"Do you wish we were fucking?"

Ford lets out a noise like he's choking. "What?"

"Well, this is ridiculously G-rated compared to what you're used to."

"There's nothing G-rated about what's going on in my pants." He shifts slightly, and his hardness digs into my back. "But no. I meant it when I said I was okay with nothing more than this happening."

"Maybe I'm not."

"What?"

I roll side-on so I can face him. "Maybe we should try this with our shirts off?"

The only sign he gives me that he's registered my words is his gaze dropping to my lips. "Thought you'd never ask."

I sit up, and we both make quick work of stripping out of our T-shirts. I'm about to lie back when I pause, taking a moment to check him out. Tattoos from his neck to the waistband of his pants, that sexy barbell threaded through his nipple. Hair that runs from his chest and down over his solid belly. He's stocky but hard. My cock pulses as my gaze meets the solid outline against his fly.

"M-maybe without pants," I manage to get out through the nerves and raw want.

Ford grunts and pulls me back against him. The heat from his skin is like a furnace. "Soon. Just relax again."

"You think I'm scared, don't you?"

"You trying to tell me you're not?" His hands settle over my abs, thumb gently tracing the line between them. "It's okay to be scared. It's okay to stop yourself doing things because of it, but it's also okay to do things even though they scare you. I'm not in a hurry, Orson."

Hearing him say my actual name sends shivery happiness over me.

"You said you don't really have a type …"

"Mmm."

"So what's your favorite thing about being with a man?"

"That's a bit of a loaded question because I can't compare it to being with another gender."

"True … okay, well, what's your favorite part of being with someone. Besides them having a great butt or a nice-tasting cock—"

His laughter is loud in my ear. "You've obviously never tried to pick up a man. Do me a favor and if you ever suck a cock one day, make sure you tell the dude it's 'nice-tasting.'"

"You can remind me when I suck yours."

That shuts him up.

And yeah, I said *when* because I'm pretty sure I mean it. The more he touches me, the more his hands explore, the more I want to do the same to him. I'm relaxing into it and switching off some of those doubts and dumb conditioned thoughts. When I'm with him, I want him. It shouldn't matter what gender he is. I wish I knew *how* to take control

—it's like I'm back in high school and trying to lose my virginity.

"You didn't answer me," I say.

"My favorite part?"

"Yeah …"

"I love knowing that I'm turning them on. That I'm making them feel good. There's no more amazing feeling than being with someone and losing yourself in their body and knowing they're doing the same. I mean, yeah, dicks and butts are hot as hell, I've also eaten out a trans dude, which was a new experience, but none of the physical stuff compares to the …" Ford's fingers dance along my V, and a spear of blinding hot lust shoots straight to my dick.

Goddamn.

"To that," he whispers hoarsely. "There's nothing I want more than to make your body sing."

He's doing it too. Barely touching me and I'm jelly for him.

"What about you?" he asks. "What's your favorite part?"

"I don't think I want to say."

"Why not? Love eating pussy and you don't want to tell me because I don't have one of those?"

I elbow him. "Doubt that will be a problem, you idiot."

"Then what is it?" His voice is softer this time. His I-can-be-serious-sometimes tone.

"The love."

"Oh, yeah?"

"It's kind of like what you said about making the person you're with feel good, but it goes beyond that. You don't just want to give them an orgasm—though you definitely want that too—it's this … *rightness*. When you're inside them and your head is swimming with how good everything is and your chest feels like it's going to explode under the force of all those emotions."

"Huh. I hope I get to experience that one day."

"I hope you get to too."

It seems almost impossible that I had that and lost it, but then Ford's kiss lightly touches my jaw, and I let the thought go. My eyes fall closed, and I remind myself I'm with him and I shouldn't feel guilty for that. I shouldn't feel guilty for wanting to be here. For wanting more. And not just when it comes to sex.

I want that feeling back. To fall in love. And I have a sneaking suspicion that I've taken a step in the right direction.

Ford's hand sneaks down over my inner thigh, dangerously close to my cock. I tense, wanting him to go lower, tempted to rock my hips up to give him a hint.

"Feel good?"

I reach down to cup myself, making sure Ford can see how hard I am. "I'm a fan."

The sound he lets out as he turns his face into my hair is pure happiness. His lips find that spot behind my ear, and I immediately arch my head to the side, giving him free range. His beard scratches my skin, but his warm lips are soft, and the warring sensations send ripples over my body. My sense of touch is heightened, and every kiss along my neck and shoulder draws my skin tighter around me. Like I'm being coiled, ready to let go.

I reach behind me, grip his sides, and trail my hands down to his hips, where my thumbs sneak under his waistband.

"I really want these off now," I say.

He groans. "Tell me what to do and I'll do it."

"Off. Take them off." I jump up and struggle out of my pants, turning to find Ford doing the same. He kicks out of them, hard dick jutting out the front of his underwear, and mine is doing the same.

Right. I'm doing this.

I walk over and straddle his waist. His body is like a solid wall of heat, and our erections are both straining the thin cotton of our underwear, tempting me to move closer, to press them together.

"Now, this is familiar," he says.

"Uh-huh." I swallow, staring at his lips, heart pounding loudly in my ears. "I want to kiss you."

"Whenever you're ready."

I kinda wish he'd taken over, but this is better. This gives me a chance to prove it's what I want. And it is. Even if I'm nervous. Even if this feels like too many big steps.

I'm scared, but I'm doing it anyway.

Because I want him, and I want to get past this so I can prove it to him.

I lean in, skimming my lips against his before I seal our mouths together. The kiss is world-spinningly good, like the one earlier, and I moan as I open my mouth and lick at his lips. Ford's hand dives into my hair as his mouth parts, and his tongue surges forward. It tangles with mine, hot, wet, tasting like him. And even with me in control, he dominates the kiss. My toes curl over when he crushes my body against his, kissing me like he's starving for it.

"As much as this position is a favorite of mine, I'd fucking love to feel you under me."

"Yes."

His eyebrows furrow. "You sure?"

"I'll tell you if I'm not."

"Good. If I do anything you're not comfortable with, tell me right away."

"Of course." And I don't even doubt that I'd be able to because Ford makes everything easy.

He holds me tight as he turns to lay me across the couch before blanketing his body over mine. The sight of him looming above, eyes dark and expression taken over by want, washes nerves over me again.

I feel small—which isn't a feeling I *ever* have—and almost vulnerable under his gaze. His hand runs from my shoulder all the way down to my briefs, where he toys with the elastic with his thumb.

I clear the nerves from my throat and ask, "Do you want them off?"

"Yeah," he answers honestly.

"Can you go first?"

His eyes search mine for a second before he nods and pushes up onto his knees. Then he shoves his underwear down. His thick cock bounces back against his stomach before settling, and my gaze locks onto it. He doesn't have any tattoos on his groin or his thighs, and it almost looks odd to be able to see Ford's bare skin. Intimate.

My tongue swipes my lips as I keep focused on his shiny head, but when I go to rid myself of my briefs, Ford's hands cover mine.

"Can I?"

"Yeah," I croak.

His fingers curl under the elastic, and he very slowly drags them off me. My cock throbs under his attention, and when Ford leans in, achingly slowly, to press his face against it, the only thought in my mind is *more.*

He licks a thigh-shuddering stripe up my cock before settling over me again.

"That's one nice-tasting cock you have there."

I bat at him. "That was my line."

"Also the truth. I just never thought to compliment someone on it before."

"Learning so much from me already." I twist my arms around him and ease him down on top of me. He kicks his briefs off the rest of the way.

"Ooh, I like this." He shifts so our cocks press together, and my eyes almost roll back at the feeling. "Fuck, you're a work of art."

"My heart is beating so hard I might be sick, so I need you to kiss me again."

He chuckles as I tug his mouth down to meet mine. His beard scrapes my stubble, big arms slide under my shoulders, hard body rubbing over me and creating an incredible pressure under his weight.

I sink into the kiss as his tongue takes control of mine, and everything else disappears. His taste and his confidence have made me hard as a shaken soda can and about as ready to explode. The needy pressure building is incredible. The longer we kiss, the harder it is to remember what I was so hesitant about.

My cock slides against his, dry but eager, over and over. My legs have closed around him at some point, and I'm rubbing off on him like my life depends on it.

"I have lube in the bedroom."

"Take me there."

Ford jumps up, dragging me with him, but I don't want to stop kissing him and break this spell he has over me. We stumble our way down the hall, knocking into walls, and laughing into each other's mouths as we meet for kiss after kiss after kiss.

Everywhere he touches me burns in the most incredible way, and it's been too long since I've had this. This gut-swooping, skin-tingling kind of high. I'd resigned myself to the idea I'd never have it again when Ford stomped into my shop with those heavy boots, tight pants, and attitude too big to be contained.

"On the bed, sweetheart," he pants as he extracts himself from me and goes over to a drawer. He pulls out the lube and coats himself with it as I lie back, ready to feel him on top of me again.

We're separated for maybe thirty seconds, and it's already too long. As soon as he's close enough, our mouths meet hungrily, and he grinds his slick cock down over mine. His hand closes around us both, and I bite back a moan, heels digging into the mattress.

It's indescribable, the way we feel together. I want to be cool, and I want to take my time, instead of acting like a complete fucking virgin at forty-five, but more than that, I want a chance to enjoy this. To capture this feeling, the bone-melting need mixed with that ballooning in my chest.

I'm not idiotic enough to think it's love or anything like that, but I do know I care about Ford. There's a deep affection between us, more than friendship but separate to any kind of relationship. It's incredible how far we've built it in a little over a month, and the dizzying pace we're moving at cements that certainty, deep in my gut, that this is exactly where I'm supposed to be.

Ford thrusts into his fist, the drag of his cock over mine creating a friction that's making my brain check out. My legs wrap around his thighs, hands closing over his large, muscled ass, encouraging him to move faster.

"*Mmph.* Yes." He grunts. "You good?"

"Need more. Just more," I pant into his mouth. "Give me more. *More.*"

His hips pound mine as he fucks into his fist, hand squeezing tighter with every stroke. My balls are pulling up, my grip on his ass almost punishing, and every time he thrusts, our balls are crushed together, pressed tight, delicious ripples spreading outward.

"Holy shit …" I gasp, rocketing toward the edge. My orgasm is so close, building so big, I'm seconds away …

"Grab my nipple," he begs.

My fingers close over the bar and tug.

Ford lets out a loud gasp before his teeth sink into my lip, and he goes stiff. The sharp sting of pain through my haze of desire sets me off. My cock pulses in his hand, thighs tightening as I shoot my load all over my abs. It feels like the longest orgasm in history, and as I ride out the high, I keep playing with the barbell, my grip gradually softening until it grounds me, helps me shake off the haze.

Ford slumps forward, face buried in my shoulder, and I wrap my arms around his shoulders.

Neither of us talks for a really long time.

I'm trying to catch my breath, trying to process what happened and work out where I'm at with it all. Ford stays hidden, and I'm not sure what's on his mind, but we both take the moment to ourselves.

And maybe it's the orgasm talking, but I don't regret that for a second.

It was incredible.

"We need to get cleaned up," I say when I become uncomfortably aware of the cum drying on my skin.

He's slow to appear. "We do, but … well, I'd kinda like it if you didn't run off this time."

"You want me to stay?"

"Only if you want to. I'm not done snuggling with you yet." He tries for the usual teasing smile, but it's uncertain. That's not an emotion I'm used to from him.

And his lack of confidence helps me find mine. "On one condition."

"Yeah?"

"I get to borrow the same sweats as last time, *and* I take the left side of the bed."

"Joke's on you—I would have given you anything you asked for."

20

Ford

ORSON'S A NATURAL. I GLANCE OVER AT HIM FROM WHERE I'm working with my sixteeners to see him helping one of the kids with the steering column on their car. His calming presence does well here. Where the kids are used to me being maybe *too* passionate about cars that I skip steps and start talking about things too advanced for them to follow, he slows it down. He's their quiet, and I'm their chaos.

My grin widens as I think of us like that. Two parts working together.

There's no denying Orson's got me twisted up and hardly able to recognize myself. I've always been an affectionate guy, open to dating but never getting that pull to anyone, and now Orson's in my life, I never want him to leave it.

He's like a new plaything I'm suddenly obsessed with, and I'm worried by how quickly that feeling has snuck up on me. The last thing I'd ever want to do is get bored and hurt him, but surely this kind of deep attachment isn't normal. I wanted him to stay at my place all week; I wanted to cook him dinner and watch him wash up, have some more orgasms, but mostly just spoon on the couch, watching reality TV.

Now I've got that small taste of domesticity, I don't want to give it up. When we talked about hooking up last week, Orson said he didn't do casual, but we never went into details about what that meant. Are we friends who hook up exclusively? Are we dating? More? My thoughts won't stop cycling through all the possibilities—including the bullshit ones that make no sense but late at night I'm convinced are real. That Orson is only using me. Experimenting. That it all means nothing and he'll walk away happy and sated, leaving me to doubt every move I've made with him.

That's not Orson, but my insecurities don't like to play fair.

"He your boyfriend?" Daryl asks.

I turn my attention back to the soapbox car I'm working on. I'm supposed to be checking the steering has been put together properly and won't malfunction midrace, so being distracted right now isn't great timing.

"Ignoring the question," Erin pipes in. "So that's either an 'I want him to be, and he's not' or an 'I'm not talking about my sex life with kids,' but we're sixteen, so I don't think that counts."

"Yeah, it's not like we're virgins," Crispin says.

I throw up my hands. "I'm not listening to *any* of this."

Daryl sniggers. "Never took you for a prude."

"Yeah, dude, you've been to prison. You've heard way worse things than teens drinking and having sex. The horror!" Crispin pretends to fall back in shock.

I have no idea how we got into this conversation, but it's

making me glad I never had kids of my own. They're brats. The lot of them. "I know it's hard for you smart-asses to believe, but I was your age too. I know exactly what I got up to then, and now that I'm no longer your age, I can confidently say you're too young and dumb to be doing shit like that."

"*Prude*," Erin covers with a cough.

"Can we get back to cars?"

"Once you've answered the question," Crispin says.

"What question? Have I been to prison?" I wink. "I'll never tell."

"I bet you haven't, and you never deny it because you want the cool points."

Oh, to be sixteen again and think things like being locked up is cool. I don't deny it because … it's true. I was incarcerated. I see no reason to lie about it when I'd make the same choices if I was in that situation again, but most people don't see it that way. There are good choices and bad ones. Apparently, breaking the law means you've made a bad one, and while Kilborough is good at being accepting for a lot of things, an ex-con puts that acceptance to the test.

Erin shakes her head. "You know we mean Orson. He's really nice. We voted, and we like him."

"Oh no …"

"What?"

"He's got the teen stamp of approval. I'm going to have to let him go. I can't be seen in public with someone you think is *cool.* "

"Don't go that far." She snorts. "We said we liked him. There is no way either of you could pass as cool."

"I dunno …" Daryl says. "I think Orson's a bit of a DILF. Have you seen his abs?"

I cringe. "Stop it. He can't be a DILF because he's not a dad, you're all complete asexuals as far as I'm concerned, and also, he's mine, so back the fuck up, Romeo."

The three of them snicker.

"Are you going to get *married*?" Crispin teases.

I roll my eyes. "I liked you all better when you were fourteen and communicated in grunts."

"Geez, love makes Ford cranky. I thought it was supposed to do the opposite?"

A deep scoff behind me makes my back stiffen, and Orson's hand closes over my shoulder. "You think this is bad? You should see him when I insult Darleen."

"Who's Darleen?"

Orson shrugs. "If you're not cool enough to know—"

"It's a car, isn't it?" Erin drones.

His eyes shoot to mine. "No, it's a ..."

"Ford names all his cars, and if you're getting away with insulting one of them, you guys are definitely doing it."

I swear Orson's mouth has never dropped so fast. I'd tell him he'll never win with these three, but no way in hell am I letting them know they've won.

I stand up and grab his hand, then before I steer him away, I lean back down and hiss, "You're all the bane of my existence, and I'm going to make sure I loosen all your screws before the race."

Apparently, I'm not as scary as the pearl-clutchers in town make out because the three of them laugh, and we walk away, followed by taunts like *I'd like to see you try, old man* and *get a room.*

Orson blows out a long breath when we're out of earshot. "That was ..."

"Not true. The love thing. I don't know where—"

"Relax, man. I figured they were messing with you. Tried to do the same, but …" His face crumples. "Teenagers are kinda mean."

"They are."

"No way would I have talked back to a grown-up at their age."

I was the same. "Probably why the world is in such shitty shape. None of us wanted to talk up." My gaze strays back to where the three of them are huddled over a plan, and even though they're little shits, I love that I've gotten to spend this time with them growing up. They were some of the first kids here when I offered up the land, and it'll be sad in a year or two when they grow bored with it or take off for college. "I hope those guys never lose their voice."

Orson nudges me. "Someone's a big softie."

"Surprised you're only now figuring this out."

"Don't get too excited. I had a hunch."

My lips pull up in the corner. "You okay with them guessing there's something between us?"

"Sure. I'm not embarrassed."

"But you're still figuring yourself out."

"I am." He steps closer, hand finding mine as he stretches up to kiss me softly. "But what happens in the future doesn't change what's happening between us now."

"Which is?" My gut is in my throat as I ask the question, and I don't know why I'm pushing the point. The last week has been incredible. Hanging out, getting to know each other more, lots of kissing, and another frotting session. I've been handed my dream guy, and I should be happy with that. With what we have. But the buzzing under my skin won't let it go without asking.

His lips flatten for a second, eyes uncertain. "I don't have an answer to that, if I'm honest. But it's definitely *something*, isn't it?"

"Feels like it to me."

He smiles, and I run my thumb over his silver-streaked scruff, watching the way it practically glistens under the floodlights. "Wanna come home with me tonight?"

"Yes." His eyes light up. "It'll still be early. I was thinking … why don't we spend some time with Rita and Missy?"

"Really?"

"Sure. You'll need to tell me what to do, but I'm good at following instructions."

I pump my eyebrows. "I know from experience."

"Perve."

"Geez. Called a prude a few minutes ago, and now I'm a perve. There's no winning with you people."

He slaps my ass as he walks away and tells me to get back to work. I do. Gladly. Even though I know the sixteeners are going to be even more unbearable after Orson saved me and then kissed me out in the open where anyone could see. Maybe we should be playing this thing closer to the chest, protecting it somehow, but … that doesn't feel like either of us. Plenty of people have reasons to keep their relationships private, but I don't give a fuck who knows I'm into Orson, so long as he's fine with people knowing he isn't straight.

Erin opens her mouth as soon as I rejoin them, but I shut her up with a stern look.

"One more word out of you lot and I'll wait until these cars are built, then throw them in the crusher. I'll make you watch too."

"It's cute when you play tough."

"I'm not playing."

"Uh-huh, yeah, okay ..." They share a look between themselves.

"Are we here for cars or what?" I grumble, crouching down beside Daryl's frame.

Crispin pats me on the head. "There's our Ford. I hope Orson knows your first love will always be cars. Nothing can compete with *Darleen*."

For years, I thought that was the case. Cars, work, volunteering here. It all made me happy.

But now I have another piece to fit into my life, and he's jumped in like I've always been waiting for him. Like the space was open and ready for him to walk into. Nothing *could* compete with my love of cars.

But I get the feeling Orson wouldn't try to.

And as I watch him laughing with one of the littlies, I also know ... well, he wouldn't *have* to.

21

Orson

I wake up to Ford's hand in my face and his other elbow in my back. Not the morning of lazy cuddles I'd been imagining.

Trying not to wake him, I shift away, letting his heavy arm fall onto the mattress. He's breathing loudly, not quite snoring, morning wood pressing against the sheet thrown over us. His tattooed chest rises and falls in a comforting rhythm, and I lie there peacefully, still marveling that I'm here at all.

A familiar guilty pang hits my chest, but I push it away. I know it doesn't mean anything. Tara would never have wanted me to mope forever, but it's hard to shake the feeling I'm *supposed* to be guilty, supposed to be constantly mourning. I've accepted that I was powerless in her death, that there was nothing I could do, but it doesn't help the waves of frustration that hit occasionally at how unfair the whole thing is.

And then I look at Ford.

And emotions stir in me that I haven't felt in years. It scares me. I can't fuck this up.

Last night, we came back here and got to work on Rita. It's been a lifetime since I worked on a car—multiple versions of myself ago—but it was familiar and comforting in the way a happy dream is. It reminded me of Dad.

Rough fingers brush my arm. "What are you thinking about?"

I turn toward his sleep-rough voice, and my smile is automatic. "How surreal this all is."

"Which part?"

"Moving on with my life, working on the cars last night, how relaxed we are together, and the fact you showed up at the perfect time. I haven't been interested in anything that even remotely resembled dating. Then I met you and just … wanted to be around."

Ford rolls onto his side and pushes up onto his elbow. "What about the man thing?"

"Hmm … that's less surreal, more … I'm wrapping my head around it. Like an adjustment period." I shake my head at how ridiculous that sounds. "Sorry, I wish I could jump in and be totally fine with it—and I am; there's nowhere else I'd rather be, don't get me wrong—it's just my brain struggling to add this new information. It'll get there. I guess I'm like an old dog."

It's a complete relief and not at all surprising that Ford doesn't seem offended or irritated by any of that. I'm probably more frustrated than he is.

"Don't worry, sweetheart. When you get there, I have a *ton* of new tricks I can teach you."

Relief sweeps over me, and I roll so I'm facing him. "Thanks." I lean in for a lingering kiss.

"Mm, thank me like that every time and I'll be the most understanding guy you ever met." He smacks another kiss against my lips right as his alarm goes off.

I groan and drop my head onto his shoulder. "I don't want to get up yet."

"I know, but if I don't, I'll be late for work."

"You start too early."

Ford laughs. "It's only an hour before you, and most of my grease gremlins are there before me. I'm the lazy boss."

"I don't think you've ever been called lazy a day in your life."

"Surprisingly, you're right. That's one of the few insults I haven't heard."

My gut tightens like it does every time he jokes about that. I have no idea if the rumors about him are true, but I'm finding it hard to care. Maybe he was arrested at some point, but that was a different version of him, too, because the man in front of me would have to be one of the best people I've ever met.

"Hey, hey …" he says in a warning voice. "Even looking at me like that isn't going to get me to stay in bed. You're a sneaky guy, Orson, but I'm onto you."

I try to play it off as nothing, but I'm not even sure how I was looking at him. I roll onto my back as he gets up and starts moving around the room, gathering clothes for today. His sleep shorts have slid down a little, revealing a strip of bare, light skin just above his butt. This urge takes over me to get up, walk over there, and slide his shorts down until that bubble of an ass pops out. I imagine sinking my teeth into the soft cheek, and my cock plumps at the sexy image.

We've been taking the sex side of things slow, getting comfortable with each other, and of course, the morning I'm ready to instigate and jump his fucking bones, he has to hurry off to work.

Typical.

I ignore the need and get up to take a leak before stripping out of the borrowed sweats that I'm beginning to think of as my pair. There's enough time for me to head home, shower, and change out of yesterday's clothes before opening, and I pause by the bathroom on my way out.

Ford's still in the shower, but I lightly knock on the door before nudging it open a crack.

"I'm heading out."

"Kiss goodbye?"

That's what I was hoping for. I push my way inside the steam-filled room and find Ford grinning at me from the shower. He leans out to meet me, dripping on my face and neck, wet hand holding my jaw as he makes the kiss deeper than the one we shared in bed.

Then he pulls back and winks. "Gotta make sure you spend the day thinking about me."

I'm almost breathless as I pull back. "Yep. That'll do it."

———

"WHAT ARE YOU DOING?" GRIFF ASKS, PLACING OUR LUNCH on the counter and rounding it to get a better look at the computer screen.

"Just searching."

"You getting a new car or something?"

Or something is accurate. Ford's kiss did the trick, and he's been on my mind all day. His garage last night felt empty. It was obviously built to hold a huge number of cars, so the space around his four babies was almost depressing. I loved hearing him talk about them though, especially Darleen, because he builds a real attachment to them.

Which makes it even sadder that he doesn't have a T-Bird.

Ford loves the sentimental shit, and what's more sentimental than the car he was named after?

"I'm just looking," I say.

"Half of those don't even look like they'd run."

"That's the point." I have this grand idea that we could do it up together. I'm borderline useless on my own, but with Ford directing me, I can fumble my way along. I think he'd like that, and every day I spend with him makes that need to see him happy burn brighter.

Griff settles on the chair beside mine and grabs his sandwich. "Still seeing Ford, then?"

"Yes."

"Are you dating?"

Are we? The word feels almost juvenile. "I don't know what we are." I give him more. "But I like it."

"That's awesome, man. Really."

"Don't ask me how the sex is," I warn.

Griff's jaw drops. "How did you know I—"

"Because it's always the next question out of your mouth." I laugh. "Oh, you're in a relationship? Fill me in on the sex."

He huffs. "I'm not that bad."

"You're exactly that bad."

"I'd tell *you.*"

"Oh, really?" I open my sandwich and take a bite, talking around the food. "So how is it with you and Heath?"

His eyes light up. "Constant. Always. We can't keep our hands off each other. You ever heard about docking? Apparently, there are attachments you can buy, so we're gonna get one for him and—"

"Nope. Stop. No." I hold up my free hand. "Let's agree to no details. The sex with Ford is great, but we've been taking it slow."

Griff frowns. "Why?"

"Because I'm not a cock slut like you?"

He opens his mouth like he's about to argue but then changes direction. "I kinda am, aren't I?"

"This cannot be new information to you."

"Just never really thought about it that way. Think Heath will call me that tonight?"

"What did we *just* say about details?" And even though he does tend to overshare, I'm happy for him. Only a few months ago, Griff was lost and coming to me for advice, on the verge of a midlife crisis, I swear. He's still dying his hair and worries about looking *old*, but he's definitely more settled now. It suits him.

I'm older and grayer than he is, but those things haven't been a concern of mine. Everyone ages. This is all part of it. Maybe I'd have more insecurities if Ford cared about shit like that, but then I don't think I'd like him as much if he did.

"Anyway …" I wave off Griff's comment. "We're making sure that we spend time getting to know each other. I love sex, but it's hard to move on and wrap my head around caring for someone again. I need to ease myself into it so I don't screw it up."

Griff's eyes turn sympathetic. "If I learned anything about my relationship with Heath, it's that the only people who factor into your relationship is you. I'm not going to pretend to know what you've been through—especially since you never talk about it—but he clearly makes you happy, so don't sabotage that, okay? You're *allowed* to be happy. That took me too long to figure out."

"I …" I exhale loudly and let out the thought that's been plaguing me. "I wonder what my life would be like if she was still here. Would we be happy? Have kids? Would I *want* kids? And then, if I met Ford, would I have realized I was attracted to him? Would I have ever figured out that I'm bisexual or whatever, or would I have died still believing I'm straight?"

Griff points at me. "That's exactly what I meant about self-sabotage."

"Which part?"

"Who are those thoughts helping?"

Fair point. "It's natural to wonder."

"Wonder, sure. You'll always love her and regret her dying, but it won't change anything. And if you fall in love with someone else, it doesn't mean you love her any less. She deserved everything you gave her, but whoever—Ford or not Ford—comes next, they deserve that too. It's horrible what happened, and letting go is going to be hard, but you can't expect someone else to live in her shadow of what-ifs. You say you don't want to screw this up, you say you've come to terms with what happened and moved on … so move on. Sorry if that sounds harsh, but you can still love her and honor her memory without making someone else feel like they come second."

"You're right." I cock my head at him. "You're wise when you're not thinking with your dick."

The last thing I'd ever want is for Ford to feel that way.

This thing growing between us is completely separate to anything I had with Tara, and the only one who keeps overlapping those relationships is me.

"Besides," Griff says, "word on the gay streets is Ford's a catch. He's gotten around a bit, and I know of a few guys who want to pin him down into something more permanent."

A perverse curiosity takes over me. "Really?"

"Yep. Are you surprised? Business owner, good with kids, big heart. He's like the romantic version of Art, and you know how many people have been trying to get him to commit over the years."

I turn back to the images of cars on the screen. Yeah, I knew Ford got around, but I didn't realize he'd left a trail of broken hearts behind him. Everything we have feels *real*, but what if that's only on my side?

Is that even possible?

No, the Ford I know would never recklessly hurt people. Unintentionally, maybe. But I can't compare what we have with anyone else because every relationship is different. Which is exactly what I've been doing with him. Keeping him at arm's length so I don't end up hurt.

Well, what the fuck is the point of this if I'm not all in?

Will I leave with a broken heart? Maybe. Just the thought of Ford walking away *hurts*.

But it also makes me feel alive again. Less *Zen*, more *zap*.

He's giving me everything I didn't know I needed.

So I'm going to do everything to give him the same.

22

Ford

WHILE I WAIT AT KILLER BREW'S OUTSIDE CAFE FOR MY coffee, I grin at anyone whose eye I meet. Most people are friendly, used to seeing me around town, but there are still those who are wary of me. A few people hurry to avert their stares, but at least I get a couple of smiles in return.

And even the rude gossips can't bring me down, not when their words mean shit all to me. Orson clearly doesn't care about their hatred, which is a huge relief. But I can't stop wondering if he'd feel the same, knowing the full story.

It's definitely something we'll need to talk about at some point, but it's not the kind of thing I tell just anyone. I don't want it getting out, and I'd want to be sure we're tough as nails before we go into all that.

"Hey, Ford," Beau says, placing his usual order.

I pretend to check a watch I don't have and send a smirk his way. "This is late for you. Normally, you meet Marty at lunchtime."

His face screws up. "I, ah, maybe forgot? So I'm running over to try and meet him before he finishes work. I'm the worst friend, I swear."

I press my lips together before answering because Beau is … scattered. To put it nicely. Even I know that, and outside of running into Beau now and then when we're both here at the same time, we're not really friends. He's been best buddies with Marty since they were kids, and he's now dating Marty's brother, Payne. Obviously, those Walker brothers don't mind a little absentmindedness in their lives.

After Beau orders, I lean around the coffee machine to the barista. "Excuse me, could you bump his order before mine? He's in a hurry."

"Sure thing." She switches our dockets around.

"You sure?" Beau asks.

I shrug. "I've got nowhere to be."

"God. Thank you."

I chuckle over how stressed he sounds because I'd be willing to put money down that Marty won't care, but at least this shows he isn't careless when he fucks up.

I'm about to ask Beau about his book when someone else wanders over to us.

"Hey, Fordy," Molly says with a little shake of his shoulders.

I chuckle at the dumb name he's always called me. "Hey, darlin'. How you doing?"

"Good. Will and I were going to pick up a few things from the market for Dad, and I saw you over here." He smiles big and pretty. "I wanted to come say hey."

The way he blinks innocently up at me has this sliver of *oh shit* trickling down my spine. I've always been flirty, always liked a bit of attention, and Molly's a hot guy even though he's … mid-twenties, I think? A bit too young for me. And the overall impression I get from him is that he'd get clingy fast.

Especially with the look he's giving me now.

I've always liked that look from guys, the unashamed perving, the little bit of awe and want all mixed up together, but that was when I was looking for anyone to keep me company. I have an incredible guy I'm working on starting something with, and it's not fair on Molly to let him think there's something here when there's not.

Feeling like a dick, I pull back and close off some of my friendliness. "Enjoy your shopping."

"You should come with? I haven't seen you around much lately."

And now I'm stuck. Orson said he didn't mind people knowing about us, but I still don't know what *us* there is. So I stretch the truth. Awkwardly. "Actually, I'm on my way home to the boyfriend. Gotta cook him dinner. Yeah. We're gonna have pork, maybe some beans and rice …" Holy shit, what is happening? I'm sweating like a cheater hooked up to a polygraph, desperately trying not to mess this up, and it's making me *really* mess this up.

Molly's staring at me like I've randomly popped out another appendage. "Boyfriend? *Who*?"

"It's new. We're still on the down-low."

"Nice. Congrats to you," Beau says, somehow missing the stress steam pouring from me. He picks up his coffees that have been called. "Thanks for this. See you around."

Then he leaves me one-on-one with Molly. My gut churns.

He's eyeing me like he's trying to work out whether it's

true or not, but every second we stand there looking at each other, his face falls that bit more.

He swallows and turns around, pretty lips turned down. "You have a boyfriend."

"Yeah. It's still new, so ..."

"You said."

"Right."

The sound of my name being called for my coffee almost makes me sag with relief. I hurry to pick it up and tilt it in Molly's direction, playing that this is all totally fine and cool and there's no tension at all. "I better be—"

The lid isn't on properly. And when I tilt the cup in a goodbye, the lid jumps off, and hot coffee pours over Molly.

My mouth drops. "Holy fuck."

He jumps back, hissing in pain, and I switch over to autopilot mode. I yank his drenched shirt over his head, then grab a handful of napkins and dab at his chest with them. His skin is bright red and painful-looking.

"What the hell?" his friend Will calls, hurrying across the cafe. "Did you throw your coffee at him?"

"What, n—"

"Here's some cold water," the barista says, rushing over with a cup. She looks flustered and panicked.

I immediately dunk the napkins into it and press them against Molly's burn. He hisses at the contact, but I hold him steady, one hand planted on his lean shoulder.

"What's your deal, Ford?" Will snaps.

"No, it's fine," Molly hurries to say. "I ... I ..."

"The lid wasn't on properly," I try to explain, and the barista's eyes go wide.

"Oh my god, I'm so, *so* sorry. I've got so many orders, and I thought I did and—"

Molly shakes his head. "Don't apologize. It's fine. Just an accident." His voice is strained, and it's clear he's trying to hold it together.

"The lid wouldn't matter if you hadn't … hadn't …" Will can't seem to find the words.

"It's *fine*, Will," Molly says.

"It's not fine. He burned you with his coffee—"

"By accident." I try to block Will out. "I'm sorry, Mols. Can I drive you home or …"

"I've got it." Will tugs Molly away from me.

Molly holds out a hand and practically whispers, "Can I please have my shirt back?"

It's then I realize I still have it crushed in my hand. And the entire cafe is staring at us.

I stiffly hand it back, and Molly disappears as quickly as he can, Will sending a glare back my way for good measure.

"I'll replace your coffee," the barista says, but I stop her.

"No, I'm good." I grab another pile of napkins and duck down to dry the floor; then, I grab the half-full cup of coffee and hightail it out of there.

As soon as I'm on the street, I check to see if I can find them, even duck into the market to be sure, but they've gone. What a mess.

Drop the boyfriend card on him, then burn him with my coffee. Poor guy didn't deserve that.

I groan, fingers in my hair, wishing I could reverse time and head straight home from work instead.

That was not my finest moment.

I pull out my phone and text Orson instead.

Any chance you're free this afternoon and want the company of a complete moron?

He texts right back.

Orson: *The moron can stay behind, but I'd love to see you.*

Me: *Not sure I can separate the two.*

There's no reply, and I stand there, lurking on the sidewalk, waiting. A few minutes later, a picture comes through, and it takes me a moment to work out what I'm looking at.

It's … a butt plug. Covered in lube.

My jaw hits the damn street.

Orson: *What if I made it worth your while?*

Me: *Suddenly moronless and on my way.*

I have no idea if he's suggesting what I think he is here, but my incredible clusterfuck is forgotten. I'll make it up to Molly later.

Right now, Orson has already blown my mind, and it's about time I did the same to him.

23

Orson

EVERY MOVEMENT FEELS *WEIRD*.

The plug is right up there, the base rubbing between my cheeks, and I'm equal parts nervous and excited over the fact I've booty-called Ford over here like it's the kind of thing I do all the time.

I'm torn between wanting to pace out this excess energy and not wanting to move a muscle because every time I do, the plug shifts, and zings are going off all over. My cock is rock hard, and if Ford doesn't get here soon, I'm going to have to start without him.

Just as I have that thought, my front door opens, and I hear heavy footsteps in the hall. There are two clunks—I'm guessing his boots—and then Ford appears at my living room door. His dark eyes are blazing when they lock on mine.

"So ... nice day?" His voice shakes with the effort to sound casual.

I lean—carefully—against the side of my couch. "Not bad."

"Anything, uh, different or exciting happen?"

"Hmm ..." I pretend to think. "I bought a pie for dinner."

"Right. Nice."

"And shoved a butt plug up my ass."

His gaze immediately drops to my groin, and his tongue darts across his lips as he takes a step closer. "Where did that glorious idea come from?"

"Well, I've been getting to know this guy, who I really like, and we've been taking it slow." I meet his eyes. "And maybe I wanted to hit the accelerator."

"Mm, talk cars to me, baby."

"You get my engine going."

He chuckles, stepping closer and closing his hands over my hips. From how I'm leaning, he towers over me more than usual. "Well, excuse me while I hit the brakes for a minute. You sure about this? Not all queer dudes like butt stuff. We have a whole world of sex we can explore together. Hand jobs, blow jobs—frotting is amazing. *You* could fuck *me*."

My eyebrows jump up, and I smile. "Yeah, we're definitely going to do that too, but ... I've always been curious ..."

"About anal?"

"Yeah. Guys talk about how good it is, and ... well, asking a chick to peg me has always felt too awkward to bring up, but ..."

"I'm a total ass slut?"

"Hey, you said it."

He leans down to kiss me, soft lips, scratchy beard. I love the sensations. My fingers curl into his dirty work shirt, and I tug him closer, wanting more. God, the anticipation of him being inside me is blowing my mind. The plug stung a bit at first, but I'm glad I did it before he got here, glad that I had that moment to work through it on my own. There's zero doubt in my mind that Ford would have done a better job with it and taken care of me, but I like that I got to take control and show him that I'm serious.

He moans lightly and pulls back.

"I'm filthy and need to shower." I'm about to tell him to fuck the shower and fuck me instead when he adds, "Maybe you should join me."

"Damn, you're clever." I whip my shirt over my head and start on his buttons. Each one opens to reveal that hairy, tattooed, mouthwatering body, and as soon as it's open, I can't help running my hands over him. His skin is hot, and when I lean in to tongue the barbell, he tastes like salt.

Ford runs his fingers through my hair and tugs. "You better stop that, or I'm going to bend you over this couch and fuck you where you stand."

Heat floods my face. "You should."

"Nope, today I'm going to take my time enjoying you." Another soft kiss. "You can be my little *Whorson* next time."

How am I supposed to argue with that? Scratch that—I don't even want to argue. Ford takes my hand and leads me into the hall before pausing.

I chuckle and pull him in the direction of the bathroom.

"Can't believe I haven't been here before," he says.

"I like your place."

"You do?"

"Yeah … it's kind of like mine but lived-in."

He chuckles. "You don't live here?"

We reach the door, and I open it before turning to him. "I

used to think I did." But the more time I spend at Ford's place, the more mine feels like a showroom. It's neat, clean, impersonal. *Soulless.*

We watch each other for a moment, and I'm glad he doesn't push me to explain because I don't think I can. All I know is that since meeting Ford, I remember what it's like to be living. Experiencing. Having fun and detouring from the usual day-to-day.

He clears his throat, but his voice still comes out husky. "Turn the shower on, sweetheart."

I do exactly that, and with my back to him, Ford crowds up behind me. Every time before now, there's been an overall hesitation to him, but tonight feels different. The way he kisses along my neck, how his hands roam down my front. Dip into my pants. A soft growl hits my ear as he rocks his cock forward against my ass.

I card my fingers through his hair, holding his mouth against me, arching my neck so he has free range. His knuckles brush over my hard-on as he pops the button on my pants and drags the zipper down.

"Commando." He makes an appreciative sound, hand immediately closing around my shaft. Ford gives me two long, bone-melting strokes before backing off.

I step into the water and turn to watch him strip out of his pants, greedily checking him out. His cock is standing straight up and ready, thick and red and veiny; it's an incredible sight. I'm not sure his cock itself turns me on, but combined with the full package of him, I'm a bundle of need to touch it so I can make him feel good. There's no sexier sight than seeing Ford come.

Each step that brings him closer has me shaking, and as soon as I can reach, I grab his waist and tug him against me.

Water runs over us as we kiss … and kiss … and kiss. Slow and sensual, hard and deep, Ford owns my mouth, and I do everything I can to give it back to him. Between his mouth and his water-slicked cock rubbing against my own, I'm in ecstasy.

"Turn around," Ford gasps into our kiss. "I need to see it."

Shit. I do as he asked and plant my hands against the tile, tilting my hips back toward him so he can see properly, and fuck, it's a vulnerable position, but that only makes this whole thing hotter.

I watch over my shoulder as his eyes follow his fingers down my back until he reaches my ass. His fingers trail into my crease and then—

"Oh, holy fuck!"

He presses against the plug.

Ford's chuckle is low and filthy as he grabs the toy, then pulls it out so fucking slowly before pushing it in again. The nerves all around my ass are alive and sending very, very good signals to my throbbing cock.

My forehead hits the tile. "Incredible …"

"Just wait until it's my cock."

Desire shivers along my spine.

"Should I … maybe *clean* myself or—"

"Nope." A kiss to my nape. "Shit happens sometimes."

"Well, that's not sexy."

He cracks up laughing. "You can do enemas or whatever, but they're not always safe, especially if they're not done right. We can talk about other things to help with bottoming later if you want, but …" His hands run up my sides. "I want you to enjoy this. Don't focus on all that other stuff, and on the very rare chance something happens, we're both adults.

We'll pretend we haven't seen anything, and I'll tease you mercilessly about it in a few weeks' time."

"Well, I'm reassured."

Before I can turn back around, there's the click of a bottle, and coolness hits the spot between my shoulder blades.

"Just relax." Ford massages the bodywash in, kneading every muscle and ridge, taking his time to squeeze and pull open my ass cheeks before making his way down my legs.

"You're spoiling me," I say.

"I'm trying to keep control of myself." I love how breathless he sounds.

"Maybe I don't want you to."

"Maybe I need to." His lips brush my shoulder, and he reaches around to hold the bodywash up in front of me. "Your turn."

Perfect. I jump straight into work, cleaning him everywhere. It's something I've never done before, but I love every second of it. The way his slick skin feels under my hands is addictive, and I don't want to stop touching. I spend extra time on his nipples, which earns me a shuddery breath, and make sure to massage him the way he did with me. Ford's soft murmurs and rasps of "yes, there" are all the encouragement I need, and when I get to his ass, I spend time there too. It's pale and round, and something about it is so distinctly masculine. My fingers dip into his crack, and Ford gives me an appreciative hum, even as my heart thumps hard and fast.

"Like that," he says.

I press against his hole, and his back muscles bunch. A hard breath punches from his lungs, and then he spins so fast I don't see him coming and pins me to the tile.

"Careful. If you wanna be fucked today, you might not want to spend so much time back there."

I laugh, but it's not funny. "I just want to touch you everywhere."

"Oh, really?" Something lights up his eyes as he drags his thumb over my bottom lip. "There is *one* place you haven't touched yet. And it's dying to meet your mouth."

I hold eye contact as I push him back, then drop to my knees. The plug shifts deliciously inside me. This isn't where I thought today was headed, but I'm all in. I don't give myself a chance to think about it too deeply, just open my mouth and lean in. His smooth head slips past my lips, and I close them around it.

All I have to go on is instinct and what I like, so I use my tongue as much as I can while I sink lower and lower down his shaft. Every time I glance up, Ford's eyes are locked on me. His hands are balled into tight fists on the tile, his whole body pulled taut, and seeing him hold back like that spurs me on. I want to make it good. I want to make him come undone. The longer I suck his cock, the more I *want* to be sucking his cock. It's driving *me* wild, and I refuse to touch myself because this is so deliciously sexy it wouldn't take much to get me off. The way I'm kneeling has the plug pressing deep inside me. It's an incredible mix of weird and want as I clench around it over and over, and as my jaw is really starting to ache, I pull off.

"I want you."

Ford hauls me to my feet. His mouth claims mine, tongue pushing possessively into my mouth as he reaches behind me and shuts the water off. We don't stop kissing as he backs me out of the shower, blindly grabbing a towel to wrap around us both before guiding me back into the hall.

"Bedroom," he grunts.

I pull him across the hall and open the door behind me.

He moans, diving on me again and giving us both the fastest dry-off in history. His hands explore my back, dip down to press against the plug, while his hard cock knocks against mine.

"Get on the bed, Orson."

Orson.

Fuck, I love that.

I drop onto my back, and Ford walks straight over to my nightstand. "Tell me you've got condoms in here."

"Bottom drawer."

He pulls it open, pauses, and then turns an impressed look on me. "So this is how you've gotten by without sex for so long."

"I've looked after myself."

"I can see that. I highly approve, by the way." He grabs the new box of condoms and pulls one out. "I'll be sharing you with that Fleshlight another day."

My cock twitches, and I nod. "Apparently, I'm on board with that."

Ford tears open the condom, and I watch him roll it down his thick length. For the first time, doubt trickles in at the thought of taking all that, but damn do I want to try. He picks up the lube I've left on the nightstand and coats the condom with long, smooth strokes, and I watch greedily as he rubs it over the tip of his cock.

"Suddenly don't think this plug is big enough."

Ford chuckles and tosses the lube beside me before crawling up my body. "You say the sweetest things. But don't worry, we'll make sure it fits."

"Will it hurt?"

"Nope. I'll make sure of it."

I spread my legs, knees lifting either side of his hips. "I'm ready."

Ford reaches for the plug. He kisses me as he slowly pulls it out, and when it's just about removed, he slides it back in again, the same way he did in the shower. In and out, over and over, he slowly pleasures me with the smooth toy, working me up to a neediness I've never felt before. I start pressing down into it, craving it deeper, harder, when Ford pulls it out completely.

The emptiness is almost overwhelming, but before I can fixate on it too much, the plug is replaced by one of Ford's thick fingers.

He fucks me with it roughly for a minute before a second one joins it. This time, there's a stretch, a slight sting as he opens me more than the plug did.

"Push down on my fingers," he says between kisses.

I let my eyes fall closed and do what he says. It makes it easier for them to slip inside with minimal pain, but the whole thing is back to feeling *weird*.

I squirm, and Ford backs off a little. He watches my face, eyes hooded and lips swollen as he pumps his fingers inside me, slowly stretching and massaging. It still feels good, but my cock has started to wane with the concentration it's taking me, and one glance down is all it takes for Ford to notice.

He pushes up onto his knees, presses my leg open wider with one hand, and dives on my cock. He swallows me right down the back of his throat, beard teasing my groin and fingers moving faster.

My eyes roll back with the onslaught of pleasure, and it takes all of my self-control not to fuck Ford's face—self-control that's tested when he adds a third finger and presses down on a spot inside me that lights me the hell up.

He backs off immediately, but I need to feel it again. "Fuck me."

And while I love how every time before now, Ford has checked in to make sure I'm okay with everything we're doing, tonight, he doesn't question me. He's given me full control.

"Spread your legs open more ... yeah, like that." His gaze is fixed on my ass as he leans forward to guide my knees up higher. They press into the mattress on either side of my shoulders, leaving my ass in the air. If I thought I was vulnerable before, it's nothing on right now.

"So flexible."

"Years of dancing."

He slaps an ass cheek, giving me a delicious sting. "You ready for this?"

"More than I've ever been ready for anything."

Ford shuffles forward, hand rubbing over my balls as the other grips his shaft. "I'll go slow."

"I know you will."

The pressure of his cock at my hole is exciting. Precum dribbles onto my abs as I bear down, and then Ford's cock slips inside. It's a stretch like nothing else, delicious and a little painful, but mostly satisfying in a way I'll never wrap my head around.

He opens me to my limits the further he pushes inside, his lube-covered hand slowly stroking my cock and keeping me horny.

"Feel good?"

"Amazing."

"You have no idea how sexy this looks." He grabs my

hips and snaps his forward, groin meeting my ass and sealing us together.

I take over on my cock, looking up at all that man towering above me. "I dunno. I have a sexy view from here."

He chuckles and sinks down, setting my ass back on the mattress and covering me again. Every small move sends ripples of pleasure through me.

Ford pulls me into a lazy kiss, his hips making small circles, testing me out.

I moan into his mouth to let him know that everything feels amazing. I wasn't lying when I told him I've always been curious, and now I know why. It's a feeling like nothing else. Being filled. Being owned. I'm more or less helpless as he spears into me.

Ford's thrusts pick up, grunts becoming hoarse, and I keep stroking myself to his rhythm. Knowing that he's using my body, that it's driving him insane and making him feel as needy and floaty as I am, is addictive.

Especially when I know that all it would take is one word from me for all of this to be over. But I'd never torture either of us like that because if Ford stopped, I really might die.

His cock is hitting all the right things inside me, and I feel filthy and dirty spread open for him, but almost cherished by the way he doesn't stop kissing me. I swallow every one of his grunts and gasps, loving the taste of his need, loving the way he's using me. My limbs feel oxygen-less, tingly, little prickles breaking out all over.

I need to come, but I don't want this to end. Not with the way he's pounding into me. Not with the way he smells like fresh sweat and sounds like he's desperately on edge.

My hand picks up, jerking off faster, but before I can

reach my orgasm, Ford closes his arms around me and flips us.

He ends up on his back, me hovering above him, and then he takes my hips and goes to town. He fucks up into me so hard and fast all I can do is hold on for the ride and try not to come.

His beautiful body is coated in a thin layer of sweat, and I love watching his arm muscles flex as he grips me hard. Harder. Firm enough to leave bruises. I want them. The reminder that once this is all over, that's how much he needed me in the moment. Ford, the man who's always so sweet and considerate, needed to come so badly that he forgot himself.

My balls pull tight at the thought.

"Ah, fuck me, I'm close."

"Trying here, sweetheart," he grunts. His grip digs in, blunt nails biting painfully against my skin. Every thrust sends a soft slap echoing through the room, over and over, mixed with his deep moans, his harsh breathing. I try to ride him, but he's moving too fast, so I fist my cock and jerk off as hard as I can. I've never precumed so much in my life, and my cock thickens in my palm. It's getting too close. Too ready. I'm *aching*. My skin itchy. Tight. Needing to get there. Almost able to feel it, to fall into it.

Ford cries out, head tossed back, tendons standing out in his thick neck as his cock pulses inside me. Feeling him unload sets me off, and finally, that amazing high crashes into me, taking over my entire body.

I slump down on top of him, not able to keep myself upright any longer, and Ford's arms immediately close me in.

He's sweaty, covered in my cum, and breathing hard, but

I curl around him, loving the closeness after all … *that*. Sure, I've had dominant partners in the past, but I've never just *given* myself to someone.

Ford presses a kiss to my forehead. "You good?"

I hum, letting my eyes close. "Very."

"We probably need to shower … again."

"Soon." I wriggle up to press my face to his throat.

He chuckles, then reaches for my other nightstand and pulls out a fresh pair of my underwear. He uses it to clean us up and then pulls me against him again. "That will buy us a bit more time."

24

Ford

Oh, yeah, my mind is blown. I'm still struggling to catch my breath as I hold Orson close, not wanting to break contact for a second.

For the first time in my life, I understood what he was talking about. That desperate need for someone, not only in my cock, but my chest as well. Seeing him ride me in all his muscle-twitching, thigh-tensing glory, I was hit with this moment where it wasn't enough. I was *inside* him, and it wasn't enough.

I get the feeling I'll always want more when it comes to him.

He kisses my throat softly, lazily, spiky scruff rubbing the skin below my beard. It's so nice I could up and fall asleep, no worries, even though I'm sticky with sweat and my gut is starting to niggle with hunger.

My hand runs along his back to his hip, where there are angry red marks there.

"Did I hurt you?"

"Yes," he says dreamily. "It was perfect."

I rub the spot gently, and this weird, possessive satisfaction rises inside of me at him being covered in my marks. "Sorry."

"Don't be. I hope it bruises."

I hesitate for a moment before confessing, "Me too."

He chuckles softly.

"I don't want to hurt you though, just … mark you up a bit."

"When I'm that turned on, you could probably punch me in the face and it wouldn't hurt."

"Well, we won't be doing *that*, but good to know I didn't ruin things."

"Far from it." His voice has a soft, dreamy quality to it, making me think he's close to sleep himself.

My hands keep exploring, touching, kneading his muscle. I work my way from his shoulder down to his forearm and pause, thumb grazing one of the scars. They're smaller and shiny white, all up and down both arms.

I've asked him before about them, and he shut me down, but I can't help but be curious.

He shifts, turning his arm over so I can see them better.

"You have a lot," I say, hoping he'll catch on to the thoughts running through my head.

"Yep."

I laugh. "Fine, keep your secrets." We fall quiet while I continue to trace them.

"I don't want you to think less of me," he finally says.

"Less of you?" I'd shake my head if I could. "There's no way."

"Eh, I was out of control for a while there."

"Not surprising considering what you went through."

I take a deep breath, brushing his scar again, and say, "Just because I'm curious doesn't mean you have to tell me. I like who you are—more than like, if I'm honest. The other stuff doesn't matter; I only want to know so I know *you* better." I kiss his head. "But I understand keeping things to yourself."

He pulls his arm away and shifts. I'm expecting him to put distance between us, but instead, he presses up onto his forearm to look down at me.

"I've told you a bit about what a mess I was. Went into a lot of the pain-numbing activities. Alcohol, mostly; sometimes, uh, *harder* things when that didn't work. I slept with a *lot* of women in that time because it was the only thing that gave me a momentary high—followed by the lowest lows I've ever felt. Sometimes, I felt like ending it—"

"Is that what—"

He shakes his head. "Heh. No. *Those* are the result of a glass bottle. He was aiming for my head, but I got my arms up in time, and when it smashed, he slashed at me with it. Luckily missed anything major."

"Holy shit." I can't imagine how he got himself into that situation. "Can I ask how it got to that point?"

He nods but doesn't answer right away. "I slept with his wife."

My gut clenches. "Did you know?"

His eyes meet mine suddenly, hold my gaze, challenging me, and he doesn't have to answer because I can read the guilt on his face, but he does anyway.

"I knew. I just wanted everyone to hurt like I did."

"Wow." I swallow, trying to think up something reassuring. "I ..."

"Nope. It was horrible. Tara was taken from me, but it wasn't anyone's *fault*. Whereas I fucked up that man's life. *Me*—and his wife, obviously—but I played an active part. It wasn't some universal tragedy, just me being selfish and making a fucked-up decision." He rubs his jaw and looks away. "It hit me, when I was sitting in a hospital bed, bandaged to the elbows, no emergency contact on file, that … I hated myself. They said I was lucky, but I just wished the guy had better aim."

My heart aches for him. "So how did you go from that to … this?"

"Art."

"As in … drawing and painting …" I trail off as he shakes his head.

"No, Art as in the pain in the ass."

That's literally the last answer I'm expecting.

"I was fired from my job since I brought drama there, which meant there was no way I could make payments on rent in Boston since I refused to touch Tara's insurance money. So I swallowed the tiny scrap of pride I had left, picked up the phone, and called him. I told him everything. We'd been friends before I left but not super close, so the fact he was the only person I had was depressing. Maybe that's what made it easier to admit everything, I dunno. I'm not sure what I wanted out of the conversation, but no way in hell was I expecting him to show up a few hours later with a U-Haul, ready to pack up my place."

"Did you know he was coming?"

"Nope. Got an Uber when I was discharged from the hospital and found Art outside my apartment, where he gave me shit about leaving him waiting." Orson's fond smile warms me. "He roped in the neighbors to help him, and they had my place packed up in one afternoon, and before I knew it, we were on the way back here."

"You didn't fight him on it?"

"Nope. I was on good painkillers, but mostly, I was exhausted. Lost. Needed fixing. The asshole did it too. Somehow, he got me to therapy, got me socializing, even had me use the insurance money to buy the shop." Orson's eyes have gone kinda glassy. "I … I owe everything to him."

I swallow back the emotion building in my chest. Knowing Orson went through all that is hard, but realizing that *Art* is the one who pulled him out of it? Who didn't write him off as too much effort and put in the work to help him?

Looks like I owe everything to that bastard as well.

"Never thought Art would become my favorite person."

He huffs a laugh and ducks his face into my chest. When he reappears though, his expression is tight. "I've put in a lot of hard work to get to where I am. But I know all that's a lot. I made some shitty choices, and I totally understand if it's too much for you."

"I get the feeling you're trying to scare me away, so I'm gonna be clear here. I don't scare easily. You made a mistake. That doesn't make you special—people make mistakes all the time. Fuck knows I've made some big ones. Good people can do shitty things, and yeah, what you did *was* shitty—we're not gonna skirt around that—but answer this: If you were in that same situation today, would you do it again?"

"Hell no." His face twists angrily. "I still feel like shit over it."

"There you go, then. You made a mistake, and you grew from it. *That's* what makes you special."

His expression is full of relief as his head drops onto my chest. "You are way too good for me."

I cringe, and thankfully, he doesn't see it. It's easy not to hold all of that against Orson when he's not the same person, but would he hold my past against me when he realizes I am? I haven't changed.

And I don't want to.

AFTER THE HEAVY AFTERNOON, ORSON AND I HAVE A QUICK shower, order in, and then spend the night on the couch together. It's perfect. Unlike him, I can't borrow clothes, so I leave early to duck home and get changed, then make my way over to his shop.

He's surprised to see me, but I peck him on the cheek and get him to show me his biggest and best bouquet that says *thank you.*

"Who are these for?" he asks.

I shrug. "My cousin's friend's sibling's dog."

He looks blankly back at me before throwing up his hands. "Don't wanna know. The white and pink ones would work."

"Got anything in yellow?"

He arches an eyebrow at me but plays my game. We wander around the store, him making suggestions and me shooting them down until I point to the original bunch. "What about those? They'd work nicely."

He rolls his eyes. "Pink and white coming right up."

"You'd think you'd be better at your job by now. They really should have been your first suggestion."

"How silly of me."

I follow him to the counter and watch him work, wrapping the bunch in that flimsy brown paper and making them look all fancy.

"Not going to tell me?" he asks.

"Nope."

The corner of his lips hitches up. "Will I see you later?"

"Undoubtedly."

I pay him for the flowers and leave as a couple walk in, then cross the street toward Killer Brew. The old brewery is a huge, intimidating structure, sitting on the water with the mountains and Kill Pen behind it. If Art isn't here, I'll eat my left nut—he practically lives at work. I'm ninety percent sure the door inside his office that is always closed leads to a bedroom or something.

Sure enough, when I walk inside, he's sitting at a booth, laptop open in front of him, with a pile of papers beside it.

"Hey, darlin'."

"Don't call me darlin'," Art says. "I'm not one of your booty calls."

"I call *everyone* darlin'," I throw back. Booty calls, servers, strangers in the street.

"Yes, but you don't have to try to act less menacing with me. I know you're a softie."

Of course he'd know why I do it. Pet names are an immediate ice breaker with most people and help them feel comfortable around me. I point to his work. "Don't you have an office for all that?"

"Yep. Was feeling social today." He looks up, and his gaze lands on the flowers, causing a slow smile to spread across his face. "It's almost like I knew handsome men would come bearing gifts."

It's a struggle not to turn on my heel and leave, but instead, I hold them out.

His face drops. "Wait. They're actually for me?"

"Not if you don't hurry up and take them."

He claims them and sets them on the table beside his work as I take the seat opposite. "Do I need to remind you that we've tried this once and it didn't work? You're a fine man, Ford Thomas, but I'm a wild stallion, completely untam—"

"Nope. Not what this is."

"Hm. Unlikely, but continue."

I look at the beautiful man across from me, the one who tries to pretend he's all surface, no substance, and it feels like I'm seeing him for the first time. I've known Art most of my life, and sure, he has his divorced club and does good things for them, but I never would have imagined he'd go out of his way for someone the way he did for Orson.

"Thank you."

He cocks his head. "For what?"

"Orson."

Understanding brightens in his dark eyes. "He told you?"

"Everything."

Art's usual teasing expression relaxes. "I can trust you to keep it to yourself?"

"Of course." His words catch up with me. "Wait. What he went through or what you did for him?"

"Both."

"You don't want people to know?"

"I didn't do it for the acknowledgment. Would have done it without even him knowing if I could have gotten away with it, but he needed a familiar face."

"Was it bad?"

"That's not my story to tell."

Given what I've pieced together from Orson, I already know the answer. "I respect that."

He nods once. "Wouldn't matter to me if you didn't."

He's got a point there.

"So you two … he told us things were happening. Is it getting serious?"

Even though we haven't sat down and talked it through, I feel like it is. He hasn't freaked out over anything we've done sexually, and he craves the same amount of time together as I do. If things keep up, I'm going to have myself a boyfriend or … a partner? "I hope so."

"Good." A dreamy look crosses his face. "More of my men finding love again. One by one, they're growing up and sprouting wings …"

I snort at the imagery of Orson with wings. "Dunno about love, but it's exciting, huh?"

"Sure is."

"So when's your turn?"

Art's laugh is loud. "That will be the one journey I never go on." He looks across the room, toward the bar. "Why fall in love once when you can fall in lust a million times over?"

I think of last night with Orson, that warm feeling spreading through my chest, my need to have more. "Because it feels pretty damn wonderful."

Art blinks at me. "Come again?"

"Nothing."

"Oooh, that wasn't nothing."

I stroke my beard, realizing that no, it fucking wasn't. "Maybe I'm sprouting some wings of my own."

"Well, while you do that, I'm going to get my pain-in-the-ass employee to put these flowers in some water." An evil glint sparks in his eyes. "Do me a favor and blow me a kiss on the way out."

"So long as you keep this little conversation all to yourself."

"Deal." He jumps up and grabs the flowers. "Wait until I'm at the bar."

I have no clue what it's all about, but once he's there, I get up, blow him a kiss, and leave.

As much as my respect might be through the roof for him, I'll never pretend to understand Art and the way he operates.

DMC GROUP CHAT

Orson: *How do you know if you're dating someone?*

Griff: *Ask them?*

Payne: *Have feelings and hook up a few times and keep stubbornly putting it off for their benefit ... no? Just me?*

Griff: *How did you end up with Beau, again?*

Orson: *Because they're in love.*

Griff: *I'm just saying, Heath had me hooked after weeks, I couldn't imagine being Beau and dealing with TWO DECADES of unrequited love.*

Payne: *Yes, but we all know you struggle to keep it in your pants at the best of times.*

Art: *Are you and Ford dating?*

Orson: *I have no idea. It feels like yes but neither of us has actually confirmed anything.*

Griff: *Do you want to be dating?*

Orson: *I think so.*

Griff: *Then tell him.*

Payne*: Agreed.*

Art: *I don't agree! You've only just found this dick-loving side of yourself. Share the love around!*

Orson: *I'm not going to sleep with you.*

Art: *Huh. In that case, I agree too.*

25

Orson

Ford wanted to get up and come with me to the market, but he hasn't had a single day off in weeks, so I told him to park his ass in bed and threatened to withhold sex if he showed his face before nine.

I miss him as I set up my stall, but it's for the best. There has barely been a day this week where I haven't seen him, and our sleepovers are becoming regular things. His scent is on my clothes, in my house, in my car. It's calming. Warming. I haven't been this happy in a long time.

Amber and Steve are setting up their produce stall just down from me, and now that we've reached October, they've set up a second stall to sell pumpkins out of. They're huge and orange, and I have this ridiculous moment imagining Ford and I carving one out together, wearing matching costumes … My gut swims happily at the stupid image.

"Morning, Orson," Amber calls.

"Morning." I point to her stall. "Make sure you remind

people that flowers look amazing behind jack-o'-lanterns in their social media photos."

She laughs. "Will do. You've got some very seasonal ones happening."

I nod and look at the orange and black flowers set up along the front. They were a pain in the ass to get in, but I know I'll sell every one of them. "Look great, don't they?"

"If you have any left, I'll send Steve over once we're done."

"Don't count on it. These ones are always popular."

They finish setup, and we spend a couple of minutes making small talk about their son in college before Amber tilts her head and asks what I can tell she's been trying to hold back.

"No Ford today?"

My smile springs to my face. "He said he'll be by later."

"It's sweet that he's been helping you. I didn't realize you were friends."

"Yeah, it's only been a few months now, but sometimes you meet those people who fit seamlessly into your life. That's Ford."

"Ford Thomas?" Leeandra pauses by us. "The ex-con?"

It's a real lesson in self-control to stop myself from telling her to fuck off. "Ford the mechanic, yes."

She exchanges a look with Claude, who she runs the pretzel stand with. "I take my car up to Springfield to get seen to. Most of us do. We don't want to support a criminal."

"A criminal?" The words are out of my mouth before I can stop them. "What proof do you have?"

"I was friends with his parents," Claude says. "They were heartbroken when he was sent away."

"I think we've had enough town gossip for one day." Steve's tone is firm.

"Not gossip." Claude straightens. "It's true. What he did to that poor kid—"

"That's enough." Where Steve was firm, I'm angry. I glare Claude down. "Ford is nothing but a good person, and no one here gives a shit that you guys don't use his garage. He has great business without you, and he's not going anywhere."

"If he had good sense, he wouldn't show his face around here," Leeandra throws back.

"He has as much right to be here as anyone, and when he shows up to help out at my booth today, you'd better keep your opinions to yourself."

Leeandra and Claude give me pitiful looks as they leave, and Amber lets out a long breath.

"Rude old bat," she says.

"It's fine."

"No, it's not. Things were really bad for Ford when he first moved back here. The last thing he needs is for that nonsense to keep coming up again."

"I don't think I was around then."

She shakes her head. "It was before you and Tara moved here."

"So … he *did* go to jail, then?"

She shrugs.

Steve rests a hand on her shoulder. "It's never been confirmed. By anyone. People are sure they know what happened, but Ford's never said a word, and his parents don't talk about it. Mostly it's old news by now until assholes like that get involved."

"Right," I say, forcing a level of calm that I don't feel.

They wander away as the market doors open, and I'm left by myself, feeling this lump in my gut. I'm not even sure what the feeling is from. Sure, the thought of him doing time isn't a happy one, but I've heard those rumors before, and they don't line up with the man I know. I'd been sure it was all talk. Small-town gossip.

But Claude had been talking like he had details. And if there was a *kid* involved?

My mind runs away with the idea, and the sickness settles deeper. It infects my mood. Makes it hard to focus. Ford didn't judge me for my past, and I have every intention to do the same, but … but. There are some things I can't get past, as hypocritical as that might be.

Hurting kids is one of those things.

In a lull between customers, I double forward, hands on my knees, and try to *breathe* through the panic. Ford will have an explanation. He has to.

The man I know wouldn't hurt *anyone* … I think of him looking up flowers and being wary of the water and so patient helping the sixteeners with their soapbox cars.

And … wait. If he'd been to prison for something to do with kids, there's no way he'd be allowed to work with them now. Right? *Right*? It's possible the parents don't know, but I hold on to the hope that Claude was exaggerating.

I'm just not sure what the hell to do about it now.

Ford let me talk through my past when I was ready, so it's not like I can go to him and demand the story. Especially when, according to Steve, he doesn't talk about it with anyone.

I mean, Art's the biggest information source in town, and he *knows* there's something going on with me and Ford. If he'd had even the faintest whiff of Ford being bad news, he never would have encouraged me.

Fuck it. I need to know.

I set my "Back in 5" sign out and head into the bar side of the brewery. It's quieter in here, only two people behind the bar and one person in a booth watching whatever sport replay is on. I ignore them all and take the stairs behind the bar to Art's office two at a time.

But when I get there, it's locked. I knock, then lean close to the door to see if I can hear anything, but it's quiet. He's not here.

Art is *always* here.

I scrub my hands over my face and pace back out to the mezzanine, feet turning toward the large mullioned windows.

The sky stretches over Kilborough, periwinkle blue and cheerful, despite how cold it's been this morning. It's one of those crisp fall days that people hang on to and take advantage of, knowing winter will be here soon. My breathing evens out, the panic taking root in my chest ebbing with each exhale.

Ford completely supported me no matter what, didn't even need to think about it. What I did was fucked-up—it ruined two people's lives, even though she played a part too. What Ford did … unless it's something completely evil, I'm going to support him too.

And knowing Ford the way I do, I can't believe it *could* be something evil.

I let myself get lost in the vastness of the sky, letting the reminder of my own insignificance set in. Even the things that seem too big for me to handle are minuscule when I put them into perspective.

"What are you doing up here?"

I turn at Art's familiar voice and offer him a smile. "Had a question for you."

"Oh, yeah? Hit me."

It's on the tip of my tongue to ask, but I change my mind. "You know what … it's not important."

"Really?"

"Really."

I tell him I'll see him later, and when I get back to my booth, the sign is gone, and Ford is helping out some customers. As I approach, I watch him. He's so friendly, so welcoming. He's talking about my flowers the same way he'd talk about his cars, and it makes my chest ache at how amazing he is.

Someone with a heart that big doesn't belong behind bars.

Then again, he wouldn't be the first guy to be locked up who didn't deserve it.

I wait for him to ring them up and say bye before I step into the booth behind him. "You're two minutes early."

"I couldn't stay away." His grin is so large when he turns to me that despite all my confusion, I return it.

Do I want to know the truth? Yes.

But do I trust Ford, no matter his past? He hasn't ever given me a reason not to.

I step closer, place my hand on his chest, just as Ford's gaze slides off to the side.

His face falls as he staggers back a step.

"Ah … I've … there's something I've gotta …" He hurries to take off his apron and grab a bunch of flowers, eyes fixed on something behind me.

"Are you okay?"

"Fine." He holds up the flowers. "I'm buying these."

I'm having whiplash that he's here and gone again so fast, but when I turn and try to work out what the hell got that reaction from him, I watch him jog up one of the aisles between booths. It's busy, but we're not at our peak yet, so I see exactly who he's spotted a moment before he reaches them.

Molly.

My gut bottoms out as I watch Ford hold out the flowers.

26

Ford

IT'S BEEN A WEEK SINCE I HURT MOLLY, AND I HAVEN'T seen him around since. Considering the little flirt has always gone out of his way to approach me, I knew it could only mean he was avoiding me.

So the second I see him here, I know I have to hurry.

Thing is, I might not be interested in Molly, but I don't want him to hate me either. He's a nice guy, and he deserves to find a nice guy of his own.

That person isn't me, but I still want to make sure he knows it. I want to do what I should have done the other day and make things clear in an amicable way.

"Wait up," I call, and his eyes fly wide at the sight of me.

"Are you serious ..." Will says, but Molly shakes his head.

"Give me a minute."

"But—"

"Go catch up with Dad. I'll be right there."

Will opens his mouth like he's going to argue, then turns his attention the way Molly indicated. "Fine, but if he hurts you again, kick his ass."

Both Molly and I laugh at that as Will hurries away.

I hold up the flowers. "I'm so sorry, darlin'."

He stares for a moment, lips turned down, before he slowly reaches for them. I'd grabbed the flowers in a hurry, but they're a gorgeous bunch. Of course they are. Orson's good at what he does.

"What ... what are these for?"

"Throwing my coffee at you for a start. It really was an accident."

"I know." He looks up at me through his eyelashes. "You'd never purposely hurt someone."

Well, not someone who didn't deserve it. I shift under his gaze and offer an uncertain smile. "I don't want to be a dick here and say the wrong thing, but everything else I said the other day was the truth."

"The boyfriend ..."

"I'm sorry. I know ..." God, how is it so mortifying to say? "I know that you maybe hoped something would happen here, but I needed to be clear with you. You're a great guy, and I know you probably have men lining up to take you out—"

"I don't. I don't have anyone. Because every time I think I have a chance with a guy, he decides I'm not good enough."

Ouch. The first thing I want to do is point out that he's still young and has plenty of time to find someone, but fuck me, that only makes me sound old. I remember being sure I had the world figured out in my twenties. I would have hated for someone to underestimate me. "I'm sorry. I really am."

His lips turn down even as he tries to look okay. "Fine."

I guess that's it, then. I turn, about to head back, when he talks again.

"Is that him?" Molly's eyes are narrowed in Orson's direction.

I follow his gaze to where Orson is watching us, hands on his hips and looking ... worried? Ah, shit.

Better make this fast and fill him in because it's just hit me what this looks like from his perspective. He distracted me with sex before I could tell him about what happened at the cafe, and then it slipped my mind, so I can understand why he'd be confused over me giving another man flowers.

I'm not sure how to answer, though, since we still haven't defined shit. So I go with a "We're new" and hope that covers everything.

"But he's so *old*." Molly wrinkles his cute nose. "Can he even keep up with you?"

"He's only a few years older than me, and also, don't. Being mean isn't you."

"Guess we didn't know each other very well at all, then, did we?"

My jaw tightens as I hold back from saying anything. He's hurt, had a bit of a setback, but I have no doubt that he'll recover and move on quickly. There was nothing more than flirting between us, which I'm regretting now. Flirting with everyone is fun until someone gets hurt.

Molly's always been a nice guy, but I sensed that undercurrent of possessiveness from a mile away, and I am so glad in this moment that I never gave in to the temptation of an easy lay.

"Goodbye, Molly."

"Goodbye, Ford Thomas."

The whole way back to Orson's booth, I'm trying to figure out how to explain all … *this*. It's pretty straightforward, and Orson's a reasonable guy, but you never know what's going to trigger someone to unnecessary jealousy. All I know is I'll grovel if I have to.

"Sorry," I say, running a hand through my hair as I step back into the booth. "The other day, I—"

He cuts me off with his mouth. A grunt echoes in my throat as Orson's tongue pushes into my mouth, his hands gripping my hair and his body pressed against me. The reaction is worlds different from what I was expecting, but I grip him and kiss him right back.

If Orson doesn't give a shit about his customers and the other vendors seeing us, then neither do I.

"Well, that wasn't the welcome back I was expecting," I say, slightly breathless, when he pulls away.

"I'm not allowed to miss you?"

"For two minutes? Nope." I rub my beard. "Gotta say that I thought you'd react differently to me giving another man flowers."

His gaze flicks in the direction I was standing with Molly, making it clear he knows what I'm talking about. "Did the flowers mean anything?"

"They were an apology."

His lips twitch. "Should have grabbed the orchids, then."

"I'll remember to consult you next time."

"Next time?" His head tilts. "You planning on giving random men flowers often?"

"I think you underestimate the high demand for me."

Orson thumps me in the shoulder and turns to pull away, but I catch him before he can. My arms circle his waist, and his back thumps against my chest.

"I told him about you."

Orson stiffens. "You did?"

I frown at the weird tone. "Was that not okay? You said—"

He twists back to face me, smile lighting up his eyes. "What did you tell him?"

"That I was seeing someone."

"Oh, really?"

Butterflies dance through my gut as I add, "He assumed you were my boyfriend."

"And am I?"

"I think you are."

"I think I am too."

My forehead rests against his. "Fuck. I've been stressing about that for days. If I'd known the conversation was gonna be that easy …"

"You should have. You can tell me anything." His eyes search mine for a moment, and even though he's brushed off this whole thing, I swear I detect worry in them.

I lean down and graze his mouth with a kiss. "In that case … I'm growing pretty damn fond of you, sweetheart. I hope you stick around."

"I'm scared."

His words take me aback. "Why?"

"Because there's not a single part of me that wants to walk away."

"Isn't that a good thing?"

His laugh is dry. "Most people haven't had their hearts broken. I have. I should be smarter than this."

"Smarter than what?"

"Than risking it happening a second time."

27

Orson

ADMITTING TO FORD THAT MY FEELINGS RUN DEEPER THAN casual dating or some fun sex leaves me feeling raw and vulnerable. We don't have much time to talk about it at the market, and then by the time we pack up and drive back to my place, I'm tired and drained. Between the stupid gossip and then seeing him with Molly, the day was a lot to process, but one thing sank in loud and clear: I'm in love with the man.

Seeing Molly touch him, seeing any kind of connection between them, it hit hard. I wanted to walk over to them and make it clear that Ford and I are an item, and if it's up to me, he won't be going anywhere.

But Ford's a big boy who can handle himself, and the last thing I'm going to do is *make* him stay. He's a flirt—I love that about him, and that will never change. If I can't trust him to be himself, then I can't trust him at all. It's not like I'm going to walk around following him everywhere to make sure he behaves himself.

He's a grown-ass man.

And I'm an idiot.

Because if this relationship ends, I'm not sure the pain will ever leave me.

A few months ago, I would never have looked twice at another guy, and now here I am, wanting to hold on to this one forever.

My phone dings with a message, and I pull it out to check. It's a response to one of the car enquiries I sent out the other day and … hello. The price they're asking is reasonable.

And doable.

I scroll back up to the picture of the T-Bird. It's a mess, but I know Ford will love the rust off the damn thing, and I keep imagining his face, coming home one day and seeing this girl parked in his driveway. I meant it when I said life was too short to put things off, and this is important to him.

My imagination is running away from me as I picture us both shirtless and working under the open hood. It's what possesses me to hit Reply and make an offer.

Fuck it. I'm already all in anyway.

Ford pulls into the Killer Brew parking lot and cuts Momma T's engine. When I told Art last week that Ford and I were heading home to carve a pumpkin together, he took it from me and refused to give it back, announcing he was having a friendly carving that we had to come to.

The way he emphasized the word *carving* and refused, point-blank, throughout multiple conversations to call it "pumpkin" carving has me walking into the brewery tonight, slightly on edge.

Until Ford takes my hand.

It gets me every time. That settled happiness that I never thought I'd have again.

"How much are we wagering that Art jumps out at us, wielding a knife like in *Psycho*?" Ford murmurs as we cut through the bar to the stairs.

"I think the odds are higher that he'll have a pumpkin on his head."

"And mess up his hair? Never."

We climb the stairs to the mezzanine level, where Art's holding the carving. Anything social that we do is always here, even when it's only a few of us, and if I hadn't stayed with Art for a few weeks while I was getting back on my feet, I wouldn't even know where he lived.

Art brings his hands together in one loud clap as soon as he sees us. "About time. You're late."

"We wanted everyone else to get here first so if we walked in to find a bunch of carved-up corpses, we at least had time to run."

He sniggers. "You know I'd have the decency to clean up after myself."

I glance around at the people gathered. There are two DMC guys here—ex-husbands—who I don't know well, but they're both friends with Keller, who's also in the circle. Payne and his boyfriend, Beau, are sipping their drinks on the couch, and there's another handful of guys hanging around who I assume Art knows but I've never met before.

"This everyone?" Ford asks.

"Yep." Art nods to where the cute barman is serving two guys from the small bar up here. "Once they're back."

Suspicion prickles along my neck at the familiar light

brown mop, and when Molly turns, my suspicions are confirmed.

This fun night just went down the drain. What the fuck is he doing here?

Ford goes tense beside me, and I know he's spotted Molly too.

I'm about to ask Art how the hell they were invited when Molly and the other guy approach, and he sets a drink down in front of Keller.

"Here, Dad. I would have gotten you one too, Daddy Ford, but I didn't know you were here already." Molly bats his eyelashes, but I'm still too in shock that *he's* Keller's son to process the flirting.

"He's your kid?" I ask, rudely pointing, but wow. They look nothing alike.

Keller's a Jason Momoa look-alike. Longish hair, dark beard, calm presence. Molly is a slight, doe-eyed twink, who looks like he's plotting how to off me.

"Yep," Keller says.

My quick math puts Molly older than I thought he was since Keller is forty-two and had Molly at sixteen.

"And you've met Will." Keller gestures at the tan guy with the backward cap and sweet smile.

I force a smile in return, my hand tightening around Ford's as we take the only spare couch.

Which happens to be next to theirs. Molly sits on the side closest to Ford, leaving Will to squeeze in between him and Keller.

"Carving time!" Art calls, pulling out two thin knives and stabbing the air like he's letting off pistols.

"Someone take those off him," Payne mutters.

"I'm interested to see where this goes," Beau replies.

Hey, at least if there's a medical emergency, this whole night comes to an end. I clear the thought away and remind myself to be nice.

"All the pumpkins are over there," Art says, using the knives like an air hostess pointing out the emergency exits. "Grab whichever one you like and get to work. I've got stencils and photos you can follow, plus a whole craft table if you want to get creative. Whatever you make is going to be decoration here for my Halloween party, so don't fuck them up." His face is lit up with excitement, the way it usually gets when he's in the throes of a hair-brained idea.

"I'll grab ours," Ford says, squeezing my thigh.

"Sure. Want me to get drinks?"

"Thanks. I'll have whatever you're having." He drops a kiss on my head and walks toward the table.

A second later, Molly scrambles after him.

My eyes meet Keller's, and he jumps up to follow me to the bar.

"What's going on there?" he asks, nodding across the room.

"I have a feeling your son might have a thing for my boyfriend."

Keller's face screws up. "No way."

"Yes way."

A full-body shudder runs through him. "It still fucks me up to consider he's a grown-ass adult."

"A grown-ass adult who probably should learn to keep his hands to himself," I say pointedly as we both watch Molly laugh and grab Ford's bicep. Ford hurriedly takes a step back.

Keller sighs. "I'll talk to him."

"Thank you." I place my order with the barman, and

something in the way Keller's standing catches my attention. He's still. Watching ... Molly's friend?

"You okay there, buddy?"

He jerks out of it and throws me a broad grin. "Sure am." He steals my drink. "Let's carve some pumpkins."

Keller walks away, and I turn back to order another one, but Joey slides it across the bar before I can.

"Thanks."

"No problem. Hey ..." He leans in. "You with that guy over there?" He jerks his head toward Ford.

Oh no. Is he going to tell me *he's* in love with Ford too?

"Yes," I grumble. "He's my boyfriend."

"How long have you been together now?"

That's a hard question to answer, considering things have only gotten official recently. "A little while. Why?"

"Curious." A smile slowly spreads over his face. "So he's *not* dating Art?"

"Art?" That would be a disaster. "No way."

"Good to know ..." Joey grabs the dishcloth slung over his shoulder and wipes over the countertop.

I'm about to ask him what's so great about it, but I stop myself. Whatever is going on between him and Art is something I don't need to know about, not when I have enough on my mind as it is.

I carry our drinks back to where Ford is waiting, and he starts bouncing in his seat.

"Can we make this? Can we? Can we?" The picture he holds up is of a pumpkin that's been carved to look like a Volkswagen van.

I study it a minute, knowing it's well beyond our range of competency. "We can give it a go."

At first, it's actually fun. We hollow out the pumpkin

onto long trays Art has provided and bicker happily between ourselves on our plan of action. But the whole time, I'm aware of Molly. Aware of the looks thrown our way, aware of his presence, aware of how he leaves Keller and Will to finish the lantern they were all working on together to go and get his own.

Aware of him when he moves closer and nudges Ford. "Sorry, Ford, can you help? I'm struggling with the top." Then he chuckles. "Not a problem I can say I've had before."

Holy fuck.

"Sorry, I, uh …" Ford holds up the knife in one hand and pumpkin insides in the other and shrugs.

But instead of taking it for the no that it is, Molly sets his hand over Ford's and slowly scrapes the pumpkin away. Every second his fingers drag over Ford's palm has my pulse rocketing higher.

Ford's stare cuts to me, clearly torn on what to do. On one hand, be the friendly person he always is. On the other, put Molly in his place.

I hate that Ford's being put in that position at all.

He snatches his hand away and forces a laugh. "Sorry, darlin'. We've got our own pumpkin to wrestle with. Lucky it looks like Orson has the top under control."

"*Molly.*"

The three of us turn to Keller.

"Get your ass over here. They're on a date. Let them be."

Molly hesitates for a second, like he might argue, and then he walks away, shoulders pulled back. My gaze follows him even as Ford and Keller turn away, so I'm the only one who sees the pinched look on his face as he tries to stop his lip from quivering. Our gazes clash for a second before he looks away.

This gross, soft feeling comes over me. Sympathy.

I hate it.

I wish I could be content to ignore him and tell him to back off my man. When it comes to Ford, I'll fight for him if I have to, but if I felt this way and saw him with someone else? Yep. That would kill me.

So even though I don't want to, I shift to put some distance between us.

"What's the story with you two?" I lower my voice so we're not overheard.

Ford's eyes flick in Molly's direction and away again. "He's been flirty since he got back from college."

"And did you know him when he was younger?"

"Nope." Ford hacks at the pumpkin. "Knew Keller from around town, and knew Molly was his kid, but I didn't know Molly at all until he got back."

"And you really never …?"

Ford sets down the carving knife and turns his full attention on me. Those dark eyes still set my pulse alight. "A whole lot of flirting, but nothing more than that. There are a lot of guys who fall into that category, but Molly took it for more than it was."

"Is it weird that I feel bad for him?"

"Nah, you've got a big heart, so that doesn't surprise me at all." He leans in as though he's going to kiss me, but I pull back.

"Maybe not here?"

His indulgent smile warms me. "See? That's exactly what I mean."

It's hard to get through the night without touching him in

some way, and I didn't realize how much I'd started to rely on it. His hand on my thigh or shoulder pressed against mine. Having his warmth and strength to lean into whenever I needed the comfort. But I keep a friendly distance, and he does the same, both of us overly aware of Molly watching. There's still a side of me that wants to tell him to fuck off, but that would give him too much power in our relationship.

The only people who matter are me and Ford, and judging by the looks he keeps giving me, I'm confident that I don't have anything to worry about there.

28

Ford

WITH THE ACHE OF A LONG DAY BEHIND ME, I TURN ONTO MY street, buzzing with anticipation. Orson came by the garage to pick up my house keys earlier, and I can't wait to see what surprise he has in store for me.

Only when I pull up out the front, it isn't my house that's lit up and waiting; it's my back shed. The roller door is open on one side, and the bright lights are spilling out into the darkening yard.

Interesting.

I climb out of Momma T into the cool air and make my way round back.

I'm completely unprepared for what's waiting for me.

There, sitting in the middle of the garage, is a '73 Ford Thunderbird. My jaw drops as my gaze slowly swings toward my boyfriend, who's radiating a smugness I've never seen on him before.

It's *hot*.

I clear my throat. "What's, uh … what's this?"

"This—" He moves closer, running a hand up the battered T-Bird body. "—is our first baby. I thought we could work on her and name her together."

"*What*?" I'm so excited I cross the distance between us and haul him off his feet and into my arms. "You gorgeous, clever—"

He cuts off a sound that's half gasp and half moan.

I slowly set him back on solid ground. "What was that?"

"Nothing."

"Orson …"

He drops his forehead onto my shoulder. "It's a surprise."

Curiosity well and truly piqued, I think I have an idea of what could have brought that sexy fucking sound out of him. My hand slowly roams down his back, over his ass, and my fingers run along the seam. They brush something hard under his pants.

"Tell me you're not wearing a butt plug." My voice comes out in a low growl.

He shoves me off him. "We have work to do."

"Are you serious?"

He gestures to the car. "She's not going to feel our love just sitting there."

"You little tease." My head drops back, and I send a silent *down, boy* to my cock. It's raring for some action. If Orson wants to play cars first, we'll play, because I have a good feeling about where he's taking this.

We spend the first little while taking stock of where the car is at, the parts it needs, the pieces we can salvage. Overall, the engine looks decent but could use some work; the chassis is solid, but the poor body is going to take a while.

It's a good find.

But no matter how impressed I am by the car and how touched I am by Orson finding it, my attention keeps slipping back to him.

To his round ass as he leans into the passenger-side door, taking a look at the interior.

To the bounce of those delicious biceps when he props open the hood.

To the rippling flex of his abs as he lifts his shirt to scrub at the grease mark on his forehead.

He spends a long time on that grease mark. A long, long time.

I yank my gaze away from his V that I'm dying to run my tongue over and meet his eyes. The heat in them tells me all I need to know.

That sexy fucking tease is amping me up on purpose.

My cock is trapped uncomfortably, and we've done about all we can on this car tonight, and so now, it's time to bring those fantasies of mine alive.

Orson drops his shirt, the playful spark gone, and we both move at the same time. Our bodies slam together, mouths seeking, hands groping, pulling, touching wherever we can reach.

His T-shirt is over his head a second before mine, and even with the chill from outside, his hard body keeps me warm. I can't stop touching him. Needing him. And then it happens again. That growing warmth right in the center of my chest that makes everything feel heightened and nowhere near enough.

I go to back him up into the T-Bird, but one look at the hood tells me that rust bucket is nowhere near stable enough to hold his weight.

"Damn, sweetheart, you're going to be the death of me."

I yank Orson off his feet and set him on the hood of my Dodge instead. "Watch the scoop."

His kissing turns desperate, messy, all tongue and teeth. "It's okay," he pants. "You're going to fuck me bent over it anyway."

I groan as he nudges me away, slips off the hood, then turns around and drops his pants. He leans forward, bent at the waist, that gorgeous toned ass angled high and wrapped in cotton briefs.

My hands seek out his cheeks like they're magnetized. So firm and round. I squeeze them, massaging the muscle and loving the way Orson squirms under my touch. Oh yeah, the horny fucker is definitely wearing a plug.

Painstakingly slowly, I draw his briefs down over his ass and along his thighs until they join his pants at his ankles.

I get my first real look at him—

and burst out laughing.

The plug he's wearing is emblazoned with the Ford logo at its base.

"Where did you find this?"

"Had it made." He glances back at me over his shoulder. "You like?"

The amusement is wearing off the longer I look at it, and I shift, easing the pressure on my throbbing cock. Do I *like*? Seeing my name guarding his hole like that? This dark, animalistic lust sweeps through me, and I step forward to take hold of the base. "I fucking love it."

And like last time, I take hold of the toy and start to fuck him with it, only unlike last time, there's nothing gentle about it. Short, shallow pumps with the plug, over and over, making sure I miss his prostate but keep the whole area feeling good.

Orson's shuddering against the car, gorgeous-as-hell back muscles rippling with every movement, shoulders tense with the grip he has on the hood.

"I assume you have a condom?"

"My pocket."

I duck down behind him, rummaging around until I find it. From this angle on my knees, his ass is right at face level, and I can't help leaning in and sinking my teeth into the meaty part of his ass.

"*Ah.*" Orson twitches, but I quickly let go. Flatten my tongue over it.

Then I turn back to the plug and slowly draw it out.

It's thicker than the other one he had, and when it slips out, it leaves him open. The sight is so sexy I lean forward and use my tongue there too.

Orson jolts so hard I swear the car shakes. "Oh, fuck."

"Let me show you just how much I liked my surprise." I spread his cheeks and dive in. He tastes like lube, but I don't give a shit because seeing him squirm and tremble is my favorite thing in life. My cock is so hard it's painful, and I have to reach down to free it from behind the zipper. As soon as it's out and in my hand, I stroke myself in time with my tongue spearing into him. His moans are loud, shed door still wide open for all my neighbors to hear, and I don't have it in me to care.

"Oh, fuck me, please fuck me," he rambles.

I wipe my face off on my arm and scoop up the packet of lube as well. Then I suit up and lube excessively before stepping up behind him and sliding two fingers inside. He's good and stretched. Perfect.

I'm so ready for him that I don't even pause to shove my

pants down. The denim strangles my thighs as I grab my cock and press it to his hole.

"Just saying, this is everything I hoped it would be and more."

"You haven't even started yet," Orson points out.

"That part is just the icing, sweetheart." I push inside with one long, firm thrust.

Orson arches up, cry cutting through the air.

"You good?" I ask as his hole clenches around me.

"That's exactly what I needed." His voice is a low rasp. "Fuck me like your fantasy."

I almost come at the request and draw out of him slowly before slamming home again. His ass sucks me in, the pressure indescribable, and every hard thrust sends him sprawling across the hood.

For someone who's never bottomed before me, he's taking it like a champ. That's one of the things I admire about him. How he jumps in headfirst. He's the calming breath you take before a deep dive, the first gulp of water after a long run, the low rumble of a V8 engine right before it accelerates. Everything about him has set up camp in my chest and lit a warm fire that refuses to go out.

If this isn't love, I don't think I'll survive the real thing. It can't get much better than this.

I set my hand on his lower back, the other grips his hip, and then I lean back a little to watch the show. My cock pistons in and out, as fast and hard as I can go. My muscles are locked up tight, and my belt buckle rattles in time with my grunts. My thighs are straining against my jeans, wanting to go wider, harder, faster. No matter how desperately I plow him, it's never enough. I want to be wrapped around him.

Melded with him. Until his breaths are my breaths and his heartbeat sounds in my ears.

"I'm so close," he chokes out.

Yesss.

Hauling him upright, I wrap my arms around his chest and close my hand over his dick. Orson pushes back into every thrust, takes me deep, drives me wild. Our bodies move together seamlessly, my hips snapping into him as he fucks my fist.

Then his cock thickens in my palm, and he groans as he comes, twitching with each spurt. Thick ropes of cum shoot lines across Rose's shiny black paintwork, and the sight of him dirtying up something so pristine, combined with the way his ass tightens around my shaft, sets me off.

My balls pull tight and then unleash, rolling waves of sheer fucking ecstasy unloading into the condom.

My moan rumbles in my chest for longer than my orgasm lasts, and when my brain switches back on, I drop my forehead to his shoulder.

"As much as I love taking my time with you, there's nothing like a quick and dirty fuck."

He hums, hands running around to grab my ass and hold me against him. "Now you get to clean me up and feed me."

"After that, I'll give you anything you want." Always. Because I'm never letting this man get away.

29

Orson

"MY ASS HURTS," I GRUMBLE AS I WATCH FORD COOK.

His deep chuckle makes his shoulders bounce. "Yeah, I got you good. The name *Whorson* suits you."

That he did. I'd never realized taking a pounding could be such a freeing experience. Both of us trying to get to the finish line, not worried about anything outside of getting off … magic.

"We'll be going to Art's party together, right?" I ask.

"Yep." Ford throws ingredients in a pan. "It's a costume party. Got any ideas?"

"None. Dressing up in costume isn't a strength of mine."

"Could have fooled me. You were perfectly accessorized earlier." Ford throws a wink back over his shoulder that makes my cheeks burn. "Speaking of, what do I owe you for the T-Bird?"

I'm shaking my head before the question is out. "Nothing. It's a gift."

"You're gifting me a car?"

"Calm down. I obviously got it cheap." I shrug. "But when it's something you really want, I don't think you should wait. There's always a reason not to do something, but time is finite. It's not going to wait for you to make a decision."

He pauses in stirring whatever he's frying up and sets the spatula down. "That's a good point."

"It's true."

Ford doesn't move for a moment, back to me, and I watch the way his back moves with each breath. Then he turns suddenly and crosses to where I'm sitting on the counter. At this height, he's a little shorter than me, and it's disorienting looking down at him.

"In that case, there's probably no real reason not to tell you this."

My mind flies through what the hell it could be, and it doesn't escape my notice that they're all worst-case scenarios—that he really was in prison, and the reason isn't one I can accept, that he's decided he wants to be with Molly, that things aren't working out between us—so when he cups my face, relief rattles through me.

"I'm in love with you."

I almost fall off the damn counter. "What?"

He nods. "Pretty sure that's what this is. And you're right that time won't wait for me to get my shit together to tell you that." His inhale is as shaky as the nerves in my gut. "You coming into my life has been the most incredible thing, and I know I've never felt this before. So even if you don't feel the same way, thank you. I had no clue what I was missing."

Every word he's saying is terrifying and amazing. I'm

flying under the way he's looking at me and so happy that he isn't playing games, isn't messing around.

My heart hurts because I know I'm in love with him too.

And going through that again is a scary fucking thing when you've already been so high and crashed so low. I've been here before, this dizzying all-encompassing feeling. Being overwhelmed by how much I can love one person.

I clutch Ford to me, not wanting him to walk away before I can find the words to tell him what's going on in my head. The skillet on the stove is spitting angrily, but Ford doesn't try to pull away.

"Was that the wrong thing to say?" he asks.

I shake my head, throat feeling tight. "No. No, no. It's … you're amazing. And I feel it too, but I don't know what I'm supposed to do with that. What if I lose you?"

He pulls me close, wrapping me tightly in his arms, waiting for me to calm down. My breathing is all erratic, and I have this strong urge to cry that I keep having to push back down again.

His big hand running up and down my back helps center me.

"I got you. I'm not planning on going anywhere anytime soon, but I know that's not always up to us. I'm so sorry you lost her."

"Me too," I say, pressing a kiss to his neck. "But I'm so thankful I found you."

Ford pulls back, thumb running back and forth over the scruff on my cheek. "I'm not gonna talk about meant to be and all that other shit people bring up when they're trying to make people feel better. What happened will never be easy or for a reason, but you're allowed to have your second chance. You're flipping the world off with both hands and taking back what you deserve. Someone to love you. Completely. And I wanna be that someone."

"You deserve that too. I can't pretend I don't love her and miss her—she was my wife—but I hope you know that my heart is big enough to love both of you. For me to give you all of me, to show you every day how amazing you are."

Ford's smile is soft. "Orson, there isn't a person who's met you who doesn't know that."

That warms me from my toes to my face, but I want him to know how serious I am. "I don't want you to think this means less. Because you're everything to me. There's no competition."

"I'm not looking to compete with anyone. I bet Tara was a great person, or you wouldn't have been with her. I don't care what you had before me. I only care that we're here, that we're together, and that, hopefully, we'll be able to build our own lives together one day."

"You have no idea how much I want that."

Our mouths meet in a slow, deep kiss, hands clinging desperately to each other, my heart trying to escape my chest.

I'm still nervous and terrified, but what's the alternative? Walking away so I don't get hurt again? It's way too late for that.

An angry sizzle is followed by the smell of burned meat, and Ford quickly pulls away and crosses to the stove.

"Well, that's well and truly fucked. Why don't we order in?"

"Sounds good to me."

He clears his throat and runs one hand over his face. "While we wait, there's maybe some things you should know about me as well."

I know what he's getting at without him having to say it. "Why you were arrested?"

"Yup."

"I've heard rumors." Lots of them. "But you don't have to tell me anything you're not comfortable going over."

Ford links his thick fingers through mine and leads me into the living room. "I appreciate it, but I'm not going to leave you wondering. I can only imagine the shit you've heard."

"Yeah, it hasn't painted you with the best brush."

"But you're still here?"

"Well, yeah. I might not have known you then, but I know you now."

"What if it was something bad?" he asks.

"What if you tell me instead of making my imagination do the work?"

Ford laughs and flops back onto his couch, pulling me after him. "Good point."

"Is this better or worse than me fucking up someone's marriage?"

"Depends how you look at it. We both hurt people."

I know I shouldn't ask, but I can't help myself. "A child?"

"Technically, yeah."

"What do you mean technically?"

"He was seventeen, I was eighteen."

Some of the tension I've been holding on to eases at that. Hurting someone is still hurting them, but there's a big difference between two people of similar ages and someone much older and larger, preying on someone younger. "What happened?"

"He did some bad things to one of my friends, so I did some bad things to him."

"Like …"

"Like *put him in the hospital with my fists* things."

"Wow."

Ford's jaw flexes, and he looks deep in thought. "I was an adult, so I was punished like one. Did my time, got out early on good behavior, and went to anger management classes. Not sure I needed them because I wasn't angry when I went after him, but they gave me some good perspective. Thing is, I see my sixteeners, and if anyone ever hurt them, I think I'd do the exact same thing."

Our eyes meet, like Ford is checking in on my reaction to that. And I know he believes his words, but I don't.

"It would be horrible, and I hope nothing bad ever does happen to them, but I don't think you'd hurt someone."

"Even though I already have?"

I snigger. "You were eighteen. I mean, it doesn't excuse what happened, but teenagers' brains aren't developed all the way. Have you hurt anyone since then?"

"No."

"Exactly." I draw in a deep breath. "We've both done things we're not proud of, but we're both working not to be those people anymore. You've been treated like shit by people here, and you never bite back. You think I have a big heart? Fuck, take a look at yourself."

He smiles, even though he's trying not to. "I'm glad I told you."

"I'm glad you did too." My stomach grumbles, and I drop my head onto his chest. "Especially because right now, I'm more concerned about dinner than things we can't change."

"One of the many things I love about you. You sure know how to prioritize."

I chuckle, caught up in the word. I don't think it'll ever get less scary, but I know one thing: I'll never be tired of hearing it from him.

30

Ford

NEVER THOUGHT I'D BE A GROWN-ASS MAN, ATTENDING A Halloween party as a hot dog. At least I've got my bottle of mustard beside me, and being one of those matching-costume couples isn't something I'd thought I'd be either.

Especially because I *like* it.

Art's closed off the entire bar for his Halloween party, not just the mezzanine upstairs, and there are more people here than I've ever seen in the one place. I know he's a social person, but this is ridiculous. There are jack-o'-lanterns everywhere, the lights have been switched out for red bulbs, and creepy monsters are hanging out in every nook and cranny of the bar.

"Want a drink?" Orson asks.

I nod, and he leaves, the top of his mustard bottle visible over the crowd. Making my way through the legions of superheroes, furry animals, and Disney characters, I spot Barney with his boyfriend, Leif, across the room.

They're both dressed as pirates; Barney's costume is short and tight, exposing more skin than I've ever seen my friend show, and Leif's looks like something that would be made for a movie. It's layered and detailed, concerningly realistic.

"You two look great," I say, approaching them. "Why pirates?"

Barney mutters, "Oh no," before Leif pumps his eyebrows at him.

"He's not a pirate. He's my wench." Leif slaps Barney's meaty ass, and Barney blushes out to his roots.

I laugh. "Embarrassed?"

"Turned on." Barney squirms and, if possible, turns even redder.

The connection between those two runs deep, and even if I don't love the oversharing, it's a small price to pay for them to be together.

Barney's ex-husband was a bit of a stick in the mud. He never would have shown up here in costume, let alone with Barney having half of his ass hanging out.

"I think if anyone should be embarrassed here, it's you," Leif says, pointedly looking my hot dog costume over.

I try to shrug, but I'm not sure the action is recognizable in this. "We wanted to be matching, and it was last minute finding something. Besides, I don't think I could have paid Orson to wear something that slutty."

"He's missing out," Barney says.

And so am I. Picturing Orson with that Ford butt plug in, shirttails covering his ass so when he bends over … Not an image I need to bring up in the middle of a party.

"Where is Orson?" Barney asks.

"Went to get drinks."

"Speaking of …" Leif smacks a kiss on Barney's cheek. "I'll grab you another one."

"It's like you're trying to get me drunk."

"Just wanna see my baby have fun." Leif winks and leaves us alone.

"He's got a point, you know," I say as Barney watches him walk away, love-dumb expression on his face. "I like you having fun."

"I always have fun."

"Not like now, you didn't. You've always held back. Leif's good for you."

"And apparently, Orson's good for you if you're suddenly this knowledgeable about relationships."

Well, he's got me there. "Good point. I know fuck all, only that it feels good."

"How is it, being all boyfriended up?"

"Feels like what I was born to do. But I don't think it would have felt that way with anyone else."

"Nope." Barney shifts. "I strongly believe that we don't have soul mates, specifically, more that there are certain people in this world who we mush with."

"Mush with?"

"Yeah. Like you smoosh together. Combine souls or whatever romantic shit people say."

"And you guys are mushed?"

He nods. "You too. Like one big, amorphous blob."

"You're making this relationship thing sound better by the second."

He has a point though. It's how I've been feeling. Like Orson is a part of me who I can't let go, can't be without. Maybe that should freak me out and launch me into some spiral of self-doubt, but there's nothing. One thing Orson and

I do is talk to each other. About everything. It's hard to open up like that, but every time I do, it gets easier. Every time his reaction isn't the drama I'm expecting, it makes me trust him even more. Makes me buy in to that four-letter word he reciprocated and makes me believe we could be the real deal.

"Phew, that was an effort," Mustard Orson says, joining us. He hands over my drink, and after one sip of the familiar, delicious liquid, I throw him a look.

"Beer?"

"It's been a while since you had one. I'm more than okay if you want to indulge and need to be carried home."

"Aww, you'd do that for me?"

Orson snorts and takes a sip of his ginger ale. "Fuck, no. You'll be on your own. But I just wanted you to know that I have zero reservations about leaving you on the barroom floor for someone else to deal with." He shoots me a grin. "It won't make me love you any less."

"Quick, someone grab my swooning couch."

"You'd think you'd keep one on hand by this point. I'm incredibly romantic."

We snigger at each other because when it comes to traditional romance, we are *not* it. But every day we spend together proves that there's no one way to do something. We look out for each other, trust each other, can talk about anything. He's entrusted me with his secrets, and I've done the same with him. We have fun and almost drowned together, show interest in shit the other person likes even if it isn't something we're all that drawn to, and he is *constantly* surprising me. All of him.

I never understood the term "partners," but he's one hundred percent mine.

We spend the night with our friends. He does some axe

throwing, but I sit that the hell out because with every beer I consume, I'm hitting that side of overly tipsy. I'm in my happy place.

Friends I've known forever, a boyfriend I don't have to babysit all night but who gets so excited to see me every time we find each other again, the happy vibes of Halloween, and free-flowing liquor.

Orson finds me at one point and pulls me toward the photo booth Art has rented. We take a bunch of cute couple-y photos for ourselves and then some lewd-as-fuck nipple flashes, hot-doggy-style poses, and "mustard" explosions to show everyone else.

Then, I have to kiss him. I *have* to. Our sense of humor and personalities align so goddamn well that Barney might not believe in soul mates, but it's hard for me to think that Orson might not be mine.

Only when I pull back and Orson leaves to show Art our pictures, my gaze lands on Molly. He's watching me with pouted lips and sad eyes. *Ouch.* I didn't even know he was at this party, and the last thing I want to do is flaunt my happiness in his face, but I also refuse not to show Orson affection when we're in public either. I'm not going to stop every time I want to touch him, just to check who's around.

Kilborough is my home, and Orson is my future. Unfortunately, this situation isn't one we can avoid forever.

With a deep sigh, I head in Molly's direction. I've tried being understanding; I've tried to let him down easily. Hell, I empathize with the man because I'm not innocent here—I let him go on thinking there was a chance. But that chance doesn't exist anymore.

If I have to be the asshole for him to move on, I will be.

I'm set on Orson, I won't change my mind about him, and if I have it my way, we'll still be together when we're old geezers who argue over which TV dinners to get for the week.

Even if that's not the case, I don't want someone hanging around as a backup plan. Molly is better than that.

"Hey," I say when I reach him. "Your guard dog Will around?"

"He's here somewhere." Molly sways on his feet and looks me over wistfully. "He didn't want me to come when Dad mentioned you'd be here with Orson."

I chuckle. "Think he might have a thing for you."

Molly frowns. "Definitely not. We both, uh, have certain tastes …"

I cock my head, trying to pick where the hell that could be going. Are they into BDSM or some shit?

"*Older* men," Molly slurs. "Guys our own age don't interest us."

"Ah." I should have guessed that.

He huffs and looks away. "I thought older guys didn't play games, but *clearly*, I was wrong."

I set my jaw. "I don't know how else to tell you. I'm sorry I hurt you—I knew you were interested, but I never picked up that it was anything more than friendly flirting between us. That's on me. But, Mols, I'm in a relationship now. That's not changing in a hurry. I'm sorry, darlin', but sitting there and giving me the puppy dog eyes isn't going to work. I hate that you're hurting—you're a good guy, and you deserve better—but I'm not going to be the one to give that to you."

He swallows roughly, bottom lip quivering. "Do you know what it feels like to never be the first choice?"

"No," I answer honestly. "I've never wanted to be some-one's first choice."

"It's horrible."

I empathize, but I'm not giving in. "Again, I'm sorry. But I didn't come over here to make it harder on you. I came over here to let you know that whatever you think we had is over. I think it's best that we both act like strangers moving forward."

Molly splutters, taking an unsteady step toward me. "What, you're not even allowed to be friends with me now? Did your boyfriend say that?"

"Nope. He feels for you, actually. I'm the one who made the call. You'll hate me for it now, but it'll be better for you one day."

"You want me to cut you out of my life completely?" His eyes flood with tears.

I hold strong against them, even though seeing anyone in pain makes me immediately want to protect them. "Yes."

"Ford—"

"That's enough, Molly. See you around."

I turn to leave, but before I know what's happening, Molly grips my shoulder, spins me back to him, and all but throws himself in my arms.

A muffled *oomph* leaves me as his mouth covers mine, and it takes a solid second for my brain to catch up. I shove him away, slightly harder than I mean to. Molly stumbles back into someone, who drops their glass, and the loud shat-tering cuts off conversation around us.

We suddenly have the attention of everyone nearby.

"The *fuck*!" I shout, and he jumps. "*Not* okay."

Molly's whole face floods red, small frame trembling. He glances around like he's not sure where he is, then lets out a strangled *oh, fuck* and bolts. The people around me are deathly silent, and I have no idea if they're judging me or Molly, but I can feel the weight of it in their staring.

I'm standing there for way too long, trying to work out whether to go after him and make sure he's okay, whether to find Keller and Will and give them the heads-up, or to find Orson and remind myself that *he's* my priority and I can't fix everything.

My brain is working sluggishly through all the alcohol I've drunk, and instead of buzzing high on such a fun night, I just feel sick.

Going after Molly isn't the right call—I know that, even if I'm worried for him and *so* angry—so I turn to go and find his dad when I look up and lock eyes with Orson.

My gut bottoms out.

One look at his tense expression tells me he saw everything.

Shit.

I take a step closer, prepared to explain exactly what went down, when Orson turns on his heel and walks away from me. My heart drops through my gut as I watch the top of his stupid mustard costume hurry toward the front entrance and leave.

This overwhelming darkness settles down on me hard and fast as I keep replaying the look on Orson's face. Tense jaw, flared nostrils, fists tight at his sides.

The alcohol-fueled anger from Molly's kiss ignites.

I'd wanted to make everything better, and somehow, I've managed to fuck it all up instead.

And Orson didn't even give me a chance to explain.

So much for trust.

31

Orson

NOT OKAY, NOT OKAY, NOT O-FUCKING-KAY.

My pulse is thundering in my ears, drowning out all reason as I storm out of Killer Brew and look around. I'd felt sorry for Molly, worried about him, but all that went out the window when I saw him put his mouth on Ford. He put my boyfriend in a situation that made him lose his cool for a second, and even though his reaction was minor for most people, I've never heard Ford raise his voice like that.

I know how much he would have hated it, especially with how hard he works to control his friendly image around here.

And I know how much I hated seeing another guy touch the man I love.

It's not until I turn the corner and find a figure huddled in the gutter that I slow my steps. A sob hiccups from him, and hearing that wretched noise has the anger I'm desperately trying to hold on to gurgle away.

Molly doesn't know I'm standing here, just sits there and cries, knees hugged tight to his chest, and as much as I want to force myself to hate him, to rage at him, and tell him how fucked-up that was, I … can't.

Damn bleeding heart.

I turn my gaze skyward, looking up into the inky black above. The stars are hard to see from the alley between buildings, but it has the same effect anyway.

Insignificance.

Ford loves me.

I love him.

That hasn't changed.

All that's changed is that Molly did something desperate, and now he feels like shit. As he should.

I clear my throat and approach him.

"That was interesting," I say. The bitterness is loud in my tone because while I might not be angry anymore, I'm still not happy about it.

"What the fuck are you doing here?" By the way his words all tangle together, he's very obviously drunk off his ass.

"Curious why you thought kissing my boyfriend was a good idea."

"I don't have to tell you anything." The defensiveness behind his words is weak.

I slump, wishing I could hate him. It would be easy, *so* easy to tell him he's a piece of shit and leave, but …

But.

Molly's hurting. And I can understand a little of what that feels like.

Awkwardly—because this costume isn't designed for sitting in gutters—I drop down beside him. "Sorry."

He throws me a bleary-eyed glare. "What are *you* apologizing for?"

"Getting in the way of your delusion."

"Fuck you."

"Mature response, kid."

He huffs. "Bet you feel *so* superior, playing the *kid* card. I'm twenty-six, not eighteen. It's not like I'm some helpless idiot."

"Never said you were."

"*Mature response*," he throws back, stumbling over the words. "I know exactly what you think of me."

"Oh, yeah? What's that?"

"You think I'm desperate and an idiot and that I'm some … some … home-wrecker." He hiccups a sob. "But I'm *not*. I'm just … so, so tired. I want somebody. I want a boyfriend, and I want to find love, and every time I think I've found someone who's interested, they … they …" He groans and clutches his stomach. "Forget it. You wouldn't know what it's like."

That old, lingering hurt fills my chest, and unlike every other time I push it away, this time, I let myself feel it. The pain is intense, consuming. The most desperate type of torture. "I know maybe better than anyone."

His gaze darts to side-eye me and look away again. "Why, because you've been divorced? Dad and Mom were divorced, and he couldn't care less."

"Actually, my wife died. And I care a lot."

His mouth drops. Snaps closed. Then he shifts, swiping at his face. "That's, uh … *fuck*. Okay, I guess it's my turn to be sorry."

"Don't be. You didn't know."

"Yeah, but …" He doesn't finish. I get it. The struggling to think of me as a real person. I'm the same with him.

"Losing her was easily the darkest moment of my life. I never thought I'd come back from that. Even now, I'm not sure what I was living for back then. It felt like every day I got up, powered by something or someone else. I was empty, just doing things because I was supposed to."

He sniffs a couple of times. "Are you trying to make me feel sorry for you?"

"Is it working?"

"A little. I don't like it."

"Yeah, well, I'm not a huge fan of feeling sorry for you either."

We eye each other for a moment, Molly's gaze unfocused as he struggles to stay upright.

"So Ford is your second choice?" he asks. "Because he's better than that."

I shake my head. "There's no competition. I loved her. I love him. Neither of them cancels out or lessens the other. She's my past. And he's my future." I harden my voice so he knows I'm serious. "He *is* my future, Molly. I'm sorry if that sucks to hear, but I won't be giving him up."

He hunches forward, wrapping his arms tighter around his knees. "I know. I get it. I'm … lonely. Even at home, with Dad and Will, I swear sometimes they forget I'm even around. Like Dad wishes Will was his son or whatever."

"I'm sure that's not the case."

"Yeah, I know. I'm just drunk and sad."

Gritting my teeth, I reach over and rest my hand on his back. "I know."

"I wasn't planning on kissing him. He said that we had to

ignore each other from now on, and I got so upset, and it felt like I was drowning, and I … I just …"

"I *know*," I say again. Because I do. I understand that feeling, that pain, way more than I ever want to. He was hurting, so he wanted everyone else to hurt with him.

Been there, done that.

Got the literal scars to prove it.

"How are you going to handle seeing us around?" I ask. "Because it's a small town, and we're not going anywhere."

He drops his chin on his knees and answers me in a small voice. "I'll … I …"

"It's probably something you should think about. You can't go around kissing men without their consent because you're hurting or feel out of control."

"I'm a horrible person." He buries his face, and I suspect he's crying again. This is *not* where I thought my night would end up. Comforting the drunk guy who kissed my boyfriend.

"You're not horrible. Good people make shitty mistakes all the time."

"I bet that's what horrible people say about themselves."

"Want to know how you can tell the difference?"

Slowly, he shifts, head turning to face me, and yup. Fresh tears on his cheeks. "How?"

"Because good people make amends and learn." I hide the smile at remembering Ford telling me something similar. "They grow from their mistakes. They don't hide behind excuses. They acknowledge that what they did was shitty, and they make sure they don't do it again."

He takes a moment to process my words. "Is that your way of warning me never to kiss your boyfriend again?"

"Nope." I chuckle. "I don't need to warn you of that. The

fact Ford put distance between you two tells you all you need to know. He's made it very clear where he's at. And if you have any kind of respect for him, you'll never put him in the position you just did again. Because while the kiss I can forgive—*once*—what I'm the most pissed about is that you made him panic. You forced him to hurt you, and it's not something that Ford does easily."

"He's amazing."

"He is."

Molly slants another quick look at me, frown falling deep. "Are you dressed as a mustard bottle?"

"Yep."

"I'm really struggling to have a serious conversation with you like that."

"And yet you *mustard* the strength to anyway."

"Urg. Dad jokes."

I scoff and pull my hand away. "They're called puns."

"Whatever you say, Grandpa."

"Hey, if I don't get to *kid* you, you don't get to *grandpa* me."

Molly straightens, tears finally appearing to have stopped. "Actually …" He looks me over. "You're hot. Like, I didn't notice before. Would you and Ford ever … just one time …"

"Flattered, but that's a huge no." I try to stand and get nowhere fast.

Molly laughs and jumps up to help me. "I could leave you in the gutter and go find Ford myself."

"Wouldn't help you."

He sighs. "I know. I think I'm just going to head home." He clutches his stomach. "I don't feel great."

"I'll drive you."

"I don't get in cars with people who've been drinking."

"Smart. But I don't drink. Come on, you're only five minutes away."

"How do you know that?"

"Friends with your dad," I say. "I've been there plenty of times before. Need to tell him you're leaving?"

Molly shakes his head. "Nothing could make me walk back in there right now. Actually, I'll probably hide out at home for the next month at least."

"Whatever gets you through."

He follows me in a drunken stumble to the car, where I half strip out of the stupid costume and throw it on the back seat. I get what Molly means. The thought of walking back into that party doesn't sit right with me, not after all that. This town is full of gossips, and being at the center of that isn't something I have the energy for.

Me: *You okay to find a ride home?*

Ford: *Of course.*

I tuck my phone away before climbing in after Molly, more than ready for this night to be over. With any luck, Ford will wrap it up soon and meet me back at my place.

I've never needed him more.

32

Ford

WELL, LAST NIGHT WAS A CLUSTERFUCK. I STRETCH OUT THE pain in my back from sleeping on this damn couch all night. Art is on the one opposite, the buttons on his shirt half-open and his normally perfectly styled hair an electrified mess.

"Successful night," he says, voice sounding like shit.

"Why? Because we both got pissed over men and drank our weight in alcohol?" My shoulder cramps as I sit up.

"Screw you. I wasn't pissed over anything."

I give him a doubtful look that he pretends not to see. When Joey came over to mention he was leaving and hooked his thumb back toward the woman waiting at the bar, Art's face went from tan to red in about a second flat. It would have been amusing if Orson hadn't completely ditched me here.

Not that I can blame him.

Seeing someone else kiss *him* would have made me rage.

"Well, while you live in denial, I need to grovel. Hard." I

drag a hand over my face, a multitude of curse words filling my head. "Surely he has to know I'd never do that to him? I'd never encourage that."

Art's hum is gravelly, and he hasn't made a move to sit up from where he's sprawled over the couch. "Our Orson is a ten, but he feels deeply. Good when it's positive emotions, but not so good when it's negative."

"I need him to forgive me."

"Eh. He's batshit about you. The tests and trials of your relationship now are only creating strong foundations to build on."

"Unless he decides to demo the whole thing."

"I've known Orson a long time, and yours is the first dumb ass he's wanted. He's reasonable. Tell him what happened, and he'll be fine."

I hope so. It sounds easy enough when Art puts it like that, but Orson's been hurt in the past, and I refuse to be the reason he's hurt again. All I want to do is be the person he deserves. Maybe we're moving quickly, but I could see us having a life together. A good, long, happy one. Like Orson said, there's no time to waste waiting for the things we want, and he's not even a want at this stage. I need him.

I want to do something special for him. I've told him I love him, and now I want to make sure he knows it.

"How do I be romantic?"

Art lets out a husky laugh. "Look who you're talking to."

"You can be romantic."

"If you want to get him into bed, I'm your guy. If you want to romance him, Orson's usually the one I send people to."

"Well, considering he's the one I want to be all romantic for, that advice doesn't help me."

"I dunno … hasn't he ever said shit he likes? Surely you guys have covered off the favorite things checklist part of your relationship."

"Checklist?"

"Yeah, you cover off favorite things, hopes and dreams, deep insecurities you can throw in their faces later."

I eye him, trying to work out if he's serious. "I'm beginning to see why a relationship isn't on the cards for you."

"Finally, someone takes me seriously."

"Maybe they'd take you more seriously if the sexual tension between you and that bartender wasn't thick enough to cut glass."

"Anyone who thinks that little shit is into me isn't paying attention. You saw him with that woman last night."

"Bi people exist, you know. Look at Orson."

"Don't queer lecture me, asshole. I have intimate knowledge of almost all the queer identities—if you know what I mean."

"I'd have to be in a coma not to know what you mean."

His eyes are closed, hand rested in his messy hair, almost like he doesn't want to face this conversation.

"Why are you so sure he's straight?"

"Just am."

Stubborn bastard. If he refuses to see what's obvious to everyone but him, there's nothing I can do there. My own relationship needs all my attention.

I'm itching to call or text him, but I can't risk him blowing me off, and it's a conversation I want to have face-to-face. With him at work, it needs to wait until this afternoon, but my gut is twisted with nervous worry.

I think about what Art said, about Orson telling me what he likes. I'm not struck with anything genius, but the more I think about him, the more I piece together. He likes the quiet. He likes special moments. Connection. Nothing big or extravagant.

He took me out on the lake just so we could be together. He got that old car just so we could spend time together, like he used to do with his dad. The car thing isn't something Orson cares about all that much; it's knowing he's spending time with someone he loves, doing something they're interested in.

Like with his mom and sitting by the fire.

I haven't even had hot cocoa in forever.

Holy shit, that's it.

Sitting in front of the fire, sipping hot cocoa, and painting his toenails. Orson's interests are doing things for other people, so maybe if I can take him back, remind him of a happy time when he did that, that's the connection he wants.

Yes, yes, yes.

I've never painted another person's toenails in my fucking life, but it's something I'll learn to do for him. Excitement races through me at the idea because surely, *surely*, doing something so sentimental will be enough to rid him of his anger.

The whole situation is a mess, and I get why he's mad, but I want him to know without a doubt that when it comes to me, I'm a sure thing. He never has to worry or second-guess.

Now for my first problem.

I don't have a fireplace.

"No chance you've got a fireplace hidden around here anywhere, do you?" I ask.

"No." Art peeks open an eye. "Why?"

"I know what I'm going to do for Orson, and it's kinda integral to the whole thing."

"Can't think of one off the top of my head."

Well, fuck. From memory, he'd mentioned a cool night—check. Hot cocoa—easy enough to come by. Nail polish—I assume I can pick some up from the store … but a fireplace isn't something I can just come up with.

Think, Ford, think.

Unfortunately, the pounding in my head isn't helping the issue. Why did I have to drink so much last night? Oh yeah, because apparently, I'm not so great at making decisions when my heart is breaking over the thought of hurting Orson and having him mad at me.

Though it's possible I was well on my way to intoxicated before I even started on the shots with Art.

I groan as I struggle to my feet, wanting to get my plan started sooner rather than later. I'm only in a T-shirt and boxer briefs, the hot dog costume discarded over by the bar, and I figure Art can hold on to it for a little while longer for me. I say goodbye and get a grunt in return, then stagger down the stairs from the mezzanine to the bar area below. It's a mess, and already Art's staff are working on cleanup, poor bastards.

First up, I need to shower, take some painkillers, and down a large, strong coffee. Then, hopefully, I'll be able to think clearer.

My Uber driver keeps throwing weird looks at me from the front seat that I ignore during the drive, and when he leaves, I send a hefty tip his way. It's the least I can do for filling his car with the stale stench of anxious sweat, alcohol, and cigarette smoke. My mouth tastes like an ashtray, so I'm pretty sure I had a couple last night while I was fucked off my face.

It's been a long time since I've gotten blackout drunk, and I don't like it. The taste of ginger ale has grown on me, and I way prefer a night out where I'm in control and can enjoy myself properly than this slimy, sloppy feeling hanging around now.

Maybe I'll drink again, and maybe I won't, but it doesn't feel all that worth it anymore.

Once I'm feeling halfway human, I pick up the phone and call Taylor. The garage is open until lunchtime on a Saturday, and Taylor's in charge of the grease gremlins while I'm not there.

"Everything's fine here, boss. I've been going over the assistant applications and found one or two okay-ish ones."

"Ah, good, but not what I was calling about, actually."

"Oh, yeah?" they ask. "What is it?"

"Can you ask around and see if anyone has a fireplace I can borrow for the night?"

"Random, but okay."

"I'm planning something romantic for my man," I explain. "The fireplace is kinda a big part of it."

"Let me see what I can do."

They hang up, and I force down breakfast, which doesn't do great things for my already unsettled gut. I'm crossing my fingers that one of my gremlins comes through for me because without the stupid thing, I'm not sure the night will hit the right sentimental note.

My anxiousness ramps up a notch when Taylor calls me back.

"Any luck?"

"Nothing," they say. "Sorry. A handful of the guys have

one at home, but they either don't work, or they're not available. I figured you didn't want kids running around while you were being Casanova."

"Yeah, kinda would ruin the ambience." I try not to sound too disappointed, but fuck. I wanted to do something special, and the universe is going to shit on it.

"Could you use a portable heater instead?" Taylor laughs. "Or a picture of one?"

"I'm thinking it's more the fire side of things that creates the mood."

"Well, if you want fire, we've got the old drum out back that we use some afternoons." Their words are supposed to be joking, but it's given me an idea.

"That could work."

"Uh … an old drum isn't quite the same romance factor."

"No, not that." The idea is spinning in my head too quickly for me to keep up with. "I'm going to need some help though. Find out who there can stay back a few hours on extra pay. I have an idea."

"Oh, really?" I can hear the smile in their voice. "Well, count me in. And don't worry, I'll have a crew ready when you get here."

EMOTIONAL SUPPORT CHAT

Keller: *Fuck, man, I'm so sorry.*

Orson: *Why? You didn't do anything.*

Keller: *Yeah, but, he's my kid. I should ... I don't know.*

Orson: *He's a grown man. You can't be responsible for him.*

Keller: *Man or not, he's my son so I'll always be responsible for him. But I'm so mad at what he did to you, and I really appreciate you making sure he got home okay.*

Orson: *It's fine. He was drunk and if I'm honest, I felt a bit sorry for the guy.*

Keller: *He said. Also told me he hit on you so, ah, sorry about that too?*

Orson: *Don't be, I take it as a compliment ;)*

Keller: *I'm going to pretend you didn't just winky face over my kid.*

Orson: *In that case, I'll pretend like your kid didn't kiss my boyfriend.*

Keller: *Deal!*

Orson: *I'm not sure if I should even ask this but ... is he okay?*

Keller: *Honestly? I don't know. He had a boyfriend for the first two years of college and they were both talking about getting married and all that stupid young love stuff, but turns out this kid had a high school sweetheart back home who he was fucking behind Molly's back. He hasn't been the same since.*

Orson: *Fuck. Our conversation is starting to make more sense now.*

Keller: *Yeah ... I don't know what I'm going to do about him ...*

33

Orson

I'M RUN OFF MY FEET. ALL DAY, THERE ARE PEOPLE IN AND
out, and just when I think I can have a breather, more people
walk in. I have no clue what's going on today, but I'm going
to struggle to stock the market tomorrow at this rate.

Maybe I'm due a day off from there anyway.

Ford never came over last night, and I haven't heard
from him this morning either. It's making me uneasy, and
with no chance for me to stop for lunch, let alone send him a
quick text to check in, I can't even get excited over what has
to be a record sales day. The way we left things last night
wasn't ideal, but I thought he was okay. He said he was fine
to get home, and I dropped Molly off, so I knew he wasn't
bothering Ford, but now I'm worried I got everything wrong.

Is he okay? Should I have stayed and comforted him
instead of running after the guy intent on ruining my relationship? Ford *has* to know that I went after Molly for him
… right?

Fuck.

If only I could catch a spare five minutes to pick up my phone and call him. Make sure everything is okay. This knot of unease in my gut is the only thing I can concentrate on.

"Just these, thanks," a man says, resting a bunch of flowers on the counter.

"No problem. Do you need them wrapped?"

"Nope, like that is fine."

He's the umpteenth person today wanting to take his bouquet bare, and that's … odd. It's rare that I have one bunch taken without wrapping, let alone more than half.

I eye the guy. "Where do I know you from?"

"Nowhere, I don't think." He shifts his body weight from one side and back to the other.

Looking suspicious.

I take in his black zip-up hoodie, navy cargo pants, and grease-stained hands. His fingernails are painted blue. "Do you work at the garage?"

His eyes immediately dart to the side like he's hoping the wall will give him his answer. "Ah, yeah. I do. Just finished up. On my way home. Buying some flowers for a special someone …"

"Okay." Not at all the information I asked for, but he's clearly up to something shifty, so I want him out of the store as fast as I can. I ring him up, and he leaves, only to have another person walk in right away. They're familiar too. The same thick pants, heavy boots, and stained hands. And blue fingernails? That's odd. They're wearing a sweater, and I'm sure that under it is one of those Ford's Garage embroidered shirts.

"Taylor," I say, realizing I've met them a few times when

they've come to help out with the soap box cars. "Back for more?"

Their dark eyebrows jump up. "Umm … yeah, I—"

"How many people do you need flowers for?"

"Oh, no, these are … I'm buying for … for someone else."

I give them a doubtful look.

"Ford. They're for Ford. He said something about a cousin's uncle's classmate's, uh—*aunt*? Grandma? I lost track."

"Right …" Something's going on here. I gesture to my dwindling supply. "Not a lot to choose from at the moment. What's catching your interest?"

Taylor's gaze sneaks to me and away again. "Which do you recommend?"

"Depends what it's for."

"No, like, if you could look around and be like *those* just by looking at them, which would you go for?"

Umm … today is getting strange. But it's my job to humor my customers, so I lead Taylor over to the biggest bunch I have, which is a mix of purple orchids, white roses, and calla lilies. "They're probably my favorite."

"Perfect. They'll do."

"Do you want them wrapped?"

I'm expecting a *no*, so when Taylor says, "Sure," I'm thrown for a second. Still, if these are for the grandma's uncle's cousin's dog or whatever Ford said, he probably wants them to look nice.

Taylor pays, and I swear I note Ford's name on the card they use, but I let them go without questioning any more. As soon as the shop is blissfully clear, I grab my phone and open my messages.

Me: *Is everything okay?*

I don't get a response, which I try not to let bother me too much. As it creeps closer to closing time, the steady stream of people slows down and seems to be back to my usual number of customers.

Five o'clock can't arrive fast enough, and as I'm crossing the shop to lock up, the door flies open and Ford steps inside.

Heavy boots, grease-stained jeans, a presence too big for my shop.

Exactly like that first day I saw him here. With one difference.

He's holding the big-ass bunch of orchids.

Ford's big, soft eyes look almost worried. "Ah, hey."

"Hi …" A smile pulls at my lips as I take in the flowers. "What are you doing?"

"Groveling."

A laugh escapes me. "What for?"

"Last night." He cringes. "What happened with Molly—"

"Wasn't your fault."

His mouth drops. "Come again?"

"Wait. You didn't think I was mad about that, did you?"

"You ran out. You left without me."

"Aww … Ford." I step forward and wrap my arms around his waist. "I gave Molly a lift home. I thought you were okay."

"Molly … home …" His whole face is screwed up now. "Why?"

"I was pissed over what he did to you, and I went after him to put him in his place, but … he looked kinda pathetic. It made me sad for him."

Ford chuckles and palms his forehead. "Of course it did."

"He was heartbroken."

"No, he wasn't. He barely knows me."

I brush a kiss over his lips. "He knows enough. Any man would be lucky to have you, and it so happens that man gets to be me."

"Yes, it fucking is." He draws me into a kiss that has me pressing closer, wrapping my fists in his shirt. Ford tugs at the tie of my apron, and when it frees, he abruptly pulls back from the kiss and takes my apron off. "You finished?"

"Just have to get these put away." I point at the remaining flowers.

"I'll race you."

"What—"

But Ford takes off, leaving the orchids on the counter as we compete to see who can pack away the fastest, and almost as soon as the final bucket is back in the cool room, he grabs my hand and drags me out front.

"Where are we going?" I ask.

The only thing we pause for is to grab the flowers and for me to lock up.

"It's a surprise."

"Mysterious," I say, but he still doesn't tell me.

Ford holds my hand, leading me down the street toward—

"The garage?"

He winks at me. "I've been busy today."

"I thought Saturdays were your day off?"

"I haven't been working on cars. I've actually been working on a way to win back your heart and prove how much I love you, but since you're not actually mad at me … it makes this even better."

"Why?"

"Because now I can show you with no pretenses. No reasons. Just because I really wanna."

"Show me what?"

Ford hands over the flowers. "These are for you."

"Kinda figured."

"You mean the cousin's uncle's grandma's excuse didn't throw you off?"

"Not in the slightest."

I take the flowers, smile pulling at my face. "Considering you practically keep me in business, I think this is the first lot you've ever given me."

"It was well overdue." He pushes open the reception area and leads me through it. "And you don't know the half of it."

"What do you ..."

He opens the door in the back of reception to the garage, and if he wasn't pulling me along, I would have come to a stop. There's a path of flowers and candles leading through the workspace to the outdoor area, and when we follow it and step outside, I can't believe my damn eyes.

"What the hell is this?"

A large metal cabana-like structure sits in the middle of the yard, completely covered in flowers. They're up the four metal poles, hang from the canopy above, and cover two of the sides. Along one side of the structure, a large fire burns and licks at the air from the long fire pit that's been created for it.

In the middle of the cabana *thing* is a picnic blanket, cushions, and a small table covered in food.

"Holy fuck. I guess now I know where the hell my flowers went."

He shrugs. "You said flowers should be there for all the important moments. The beginnings and ends and all those milestones in between." His large hand wraps around mine, fingers linking between my own, and I follow him over to his setup. "This might not be a milestone they write Hallmark cards for, but I hope it's a big one for us anyway."

"Why is that?"

Instead of answering, Ford gives me a soft smile. He settles onto a cushion, and I take the one beside it, not able to stop looking around at what he's done.

"You're important to me," he says, unscrewing the lid of a thermos and pouring dark liquid into two cups. He passes mine over, and I get a strong hint of chocolate. Cocoa.

It's been forever since I've had this.

"Maybe the most important person I've ever met. I know you can't say that back, and I don't want you to. Because I know that I'm the most important person to you right now, and that's all I care about."

I nod quickly, wanting him to know how true that is. "I wasn't expecting it, but you were the best kind of surprise."

"Right back at you, sweetheart." Ford grabs my legs and lifts them to rest over his. Then he pulls off my shoes and socks. "It's incredible to me how fast I've fallen for you, but it feels right. The same kinda rightness I felt about being a mechanic one day or offering the lot to help with the soapbox cars. There are things in my life I did because they felt like they fit. I've never had doubts about them." He looks up and winks, then reaches for something behind the table. "You're one of those things."

My heart feels so full, even before I register what he's holding.

A small bottle of blue nail polish. He unscrews the lid, slight concentration line settling in the middle of his forehead. "I've gotta warn you; I might have been practicing all day, but I'm still terrible at this."

And then he starts to paint my toenails.

The cocoa, the fire, the nail polish.

I have to swallow back the lump in my throat as my love for him builds so big it *hurts*. His tongue is clamped between his teeth as he works, and seeing this giant, tattooed man with the softest heart struggle to keep hold of the tiny brush and paint neatly is my undoing.

"I want to keep you."

"Hey … that was my line." His smile is fucking huge. "This isn't a proposal because I don't think I want one of those, and I have no idea if you ever would again either, but this is me saying you're it for me. I'm never changing my mind about you. I want to move in together and discover each other's bad habits. I want you to burn dinner and for me to be too messy for your liking. I want to argue and disagree, but once that's over, I want us to be stronger for it. Because nothing can change how I feel about you, and I want to work to make you mine for the rest of our lives."

"You don't need to work at it. I already am."

"And that's what makes tonight so special. It's the first day of our lives together."

We're smiling at each other so hard I'm sure I look borderline unhinged. I wriggle in closer so I can rest my chin on his shoulder as I watch him work. Every tiny little stroke, every time he gets paint on my skin and madly scrubs it off, every time his tongue pokes out again. All of it makes my heart warm.

I drop a kiss on his neck, then turn so my lips are at his ear. "Just so you know, I didn't *think* I'd want that ever again. Until you. If you ever wanted to get married, Ford, all you'd need to do is ask."

34

Orson

THE FIRE IS THROWING WARMTH AROUND US, AND I'M SO comfortable I never want to move. Other than the sound of occasional cars driving past outside the garage, the afternoon is quiet. We could be on a secluded island for all either of us know because we switched our phones off ages ago.

Ford runs his rough fingers over my abs again, sending ripples through me, and his chest moves behind me as he laughs.

"Thought you weren't ticklish?"

"I'm not." I huff. "It's a whole other sensation."

"Oh, *really*?" His fingers skim lower, and I suck in a steadying breath. "Oh, I like that."

"Like what?" I ask.

"Seeing those pretty toes curl up."

It's my turn to laugh. "You're an asshole."

"What? They're very, *very* pretty."

"Like you can talk." I nudge his bare foot, the nail polish I put there catching the light from the fire.

"Mine are pretty too. Obviously. They were before you painted them though—*oomph*!"

He flinches at my elbow digging into his ribs. "Now who's the asshole?"

"Speaking of assholes …" I turn in his arms. "I've been thinking about yours a lot."

Ford's face lights up. "Tell me more."

"I've never actually seen it, which seems like a missed opportunity. What's the point of having a boyfriend if I never get to see his ass?"

"I can bend over for you right now if you want."

"Would you?"

His teasing dries up. "Are you serious?"

I lean in to brush my lips over his. "It's not my fault you got me all hard."

"Here I was thinking we were snuggling."

"You knew what you were doing."

The mischievous spark in his eyes tells me I'm right on the money. "And you, what? Want to fuck me in the middle of my yard? Where anyone could come by?"

We both know the side gates are locked, and no one is coming in the front unless they're up to no good. The fences around here are too high for anyone to see in. "I don't think I can wait until we get home."

"Why's that?"

"Because you are too sexy for your own good."

"Luckily for you, I showered earlier, otherwise you'd be having sex with a brewery."

"It's hilarious that after all my stories you somehow still think I have standards."

"It's my exceedingly high opinion of you."

"I know you're being a smart-ass." I stroke his face. "But thank you. For seeing past all that shit."

"Right back at you, sweetheart."

My hand rests on his bare chest and slowly moves south. "Now, speaking of things I want to see …"

"Hold that thought." Ford reaches into the basket of food and pulls out a condom and some lube. "I'm a mind reader."

"Or maybe you had a plan to get me into bed all along."

He cups my face and draws me into a deep kiss, beard scraping my stubble. "Damn, you taste good."

"It's the strawberries."

He hums into my mouth, and then the talking is over. Neither of us comes up for air for a really long time. We kiss for what feels like hours, enjoying the slide of his tongue over mine, his soft lips working mine open, the small nips and licks he gives my bottom lip before sucking it into his mouth.

I'm so hard my cock feels like it's trying to drive a hole through my pants, but I'm determined to ignore it for now. Now the only thing I can care about is that I have the freedom to do this whenever I fucking want. I don't need to rush. I can enjoy him and everything he's offering me.

We lie back into the cushions as our hands get in on the action. We're both already shirtless, miles of skin exposed for our hands to map out every curve and bump. Ford scratches his nails through the light hair between my pecs as I give his nipples attention. Light flicks and short, sharp pinches. They're already rock hard, and the small shivery breaths Ford lets out tell me I'm on the right track.

I finally break from the kiss, duck down, and sink my teeth into the flesh around his pierced nipple. My tongue flicks the barbell back and forth a few times before I release him, and Ford immediately flips me onto my back, his body blanketing me a second later.

"You're going to pay for that."

"Oh, yeah. What have you got for me?"

His filthy smile tells me that while he might have torture in mind, I'm going to enjoy every second of it.

Ford pops the button on my pants, pulls down the zip with his teeth, and then yanks the material down hard and fast. My briefs follow until they're bunched up under my ass, and then Ford sinks his mouth down around me.

It's exquisite. The warmth, the suction, the sloppy sounds he's making. I want to thrust, force him to take me all the way down, but I lie there fighting against the instinct and give Ford complete control.

It's a wonderful fucking thing.

He must have sucked a lot of cock in his day, and I thank every one of those people who came before me because it's the most incredible blow job of my life.

So good, in fact, that I'm about to—

Ford pulls off with a wet *pop*, and I tilt my hips higher, chasing his mouth.

"No fair," I complain.

"Yeah, you're not coming in my mouth when you can do it in my ass instead."

He makes so many good points, but his breath brushing the head of my cock is making it hard to agree with him. My orgasm was *right there*, and now I'm stuck in that frustrating limbo of being turned on and denied.

"I could kill you," I complain.

"I know, but trust me when I say I'll make it worth your while."

"You better."

Ford pushes up onto his knees and makes fast work of undoing his pants. He wrestles them down, standing long enough to strip them off before finishing the job with mine. Both pairs of pants end up in a pile on the opposite side of our cabana to the fire.

He leans down again, pressing his cock against mine, and gives a solid thrust.

My eyes almost roll right back. I'll never get tired of how his cock feels. So large and rock hard, leaking enough precum that it's sticky against my own.

Ford sets a slow, steady rhythm as he thrusts against me, the lazy hip movements of a man in no hurry.

But I *am* in a hurry. Unlike him, I've been so close to blowing my load already, and now that edge is slowly receding, I'm thankful for his self-control. If I'd blown in his mouth, it would have felt incredible, but I would have been pissed the hell off at myself.

Especially with what Ford does next.

He pulls away and turns, planting his hands on the floor and tilting his ass up toward me. The bare skin of his ass looks perfectly stark against the artwork covering his entire back.

"You know what you're doing back there, right?"

"I've had some practice." And while shoving my fingers up my own ass is a world different to doing it to someone else, the mechanics of it are the same. I'm still nervous though. I use too much lube and press my first finger in faster than I mean to.

"Ease up," Ford says, voice strained.

"Sorry. It's possible I'm excited." Excited, shitting myself, same difference.

He chuckles. "Me too, but if you want your cock in there, you'll have to play nice. Romance it a little."

I drop a kiss to his back. He's ridiculous. But while he might be messing around, his advice applies. I'm gentle as I work my finger in and out, loving the push and pull sensations against me, and when I slowly work in a second finger, the tightness makes my head spin. He's going to feel so, so good around my cock.

I spend a lot of time stretching and getting him used to the feeling of being full, and while I fuck him with my fingers, I skim my free hand over his balls. Massaging them and squeezing gently, alternating attention to his balls and wrapping my hand around his thick length.

Ford's back muscles are straining, biceps on full display as he holds himself up, and when I get another finger inside him, searching around for that bundle of nerves, I know the second I find it. Ford lets out a hoarse cry and starts riding my fingers like he'll die if he stops. Seeing the large man blissed-out and desperate makes my cock throb. Getting inside of him is less of a want and more of a need at this point.

I pull my fingers out, tear open the condom, and roll it down my shaft. I'm oversensitive already and even covering myself in lube is an effort in restraint.

"You ready?"

"Fuck yes." He growls.

I slap his ass. "On your back."

"Really?"

"Yeah. I want to see your face."

Ford flops back onto the blanket, and I immediately cover him. My mouth closes over his as I grab my cock and steer it toward his hole. The second I push forward, Ford bears down, and I slip inside with only a little resistance. It's clear he's experienced at this, too, because he grabs my ass, and with one pull, I slam home.

The pressure is unreal. Incredible. I give a small thrust, and tingles race through to my balls. I'm almost cross-eyed with lust and want and the need to get off.

My mouth breaks from Ford's, and I grab his hands, fingers slotting between his, pinning them over his head.

"Hold on tight, babe."

"You're gonna kill me," he breathes, grip on my hands clenching hard. He tilts his hips upward, and it's the perfect angle for me to let loose. My self-control is at an all-time low, and I know I won't be able to hold off for much longer, so I don't. I give in. Give myself over to how amazing this feels.

I rail him.

Ford's not quiet about it. He grunts and moans, meeting each thrust, heels digging into my back. The fire feels like a wall of heat beside us, and that, combined with my erratic pulse, has sweat prickling over my skin.

I dip my head to close my lips over his neck, sucking the soft skin into my mouth. He arches to give me more room, and the taste of his skin makes me high. All warmth and a hint of salt. I leave red bruises wherever I can reach, hardly able to believe this is it for me. He's mine. This is *us*.

I might have doubted I'd ever find love again before him, but I know, without a doubt, that Ford will be my last. I'm never giving him up. And I'm so glad he decided on me, too, because I never want to imagine my life without him.

"I'm gonna come."

"Ah, fuck, do it," he gasps.

I press all my weight into our hands and fuck him with

the end in mind. I'm so checked out all I can concentrate on is the feelings building in my gut. The ripply waves of pleasure vibrating from my cock to the ends of every limb, making me feel like jelly, while all of my muscles pull tight. I'm so close. I'm consumed by the drive to get off. The pressure in my balls is building, building, pulling tight …

I release Ford's neck and clamp my teeth down over his nipple.

His roar sets me off.

My cock pulses with my orgasm, each spurt filling the condom as I unload into Ford's ass. His cum fills the space between us, and when my lust haze cools off, I flop down on top of him, smearing it between us.

I let out a long groan, not having the brain power to form actual words yet.

"That was … that was …" Nope. Still nothing.

"The first fuck of the rest of our lives."

I laugh into his shoulder as he wraps his big arms around me. "Let's see them put that one on a Hallmark card."

35

Ford

"Yes. *Yes*. Yes!" My fists are clenched, and I'm balancing on the tops of my toes as the soapbox cars fly past me. Daryl is in a good position, driving well, so fucking close to placing. This is everything my sixteeners have worked toward over the last few months, and it feels like their success is my success.

The racers approach the finish line at the bottom of the hill, and my muscles coil tight. They're close ... closer ... Daryl is neck and neck with the car beside him, fighting it out for second and third position.

Don't do anything stupid ... don't do anything stupid.

Daryl crosses the finish line, and the group around me explodes into cheers. It's too hard to tell from here if he placed second or third, but he did it. Top three is always our goal. And the clever little shit did it all in a soapbox car he made himself.

We make our way over, and when Daryl tells us he made second, my heart soars for him. I have no idea if I'll have any seventeeners next year, so it's awesome for this year to go out on a high.

Even if that thought tries to bring me down.

Orson makes it back just in time for the presentations.

"How'd your littlies go?" I ask.

"Great. A couple of places, a couple of wrecked cars, and a lot of tears."

"Sounds like a usual race day to me."

He chuckles, and I pull him in front of me and wrap my arms around his waist. We cheer when Daryl's name is called and join the parents and families in congratulating the kids—all of them. Even if they didn't win, they still built a whole damn car.

After that, Orson and I make our way back to the booth we've set up. The Springfield Thanksgiving festival is always a great day, and I love setting up my little booth to talk cars and offer free advice on issues while Orson covers the kids in temporary tattoos.

This is the fucking life. Simple and happy. Cars and Orson.

Our last few weeks together have been incredible, and even though it's a chilly day overall, it hasn't snowed yet this year, and the weak sun is doing its job enough for people to make the trip out here. The festival is full, a last-ditch attempt at enjoying the outdoors before winter kicks in and months of hibernating begin.

I love that I've been able to share this with him, and hopefully, we'll have plenty of years ahead of doing the exact same thing.

After the night together a few weeks ago, where I put it all on the line and told Orson exactly what I wanted from him, we've barely spent a night apart. Next week, we're doing Thanksgiving with some of our friends at my house, and after Christmas, we're going to start the process of him officially moving in with me.

"You okay over here, big guy?" Orson asks when the group we've finished helping moves on.

"Sure am."

"You're all … quiet. Pensive. It's weird."

I chuckle. "What? I'm not allowed to sit back and think about things?"

"Not unless those things are me."

"Oh, those things are *always* you and what I'm going to do with you later."

"Hmm, I'm listening."

"Well, first, I'm going to get you home …"

"Yes?"

"Strip you off …"

He inhales sharply. "And?"

"And dress you in my warmest clothes before serving you up hot chocolate and foot rubs."

"Urg." Orson drops a laugh against my shoulder. "That didn't end the way I thought it would."

"Let me guess, you thought I'd end with you finishing?" I cluck my tongue. "So rude."

"You started it."

"You bring out the worst in me."

And the very, very best. Orson has been an excellent study in the bedroom, and I've never met anyone so fucking shameless and excited to try new things. I can barely keep up with him.

My gaze snags on a couple a few booths away.

"Hey, Orson. Date or mates?"

He sniggers. "Definitely date."

I tilt my head, eyeing the men. "I dunno … they're looking kinda platonic to me."

"I don't think this game works as well when you don't know the answer."

"True. But I'm curious now." I step forward, but Orson hauls me back.

"You can't go around asking random men if they're together."

"Don't see why not."

"Some guys don't like that."

I pull away and throw him a wink back over my shoulder. "Do I look like the kinda guy people intimidate easily?"

Orson shakes his head as I round the counter and pretend to straighten out my display. I wait for the men to get close enough.

"Oh, hey, darlin'," I say as though I've only just noticed them. "Nice day out."

The blond one huddles down into his scarf. "Are you kidding? It's freezing."

"Don't worry about him," the redhead says. "He's cold-blooded."

I chuckle and look over the blond again. His cheeks and nose are bright red. "Probably need to move somewhere south."

"Actually, we noticed your sign. Kilborough, huh? We're relocating."

"Oh, *really*?" I shoot a glance Orson's way. "Any reason?"

"Got a job opportunity there."

I nod toward the blond. "And your partner's moving with you?"

They both burst into laughter. "Friend. Brayden is escaping a shithead family, so he's coming with me."

And … I win another one. I glance over at Orson, wondering what the chances are that I'll be rewarded with another lap dance.

"Well, if you don't know anyone," I swipe up my business card, "give me a call. Orson and I would be happy to show you around, uh …"

"Luke." His lips pull up in the corner as he reaches out and takes my card.

"Right, nice to meet you."

They leave, and I turn to Orson with a shit-eating grin. "So are you going to *Pour Some Sugar on Me* here or wait until we get home?"

"I hate how good you are at that game."

"I'm great at reading people."

"Uh-huh. Which is why you could tell that guy was totally into you."

"What?" I whirl around so fast I get whiplash, and sure enough, Luke is checking me out. He gives me an upnod that I awkwardly pretend not to see. "Well, fuck."

"It's the pet names. I might have to veto mine. Darlin', sweetheart—I don't want to be in the same box as all the other guys who flirt with you."

Ford lifts his eyebrows. "I call everyone darlin'. My postman, the barista, people who drop off their cars at the shop …"

"But …" I think back. "You've never used it on me."

"I haven't. You've always been *sweetheart* because you

make my heart feel all sweet. I've known you were special right from the start."

"Aww …" Orson's big hazel eyes go soft, and he leans up to brush my lips with a kiss. "I take it back. You can *sweetheart* me all you like."

"Every day, sweetheart. For the rest of our lives."

EPILOGUE

THREE MONTHS LATER

Orson

"Wait—no, *stop*. Dammit, Art," Payne cries.

Art unleashes a guilty smile. "Oops?"

I stare in dismay at where Art's put the couch leg through the wall. Considering he and Payne were the only ones who volunteered to help us move in, I can't even be angry. "Ford's gonna kill you."

Instead of supporting my warning, my boyfriend walks into the room and chuckles. "Oops."

"Oops?" I echo.

Ford and Art glance at each other and in complete unison say, "Oops."

I'm going to go gray at double time with those two spending so much time together. "Everyone will be here in a few hours."

"And they'll find a hole in the wall," Ford shrugs. "No biggie."

At least he's not getting pissed and blaming me for it.

Not that he's ever given me a reason to think he's that type of person, but this is my home too now, and while I might be another version of myself, in another home, I still need the calm that clean and orderly brings.

Ford is getting rid of his old couch, and we've got my navy one to replace it, along with all the brown and white cushions. He's replaced his bedspread to be more calming colors and has gotten a lot better about picking up after himself.

Today will be my first official day living here, even though I can't remember the last time I spent a night at my place.

The thing about Ford is he makes me want him around. Always. And if that means moving out of the place I thought I'd die in, I'm more than happy to. We have his garage here and already so many memories that it just makes sense.

I love that life with him has taught me that sometimes things don't happen the way you expect them to, and *sometimes*, that's for the best.

"Dinner is seven, right?" Payne asks as he and Art set the couch down.

"Yup."

"I'll text Beau a reminder. I've already set three alarms in his phone, but he was in hyperfocus mode when I left. Didn't even register when I kissed his head goodbye." There's a dopey amount of affection in Payne's tone that immediately makes me glance over at Ford.

He's grinning back like he can read my mind. It's not like I make it hard on him. I'm either thinking about sex, how happy I am, or that he needs to get his damn empty mugs off the counter.

It's pretty easy to pick the difference.

"We all know you'll end up having to pick him up," I say to Payne.

"Without a doubt." Payne walks out, phone in hand.

Art and Ford both collapse onto the couch. "Yeah, don't get too comfortable. There's still lots to do."

Art groans. "Why did I volunteer for this?"

"Because you like to pretend you're an asshole, but the people in this room know the truth."

He mutters something under his breath, but I don't bother getting him to repeat himself. He's being a surly shithead today, which I'm sure has nothing to do with him finding out that Joey has a girlfriend. Instead, I head through to the kitchen, grab a beer out for him and Ford, and hand deliver. Ford barely drinks at all anymore, and when he does, it's only one or two.

I'm excited for tonight. For this part of our lives. All my DMC friends will be here, and Ford's invited Barney, some people from the garage, and Luke, who we met in Springfield forever ago. He only called Ford for the first time last week, and once I'd made sure I wasn't going to have another Molly on my hands, we all got along great.

This happiness is still something I'm thankful for every day.

No more going with the flow and waiting to see. No more letting the universe make decisions for me. Ford and I have plans for our lives. Travel, volunteering, maybe even foster parenting. He wants to expand the garage, and I want to buy more cars to work on with him.

Large, warm arms wrap around me from behind. "You took away my view," Ford says.

"Let me guess: my ass?"

"Damn right." His hand runs down to squeeze my ass cheek. "And your arms. Your legs. Your cock imprint."

"I don't have a cock imprint."

"Hmm … maybe I'm just that good at picturing it now."

"You have given it a lot of study time."

"Not my fault it's my favorite subject."

I laugh and turn my head so we can share a quick kiss, but my gaze catches on something on the counter.

A picture of Tara.

"What's that doing here?"

Ford bundles me up tighter. "Found her hidden away in a box in your closet. Thought she might like the view from out here better."

"My late wife. On our kitchen counter."

"She's family." He kisses my cheek. "I want her here with us if you do."

My eyes get all blurry, overwhelmingly grateful that I've found someone who accepts every little part of me. No hiding. No pretending to be okay on the days that I'm not.

Losing someone is something you never get over, but Ford makes it easier. He makes everything easier. When I'm struggling, he pulls out the nail polish, holds me tight, and murmurs filthy things in my ear until I'm relaxed again.

I feel bad for all those people who judge him just by a look because if anyone is close to perfection, it's him. Which reminds me of an idea I had.

"You know how you're always struggling to hold on to an assistant?" I ask.

"Unfortunately, yes."

"Well, what if you didn't hire the traditional way? I thought … your story isn't an isolated one. Lots of kids make bad choices, and it follows them for life. There are programs I've looked into … ways to hire people who need that second chance."

The more I talk, the more tense Ford gets. "Holy shit."

"I mean, it was only an—"

He cuts me off with his mouth. We kiss for a long time. For longer than we normally would, especially with people moving furniture into our house. My neck twinges at the awkward angle. When he lets me up for air, he turns me, large hands cupping my face.

"I am so fucking lucky to have met you."

"You have no idea."

His laugh is soft. "You don't get it. I always thought I'd spend my life alone. I was fine with knowing that's what was on the cards for me. You blew that whole goddamn plan up in my face."

"I did it with a smile too."

"And one badass lap dance."

I cuddle into his large chest. "Here's to the newest version of ourselves."

"And to all those versions who came before."

MY FREEBIES

Do you love friends to lovers?
Second chances or fake relationships?
I have two bonus freebies available!

Friends with Benefits
Total Fabrication
Making Him Mine

This short story is only available to my reader list so click
below and join the gang!
https://www.subscribepage.com/saxonjames

OTHER BOOKS BY SAXON JAMES

FRAT WARS SERIES:

Frat Wars: King of Thieves

Frat Wars: Master of Mayhem

Frat Wars: Presidential Chaos

DIVORCED MEN'S CLUB SERIES:

Roommate Arrangement

Platonic Rulebook

Budding Attraction

NEVER JUST FRIENDS SERIES:

Just Friends

Fake Friends

Getting Friendly

Friendly Fire

Bonus Short: Friends with Benefits

LOVE'S A GAMBLE SERIES:

Good Times & Tan Lines

Bet on Me

Calling Your Bluff

CU HOCKEY SERIES WITH EDEN FINLEY:

Power Plays & Straight A's

Face Offs & Cheap Shots

Goal Lines & First Times

Line Mates & Study Dates

Puck Drills & Quick Thrills

PUCKBOYS SERIES WITH EDEN FINLEY

Egotistical Puckboy

Irresponsible Puckboy

Shameless Puckboy

FRANKLIN U SERIES (VARIOUS AUTHORS):

The Dating Disaster

And if you're after something a little sweeter, don't forget my YA
pen name

S. M. James.

These books are chock full of adorable, flawed characters with big
hearts.

https://geni.us/smjames

WANT MORE FROM ME?

Follow Saxon James on any of the platforms below.
www.saxonjamesauthor.com
www.facebook.com/thesaxonjames/
www.amazon.com/Saxon-James/e/B082TP7BR7
www.bookbub.com/profile/saxon-james
www.instagram.com/saxonjameswrites/

ACKNOWLEDGMENTS

As with any book, this one took a hell of a lot of people to make happen.

The cover was created by the talented Rebecca at Story Styling Cover Designs with a gorgeous image by Wander Aguiar, and edits were done by the comma-queen Sandra Dee from One Love Editing, with Lori Parks proofreading the bejeebus out of it.

Thanks to Charity VanHuss for being the most amazing PA I could have ever dreamed up. Without you I'd be even more of a chaotic disaster and there isn't enough space to cover the many hats you wear for me.

Eden Finley, you constantly under-sell yourself but I've learned so much from you. You're the bestsest disaster bestie I could ask for, and a queen of a co-author. You're also stuck with me. Lucky you.

To Louisa Masters, thanks for constantly reining in my spirals of doom and reminding me to "stop borrowing trouble". I'd be an anxious mess in the corner at least half of the time without you.

Karen Meeus, AM Johnson, Riley Hart, CC Belle thank you so much for taking the time to read. Your support is incredible and I really appreciate it!

A special thank you to A.E. Madsen and Kara Beale for helping me name Orson's florist shop.

And of course, thanks to my fam bam. To my husband who constantly frees up time for me to write, and to my kids whose neediness reminds me the real word exists.